ADDICTED TO THE PAIN

DEAD SOLDIERS VS TAILORS DUET

ROSA LEE

DIRTY LITTLE PUBLISHERS LTD

BLURB

What happens when you fall for the sworn enemies of your family?
I'm kidnapped by the Tailors, a rival gang that wants my entire family wiped off the face of the earth. After spending a couple of weeks experiencing hospitality in the Tailor's very own dungeon, I'm really regretting my life choices up to this point.
Then in walks a tall stranger, with bright hazel eyes, and something in me stirs, growing stronger as I meet each of the Tailor boys.
Aeron, the heir to the Tailor name and a dark devil.
Jude, second in line and mad as a box of frogs but sexy as f*ck.
Knox, tall glass of water with the need to rescue and protect.
Tarl, the Tailor Inquisitor with mismatched eyes, but a healer at heart.
I don't stand a chance against their soothing touches and possessive affections. We fall hard and fast, but like most dreams, eventually you have to wake up.
I just hope that they can forgive me for what I'm about to do.

Addicted to the Pain is the first book in a dark contemporary whychoose romance, where love is love and our girl (and guys) end up with more than one love interest. Swords will cross.
Be warned, love hurts.

***Warning: 18+ Please be aware that this book may contain graphic scenes that some readers may find upsetting or triggering, so please read the author's note at the beginning. ***

Disclaimer: Please note. Rosa Lee cannot be held responsible for the destruction of underwear of any kind. She recommends you take adequate precautions before reading to avoid any sticky situations.

I dedicate this book to all the fictional men with massive, pierced and inked up purple helmeted pork swords. So what if you've given us unrealistic expectations? A girl has gotta dream and what better dream than that?

Rosa Lee
Xxx

"They breathe truth that breathe their words in pain."

— *WILLIAM SHAKESPEARE*

NOTE TO READERS

Dear Reader,

Firstly, thank you so much for choosing to read *Addicted to the Pain*. I hope you enjoy it and that it satisfies all of your needs!

I let my dark inner heart take over with this one, and I became addicted to Lark and her Tailor boys. I really hope you love their journey as much as I have writing it.

As mentioned in the blurb, *Addicted to the Pain* is a dark romance. There are many subjects explored some readers may find disturbing. Please, if you have any triggers, take care and check out my website.

For a full list of triggers please visit www.rosaleeauthor.com/trigger-warnings

PLAYLIST

I love books with playlists and I listen to my compiled playlist as I'm writing. I've even based some scenes solely around one track, listening to it on repeat to really get into the vibe.

Listen to the full playlist on Spotify HERE

"Victim" by Halflives
"Numb" by Carlie Hanson
"Hey Jude" by Joe Anderson
"I Wanna Be Yours" by Arctic Monkeys
"Bad Boys" by Azee
"Scars" by Boy Epic
"Panic Room - Acoustic" by Au/Ra
"Into It" by Chase Atlantic
"Panic Attack" by Liza Anne
"Falling Too" by Veda Gail
"DEVILISH" by Chase Atlantic
"Stockholm Syndrome" by Sofia Karlberg
"Fucked Up" by Bahari

"Smother Me" by Kelaska

"Demons" by Jacob Lee

"Big Bad Wolf" by Roses & Revolutions

"Right Here" by Chase Atlantic

"Mr. Sandman" by SYML

"Midas" by Skott

"Daddy" by SAKIMA, ylxr

"Monsters - Acoustic" by Ruelle

"Can't Help Falling In Love - DARK" by Tommee Profitt, brooke

"You're The One That I Want" by Lo-Fang

"Sanctify" by Years & Years

"Please don't break my heart" by escape

"Ocean Eyes (Acoustic)" by SVRCINA

"Blood // Water - Acoustic" by grandson

"Crazy in Love" by Eden Project

"Poison" by Freya Ridings

"Contaminated" by BANKS

"Ozone" by Chase Atlantic

"Running Up That Hill (A Deal With God)" by Loveless

"Say Something" by Pentatonix

"Love Is Gone - Acoustic" by SLANDER, Dylan Matthew

"Get You The Moon" by Kina, Snøw

"365" by Mother's Daughter, Beck Pete

"I See The Light" by Brent Morgan

"Bodies" by Bryce Fox

"Growing up can go to hell" by Marisa Maino

"Play With Fire (Alternative Version)" by Sam Tinnesz, Ruelle, Violents

"Do It For Me" by Rosenfeld

"Play Dirty" by Kevin McAllister, [SEBELL]

"I Found" by Amber Run

"Sorry" by Halsey

"Arcade" by Duncan Laurence

CHAPTER ONE

"VICTIM" BY HALFLIVES

LARK

Drip.
Drip.
Drip.

That fucking sound will be the death of me. Well, you know, if all the torture doesn't kill me first. I guess there's a real possibility of hypothermia too, given they haven't let me wear any clothes for the past couple of weeks, so I've been having to make do with my birthday suit. Spoiler alert; it's fucking colder than a priest's bed.

Drip.

Fucking cuntish motherfucking drip. You'd think that with all the fancypants torture equipment these bastards have, they'd fix a fucking leaking tap.

Drip.

My eye twitches with the noise. I swear to god I've got new tics because of my stint in here. If this affects my OnlyFans income, I'm fucking suing! *Assholes*.

Drip.

Heaving over on the stained mattress, a pained groan leaves my dry and cracked lips. I look around, desperate to find the source of that fucking drip, and rip it out with my bare and bloodied hands.

Drip.

Another jerk of my eyelid.

I'll never find a decent sugar daddy with a fucking eye twitch. Especially being skin and bones as I am now having been down here for who the fuck knows how long. At least I've still got my tits. Must count for something, right?

That's about the only fucking something right now. There are no windows, and I'm surrounded by concrete and only one heavy metal door. It isn't exactly the Four Seasons. Other than the bed, there's a bucket on the floor in the corner. *Fucking animals.* You can tell a lot about a place by its toilets, or lack thereof, and I'm telling you now that my TripAdvisor review would read:

'Cold, dark most of the time, given the inadequate lighting of a single bare bulb and no natural daylight. Colder than a witch's tit, with uncomfortable sleeping arrangements lacking in any form of bedding aside from an old mattress with questionable stains. Could definitely do with a spring clean—or napalm. Appalling facilities, basically nonexistent. Zero stars.'

Drip.

The whole side of my face quivers this time, a rasping growl cracking out of my raw throat. Motherfuckers. I'm going to look like a fucking junkie if I ever leave here. Which, admittedly, is looking less and less likely the longer I'm down here.

I suppose there are regular, daily, torture sessions to break up the monotony. Silver linings and all that, I guess. Although having one's fingernails pulled from one's hands is not the same as a nice mani-cure, you know? Doesn't have quite the same relaxing quality to it.

And all this pain for what? For information that I can't—won't—

give them. These faceless men. These heartless bastards that torture a girl just because she shares a last name with a monster far bigger and scarier than they could ever be.

Drip.

Fuck. My. Life.

I swear this is another form of torture. It's almost as bad as the loneliness that keeps threatening to consume me until I'm a gibbering wreck, but then I remind myself of all my fans—*twenty thousand subscribers, bitches!*—and fight the darkness with a strength I have to dig deep for. I guess if we're really getting down to it, there's also Rook, my brother, to keep me going.

I tried to make an invisible friend to help stave off the aching emptiness of my current existence, but no one answered the ad. That's how pathetic I've become. Even invisible people don't want to know me.

The grating sound of the lock turning brings my gaze over to the door, and my head snaps up, my entire body coiling, ready for fight, flight, or hell, at this stage, even fuck if it'll help. It swings inward with an ominous creak—*they definitely need to spruce this place up a bit*—and in steps...someone new.

From my vantage on the floor, my eyes travel up from his tan work boots to his fitted dark jeans, pausing on the significant bulge at the apex of his thighs that makes my kitty kat sit up and take notice, practically purring. *Keep your head in the game, Lark.*

His abs are etched through his tight, white T-shirt and my breath shortens to a pant at the defined pecs and broad shoulders that greet my hungry stare. I resist looking at his face, prolonging the anticipation, and deciding to trail along his strong, tattooed arms instead. After all, anticipation makes your panties grow wetter, right? *And holy mother of all things hotness!* His forearms are corded and thick, his massive biceps perfect for pinning you down beneath him. My dry tongue traces my chapped lips, my teeth desperate to sink into those muscles as he fucks me hard.

"You keep looking at me like that, Little Bird, and I'm gonna forget what I came here to do." The deep timbre of his voice caresses my sore and broken body, swirling around my sex and making me ache in delicious ways that, over the past few years, I have almost forgotten.

Unable to resist any longer, my eyes swing up to his firm chin, covered in a light stubble of dark brown. My lips tingle as I trace his full mouth, which is pulled up in a sexy as fuck half smile. Moving on, I take in his ever-so-slightly crooked nose until I reach his eyes and stop dead.

Bright hazel orbs stare back at me, full of a raging heat that burns me in the best way. Not like when those other pigs actually burned me. That sucked big, hairy, donkey balls. The slowly healing blisters on my lower back twinge, the scent of burning flesh filling my nose for a moment. Shaking the memory from my head, I move past his captivating eyes to see a dirty-blond mop of hair. It's styled to look like he just rolled out of bed, shaved close on the sides and long on the top. It's also long enough to enable a good grip whilst I fuck his face.

Maybe this could work in my favor after all. Perhaps help me out of here and give my south mouth something yummy to feast on...

"Shit," he curses, and I go back to look into his eyes again, the lines around them suggesting that he's older than I am, maybe in his early thirties–hello Daddy. I give him my best sultry bedroom smile. I'm glad that yesterday was a waterboarding day so I'm sort of fresh.

"Oh, I'm not into poo play I'm afraid, but I'd let you do pretty much anything else to me, Big Daddy," I tell him, my voice all kinds of croaky from all the screaming that I've been doing the past couple of weeks, but I'm thinking it adds a new sexiness to it. Fuck, it'd make a fortune on the phones.

I smirk when his nostrils flare and his fists clench at his sides as his delicious body thrums with tension. He's younger than the others who usually come to get me, and he's fine as fuck, a tall glass of water in a dry as a nun's cunt desert.

"Are you playing with me today, big boy?" I ask, using the wall to pull myself up to standing. I wince when my nailless fingers scrape on the rough surface, the pain making my jaw clench. That shit does not heal fast, I can tell you. My legs threaten to give out as I've not eaten in a while, and when they give me food, it's mostly scraps and vegetable peelings.

On wobbling legs, I make my way towards him, feeling the scabs on my back split open and warm blood dripping down my bare back. That whipping was not fun. He stands stock-still, watching my naked form with hunger in his gaze. I learnt from an early age how to use my body on men to my advantage, so I sway my hips as much as my wounds allow. He doesn't move when I reach him, my hand darting out as a wave of dizziness washes over me, the dark room tilting.

"Steady now, Little Bird. They did a number on you, huh?" he asks in that pussy-clenching voice of his before wrapping powerful hands around my own tiny biceps to help hold me up. It's strange, but the way he asks, I could swear there's a slight inflection of anger in his tone. I must be imagining it. He is with *them*, after all.

No mind, they'll all pay, eventually.

His face swims back into view, and there are slight lines around his eyes, the heat gone, replaced with something that looks almost like concern.

That's bullshit, Lark. These psychos don't feel normal emotions.

"Not a fan of their work?" I question, leaning into him just because he smells so good. Like a cat does with catnip, I want to roll around in his scent of cloves and petrol and get drunk off it. "Personally, I think it lacks finesse and imagination, you know, that je ne sais quoi that sets it above normal, boring torture. No originality."

A deep laugh rocks his chest and my body follows the movement as I'm now practically draped over him.

"They didn't tell us you were so funny, Little Bird," he murmurs in my ear, not protesting as my head drops to that space between his neck and shoulder and I take a deep sniff like the weirdo I am. What? I've got to get my kicks somewhere in this hellhole.

"They just don't understand me, Daddy, not like you do," I tell him in a sensual, fractured whisper as I nuzzle closer to him. It's like my body has taken over, my arms lifting to wrap around his thick neck. I hiss as more scabs splinter open on my back, blood dripping down and tickling the healing wounds.

"Fuck, baby. They tore you up good," he growls, again that thread of anger lacing his tone when he glances over my shoulder at my back. He's taller than my five-foot-six frame by almost another foot, if I had to guess.

A moan escapes my lips when his fingers ghost over my torn-up back, and I push closer into him, groaning again when I feel something hard press into my pelvis. Dammit, he's too tall for me to get that hardness where I really want it. I go up on tiptoes, just managing to rub my clit on his jeans-clad length, eliciting a deep sexual sound from his throat that caresses my naked skin.

"You like that, Little Bird?" he asks, pressing a finger into an open wound on my back. His other hand comes between us and pushes down onto the tight bud at the apex of my thighs. Sharp fire races across my skin to meet the flare of pleasure flowing from my core.

"Yes, fuck yes, Daddy. That feels so fucking good," I reply in a husky, sultry voice, filled with a longing that I rarely feel when I'm with one of the Soldiers. My father's men do not inspire feelings of desire, and I find my stomach feeling heavy with the anticipation of dread that never materializes. I want him badly, and that might be the most surprising thing that has happened to me since my capture. I shamelessly grind against his hand, electric pulses zinging over my skin at the heady mix of pleasure and pain. "Please, Daddy, I need you inside me so fucking bad."

I give no shits that I'm pleading with this god-like man, one of my supposed enemies. I'm suddenly burning with a need that only he can ease.

My arms leave his neck, shakily coming down to his belt buckle and undoing it, the clanking sound loud in the room. He doesn't stop me, just holds completely still, and I pause, my gaze flitting upwards to see if he wants this. I might be willing to use him, but I'd never do anything that he didn't want. I know the feeling of being forced all too well. Seeing his hooded gaze on my peaked nipples and his tongue coming out to lick his plush lips has my fingers popping open the top couple of buttons on his jeans, a breath hissing out of me at the slight pain from my missing fingernails. I pull his hard length out and my knees almost give way at how silky he feels in my palm. At how big he is, and how delicious his cock looks.

"Little Bird..." he groans when I wrap my fingers around his length and pump my hand up and down, relishing the piercing pain of his fingers digging into my ripped-up back. "Fuck it."

In the next moment, both of his hands are under my thighs and are hoisting me up so that I have to wrap my legs around his waist. My own arms come back up, hands grasping his shoulders as I steady myself. A keen leaves my lips when he slams me up against the wall next to the door, the pain from my back ricocheting across my entire body and leaving me dizzy.

He pins my body against the wall, as one hand leaves my leg, and I look down to see him lining himself up with my entrance. I'm not quite wet enough, but my eyes roll as he forces his way inside me, inch by thick inch, the burn fucking exquisite. His hand returns to hold me under my thigh, squeezing as he pushes inside me.

"Shit, Little Bird," he rasps out, pushing the last part of his length inside me until our bodies are flush. "Your pussy feels like fucking heaven."

"Less talk, more action, Daddy," I tease him, voice breathless with just how incredible he feels. My whole body feels like it's on fire, the mix of sharp pain from my back and the pleasure of his cock sheathed inside my aching pussy a heady feeling.

It's fucked up. His people—the Tailors—have tortured me for fuck knows how long. I'm broken physically and mentally into small, shattered pieces, lying in a dungeon with a stained mattress on the floor and a bucket to piss in, but this guy, whatever his name is, makes me feel more alive than I have in a long time. Even before I came here.

"You giving me orders now, Little Bird?" he questions, his voice deep and gravelly as he holds still inside me. My pussy walls flutter round him like a moth to a goddamn flame. "Maybe I should leave you now, cunt aching for me to fill it again."

"No!" I clamp around him, my inner muscles squeezing his dick like a vise, and he lets out a grunt. "Please, Daddy. Make me scream your name and come all over your beautiful cock." I feel fraught, even more so than when I was tortured. Having this escape from my current shitty situation makes me beg like I never have before. "Please, Daddy."

He stares into my pleading eyes, his own filled with lust, and something else. Perhaps sorrow or resignation. I don't care if this is a pity fuck though. I'm too desperate for him not to stop, not to leave me so cruelly unfulfilled.

"If I were Aeron, I'd leave," he murmurs. I know who Aeron Taylor is, and pray that I never meet him in the flesh if he's that much of a cunt blocker. "But fuck, you feel too good to stop, princess."

He pulls almost all the way out before slamming my back on the hard, unforgiving concrete. It feels like my entire body is burning, the opposing sensations almost too much. A low moan falls from my parted lips, my eyes closing as I give myself over to him completely. It's something that I've refused to do when other men have taken their pound of flesh. Both here and back at Dead Soldier HQ, but I want to relinquish control with this stranger.

"Look at me, Little Bird. I want to watch you come undone on my cock," he orders, voice strained. My lids obey immediately, snapping open to stare into the hazel depths of his irises. They burn me up from the inside, obliterating me as surely as his hard length pounds into my cunt.

"Daddy, fuck that feels..." I can't even finish my sentence, the pleasure-pain reaching a crescendo until I'm just a being made from it, and everything else melts away.

The dark, dank room.

The fucking drip.

It disappears under the heavy glow of my impending explosion, and I marvel at this thing I've only ever experienced with my own hand a very long time ago.

"Knox," he groans out, a bead of sweat dripping down the side of his temple. I lean in and lick it off, the saltiness bursting on my tongue and making my taste buds tingle. "Say my name when you come, Little Bird."

Unbidden, my mouth forms his name. It leaves my lips like a prayer with every hard, punishing thrust between my thighs until I can no longer form coherent thoughts as I shatter from pleasure instead of just pain this time. A strangled cry echoes around the room as I climax. My inner walls clench and grip him, making him work harder to thrust into me, extending my orgasm until I'm a shuddering, hot mess clinging onto him for dear life.

With a deep, desperate moan, Knox reaches his own peak, biting down hard on my neck and triggering another orgasm to tear through me. I whimper, my throat even more raw than it was before.

"I see you got waylaid," a drawling voice sounds from next to us.

My heart thuds hard in my chest, but the endorphins racing around my body coupled with the way Knox holds me tightly has my initial panic quickly receding.

I languidly turn my head to find startling, ocean-blue eyes staring back at me, filled with amusement and a heavy dose of lust.

Something about them gives me pause and holds me back from falling into their watery depths. I realize with a tremor that underneath the apparent desire there's a coldness, like the fathomless deep where deadly things live. There's a deadness in his stunning, blue orbs that tells me this guy is someone to be wary of.

"Ah, shit," Knox whispers, pulling out of me and gently lowering me down to the ground. A rush of wetness leaves my pussy, our mingled release tracking down my thighs, and looking down, I see it's tinged red with the blood from my back.

"You made the Dove bleed, Knox," the blue-eyed stranger admonishes, but not like he cares much.

When I look back up, I can see that he's excited, like a shark who's caught the scent of blood in the water. His tongue darts out to lick his lower lip as he stares at the mess dripping down my inner thighs, and the move makes my core clench. His pitch-black hair is slicked back, not a strand out of place, and his tailored suit is pristine. He's even got a fucking pocket handkerchief.

I smirk and extend a trembling arm, my back smarting somewhat now that the endorphins are leaving my system in the aftermath of our violent fucking. Taking hold of the square of navy silk that matches his eyes perfectly, I pull it out of his pocket, his cold contemplation never leaving me. Breaking his stare, I look down and use the handkerchief to mop up the bloody cum, folding the fabric up messily once I'm done, and placing it back into his pocket.

"Something for later, Devil Man," I tell him with a wink. The skin around his left eye twitches—*yay twinning!*—but other than that, he gives me no reaction. The heat in his eyes flares, and I'm not sure if it's because of my challenge, or if he plans to wank off over the cum-stained hankie he now owns. "Don't say I never give you anything," I tease, feeling Knox's chest shake with laughter behind me.

"She's fucking funny, right, man?" the blond god says between chuckles, finally stepping back and tucking himself away again.

"A regular comedian," the devil man replies without so much as a twitch of his lips. "Bring her upstairs so the others can meet the Dove."

And with that, he turns on his polished heel and stalks down the dark corridor.

"It's Lark, asswipe! A completely different type of fucking bird!" I hoarsely yell after him, huffing and placing my hands on my hips, ignoring the fire that's taken over my back and making my limbs tremble. "Others?" I question, turning around and looking at Knox with my brows arched into my hairline, feeling a pooling sense of dread mixed with excitement at the word. At the possibilities.

"Yeah, they sent me down to come get you before we got—"

"Way*laid?*" I supply, unable to stop the goofy grin from lifting my lips.

"Yeah. Way*laid*," he replies, emphasizing the last part like I did, which makes me giggle. "Come on."

"Already done that, big boy," I sass him, taking a step and feeling the entire room spin, my vision darkening. *Ah shit.*

I expect the slam of my body onto the concrete floor, my body tensing in preparation, but the pain never comes as I'm wrapped up in cloves and petrol, and lifted into the air before the darkness makes me its bitch and claims me.

CHAPTER TWO

"NUMB" BY CHARLIE HANSON

AERON

My whole body thrums, my fingers itching to grab the handkerchief that's burning a hole in my pocket. I want to bring it to my nose and inhale the scent of Dove mingled with that of my brother.

Well, not my flesh and blood brother, but what the fuck does that matter with all that we've been through?

I leash the urge tightly, gritting my teeth and not letting my hard-won control slip as I walk up the basement stairs with measured steps. My lips tilt upwards when her shout reaches my ears, echoing up the dank staircase.

Stepping out into the vast, converted warehouse space, I roll my shoulders before taking in a deep inhale. It's our main living area and now that we're back from our last job, on behalf of the Tailors, it's up to us to babysit the little Dove. My father has tasked us to try to extract all of her secrets, or more accurately, the secrets of the Dead Soldiers, her own father's gang. My lip curls at the thought of that cunt, my fists clenching at my sides.

We're to get the intel by any means necessary. Though, if the look of her shaking and bleeding body is anything to go by, my father's men have already tried their best with little results. She's a strong Dove, I'll give her that. Not that it matters. I'll break her wings. I always do. It's why father gave her to me when it became apparent neither he nor his men couldn't crack her.

"Knox not with you? Where's the girl?" Tarl asks, swinging his mismatched eyes in my direction. It's always disconcerting being under his scrutiny. It's what makes him a great interrogator, and another reason why my father gave us this job.

"They're on their way. I told him to bring her upstairs," I tell him, looking away from him and towards Jude.

His eyes match that of my own as they land on me. Jude is my flesh and blood, my younger brother. We look very similar; same build, eyes, and dark black hair, though he leaves his to flop all over the place like a fucking hobo and lets a permanent five o'clock shadow grow along his jaw. Also, where I try to at least partially conceal the deadness that lives inside me, he doesn't bother, giving it free rein to rule. Even my father's men are shit scared of him.

"Why didn't you take her to the playroom?" Jude questions, his brow furrowing.

He likes the 'playroom' aka torture room we have downstairs in the basement. I'm guessing after three weeks, Lark—our Dove—is well acquainted with it. His question sits uneasily with me. I'm not sure what prompted me to tell Knox to bring her up here instead. I should have ordered her to be taken there, but I didn't.

"She looked like she needed patching up before we break her again," I tell them, the lie falling from my lips as I stroll over to make myself a coffee. I feel calmer once the deep smell of coffee beans brewing fills the space. "And anyway, she's clearly resistant to physical torture. So I'm thinking we mix in some mental manipulation too."

There, that was clearly my motivation.

"I wanted to have some fun with her," Jude pouts, cleaning his nails with a wicked sharp flip knife, one of his favorites.

"And you will, brother. Just give her a couple of days to heal a little, then you can take her to the playroom," I placate him, inwardly shivering as he grins. Suddenly, I'm not sure I want to leave her in my brother's clutches. He'll get everything she knows out of her, but his toys usually end up broken and bleeding out. It pisses me off that I'm even worried.

Knox steps through the door that leads to the basement, and we all turn to look at him. I'd left the door open, which makes me frown as I'm always careful to close it behind me. Luckily for him, it was open, as he's got a naked, passed-out Lark in his arms, her matted, red hair trailing down towards the floor. There are matching red streaks dripping down the tattooed arm around her upper back and Knox's white T-shirt is stained with crimson where blood from her back paints it.

"What the fuck happened?" I growl out, startled by the flash of anger I feel towards him. *Her being unconscious just messes with my plans, that's all.*

"She passed out, bro. Chillax," he tells me, knowing I hate when he uses that term but using it anyway. *Fucking prick.*

Striding over to the pair, I notice how still Jude and Tarl have become, staring at her naked form with hungry eyes. I can't blame them. We all like our women a bit roughed up. Some of us even crave the sweet blood that spills across white sheets. I know my dick has been hard ever since I watched Knox fuck her up against the wall of her cell, the concrete behind her back stained red from her wounds.

"Where shall I put her?" Knox asks, looking around the space at the low leather sofas and glass dining table.

"Put her in my room," I instruct without thought, taken aback at the suggestion. I was trained from birth not to show emotion, but I can see Jude's lips twitch in my peripheral vision.

"Your room?" Knox questions, his eyes narrowing on me. I can feel my blood boil at the way he holds her just a little bit tighter, like he doesn't trust me.

"That's what I fucking said, didn't I?" I snap back, sticking to my instinctive decision now that I've made it.

"Tarl should check her back. I think some wounds might be infected. She feels pretty hot for being locked in that cold cell for weeks," Knox argues, still not moving to the staircase that leads up to our rooms.

"You sure that's not from where you just fucked her?" I ask, raising a brow at him. A flare of white-hot, furious jealousy flashes through me at the mental image of him buried balls deep inside her whilst she screamed his name like a goddamn prayer to God. His jaw clenches and my lip tilts upwards at having gotten a rise from him.

"Fuck's sake, Aeron, just look at her! She's shivering and burning up all at once," he chastises hotly, my gaze immediately going to the sleeping beauty in his arms and seeing that his words ring true. Her pale skin is flushed all over, which could have been because of the sex, but the shivers and chattering teeth tell me that there's an infection raging through her bloodstream.

"Tarl, come with us," I order, dismissing Knox and this tension that runs between us.

It has been this way for the past several years, ever since June–my sister and Jude's twin–died, both of us unable to get over our blame of the other and our own self-loathing. Doesn't make him any less than my brother. After all, families don't always like each other.

My shoes clack up the metal stairs, and three sets of footsteps sound from behind me, telling me that Jude is tagging along too. Just what we need, for him to become obsessed, which I can tell he will from just a single look at the beautiful creature that now rests in Knox's arms. She's that irresistible mix of strength and vulnerability that we all find hard to resist. He's also not been the same these past few years, the darkness having overtaken him since that fucked up day, but I guess the brutal murder of your twin in front of you will do that to even the most sane person, and Jude was far from sane to begin with.

Pushing open the door to my room, I look over the ordered space with an appreciative eye, making sure all is how I left it several weeks ago. I perfectly made the bed, there is no clutter or trinkets on the desk, and everything is in its rightful place. I cringe as the others follow, my teeth on edge with them in my space, messing it up with their vibrancy.

Knox strides straight over to the bed as Tarl pulls down the covers, and my eye twitches at the mess he's just created. More gently than I ever thought him capable of, Knox lays the little Dove down, turning her so that she's on her stomach and we can see for the first time how ravaged her back really is. Earl's work, by the looks of it.

Even I grimace as I step closer, Jude next to me as we both gaze at the mess of flesh and blood. The skin of some splits is an angry red on either side, demonstrating the first signs of infection.

"Jesus," Tarl mumbles in a low tone, placing his medical bag on the bed next to her. He must have swung past his room to grab it. Knox steps away as Tarl leans closer to inspect the wounds. "There are burns down here too."

My eyes snap down to her lower back, seeing the blisters in the shape of tailoring shears, our cursed gang emblem. My breath catches as I gaze at the angry wound, my still-hard dick twitching at the brand which now marks her as our property.

"She looks so pretty, all bloody. Beautiful, broken bird," Jude says with a sigh, and I realize that he's gone from my side, having moved to the other side of the bed and laid down next to her, brushing her hair from her damp, trembling face.

Crossing my arms over my chest, I watch him, watch the obsession take root like a parasite as he gazes at her like she hung the fucking moon or some shit.

"Don't get too comfy," I tell the room, my brother's eyes never leaving her prone, shuddering form. "We still have a job to do. She has information on the Soldiers, and we need it to take those bastards down once and for all."

"Oh, don't worry about that, brother," Jude coos, a soft whimper leaving our little Dove's lips as he traces a deep cut with his fingertip. "I'll have her singing soon enough. Won't I, my darling Nightingale?" He brings the digit to his lips, sucking the bloody tip with a look of rapture on his face.

I look up to meet the worried gazes of Tarl and Knox, all of us wondering if she'll survive Jude's affection long enough to give us what we need. I fucking hope so. I vowed as I held the cooling corpse of my little sister that I would seek revenge on the Dead Soldiers, those cunts that stole her from this world.

And if I have to make their leader's daughter shatter into a million pieces, pull out all of her feathers one by one, then I will do it with a motherfucking smile on my face.

CHAPTER THREE

"HEY JUDE" BY JOE ANDERSON

LARK

Groaning, I snuggle into the soft cloud that embraces my throbbing body. The fresh scent of clean cotton mixed with an intoxicating mix of amber, sandalwood, and vanilla surrounds me and makes me want to never leave this haven. I rub my face in it, practically purring as it fills my senses.

"You like the way my brother smells, pretty broken bird?" a voice asks from next to me. I pause in my movements, slowly turning my head to see a black-haired god in bed next to me. He looks familiar, but my brain feels a little fuzzy and I just can't place him.

My eyes take him in like the tall fucking drink of water that he is. Well, I assume he's tall, given that I have to look up to catch his deep blue gaze. What I see in his orbs gives me pause though. There's nothing in their depths at all. His face might smile with amusement, but his eyes are dead, empty pits that look upon the world dispassionately. A shiver cascades over my body, my skin tingling with warning mixed in with strong desire that again surprises me in its intensity.

"Your brother?" I question, my voice cracking as my throat is dry as a motherfucking desert.

He reaches behind him, giving me a view of his naked back—*is he in the buff?!* I stifle a gasp as I take in the furrows and valleys that make up the skin there. Without thinking, my hand darts out, my fingers caressing one of the deeper scars that slices his back in two. He shudders, a small yet deep sound coming from him that makes my core ache. *Greedy bitch.*

"We match, you and I, broken bird," he says, turning back to me so that I can see his defined torso, the sheet having fallen down to his lap. His body is a mix of ink and scars. Curiouser and curiouser, and yep, looks like he's naked as the day that he was born. Not that I'm objecting to the view, though I wonder why he's in my bed and what may have happened whilst I was out. I'm not objectionable to a bit of consensual somnophilia, but a girl likes to experience if she's been fucked seven ways' til Sunday by a god, at least the first time. I don't think I was that lucky, the place between my thighs only slightly tender from fucking Knox but no more so than that. "And yes, my brother. I believe you met him yesterday when Knox was balls deep inside your pretty cunt," he continues, and my eyebrows rise as the memories flood back. I wiggle my backside as the ache in my sex makes a little more sense, a dull pain flaring across my back at the movement.

"Ah, yes, tall, dark-haired dude with a pocket handkerchief?" I question, smirking when I remember what I did to that piece of cloth.

"Bingo, birdie," he replies, holding out one of those reusable, metal bottles with a straw cap.

Lifting my head slightly, I take the straw in my mouth and suck, holding his gaze. It hurts like a bitch, but I'm too damn thirsty to care. A flicker of heat warms his blue eyes as he watches me drink, taking the bottle away when I stop.

"You can be Baby Devil then. You know, seeing as you're clearly younger than him," I inform him, looking at his boyish face and deciding that he's more my age than that of the two guys I met in the basement, Knox and his brother, who seemed older. Speaking of... "Where the fuck am I?"

"The Devil's lair, my Nightingale," he tells me with no emotion in his tone. "Or my brother's room. He insisted we brought you here to recover before we break you again." His own hand reaches out and traces my fresh wounds, a hiss leaving my lips at the contact as I flinch from his touch. Of course, my pussy clenches, reminding me of the pain from Knox fucking me while my back was rubbed raw against the wall of the cell.

"Why bother?" I ask, brows furrowed in a mix of confusion and pain as he keeps stroking my ravaged back, my hands digging into the soft as a fucking cloud mattress beneath me. "Why let me heal first?"

"All the better to hurt you later, Nightingale," he answers in that timeless voice. There's a gleam in his blue eyes, a quickness to his breath as he studies my wounds, lapping up my pained movements and gasps. The fucking psycho even gets a hard-on, the sheet tenting in his lap.

"You just like giving pain, Baby Devil? Or you enjoy receiving too?" I question, nodding to the admittedly large chubbie that's trying to make a bid for freedom.

"Both," he replies, his other hand tracing some scars just above his hip bone. The sheet slips further, his erect dick springing free, and my eyes bug as both my mouth and pussy water. Metal glints on the end and along the underside, creating the holy grail of dick piercings; a Jacob's motherfucking ladder ending in a magic cross.

"Don't hold back on my account," I inform him, my voice breathy as my heart pounds in time to the pulse in my lower lips.

"Tarl will be mad if I break you open again," he pouts, grabbing his shaft anyway and fisting it, pumping up and down until pre-cum glistens on the tip. My tongue darts out, desperate for a taste even though I'm lying prone with my back all kinds of fucked up. Escapism at its finest.

"I won't tell if you don't," I whisper huskily, wiggling a hand underneath me, my fingers hitting the jackpot as my slicked-up clit meets them.

A sharp pain in my back makes me groan as my pussy floods with excitement and my eyes flutter. I don't close them completely, watching my devil boy as he pumps his shaft, delicious noises falling from his fuckable lips as he zeros in on what my hand is doing, before flicking back up to my back. His finger pushes deeper into my back, another sharp pain sending fire racing across my skin as my fingers strum a quick rhythm on my engorged bud.

"Naughty little broken bird," he rasps out as another moan leaves my lips, bliss fluttering at the edges of my vision in kaleidoscopes of colors.

Looking up, his face is a mask of exquisite torture, his gaze fixed on my back, which, if the warmth seeping down my side is any sign, is currently bleeding. I watch enraptured as he brings a bloodied finger up to his plush lips, his eyes rolling back as his tongue flicks out and licks the crimson off, a deep animal sound of pleasure rumbling out of his chest.

My orgasm takes me by surprise, exploding over me like I dipped my finger into an electric current, and my whole body goes rigid as I cry out. My eyes flutter shut as wave upon wave of pleasure rolls over me, obliterating the pain from my wounds, as well as the fact that I'm being held against my will because of my shitty last name and a rivalry that started before I was even born.

The bed shifts beneath me, and I crack my eyes open to see devil boy up on his knees, his dick clutched in bloody fingers as he tugs at it with a furious intensity. Spellbound and unable to look away, I watch as he throws his head back, his own body going rigid and his member going rock-solid before spurts of creamy cum shoot out of him. I jerk a little as they hit my back, the slight sting not unpleasant though given all the endorphins running through me at the moment. The sight and feel of him coming all over me triggers another rush of wetness to pool out of me, a gasp leaving my lips as a second climax rips through me.

Moments pass, both of our panting breaths loud in the room's silence. The mattress moves again, and I open a single lid to watch my Baby Devil walk away, the sound of water running reaching my ears seconds later. He appears back in my line of sight, his naked body a masterpiece of pain and beauty, the entirety of his skin covered in stunning, black images and white scarring.

I clench my teeth when he cleans my back with a wet cloth, the cool flannel soothing at the same time as it stings.

"What's your name, Baby Devil?" I ask through gritted teeth as he makes another swipe.

"Jude," he answers, the wet sound of the cloth hitting the carpet rings out as he drops it, clearly having finished his task. I feel the warmth of his breath fan over the skin along my spine before the soft caress of his tongue. Holy fuck, he's licking my blood off my back, and I shiver with the realisation. *Why is that so fucking hot?*

"Thank you, Jude," I murmur, my breath stuttering with another swipe of his tongue. I'm a little unsure if I'm thanking him for the orgasm or the cleanup, but either way, a good job always deserves to be praised, I think.

"Oh, don't thank me, Nightingale. I haven't started breaking you yet."

"I WANNA BE YOURS" BY ARCTIC MONKEYS

JUDE

I watch with delight as my little Nightingale widens her eyes, the traces of languid pleasure dissipating as fear enters her emerald depths. I eat it up, relishing the heady feeling of power that I get from her terror.

She shows no other signs of fright, her breathing even and the tremble gone from her limbs. Such a beautiful, brave bird.

"You need to eat!" I declare, and this time she does flinch, then winces in pain. Fucking exquisite. "I'm going to get you some food, my little Nightingale, and you'll eat it all up like a good little pet, won't you?" My eyes narrow in a hard glare, and she just nods, a bemused look on her beautiful, pale face. "I knew you would," I praise, placing a gentle kiss on her forehead before heading out of the room.

Jogging down the stairs, I whistle the tune to "Part of Your World," my Nightingale reminding me of that sexy, red-headed mermaid.

"Please tell me you didn't fucking sleep naked next to her?" Aeron's exasperated voice sounds to my right, and I glance over to see him pinching the bridge of his nose, his eyes closed in frustration. My lips tilt upwards in a Cheshire Cat grin.

"Of course I fucking did," I reply, tsking and rolling my eyes at his stupid question. "Where else was I going to sleep? And you know I don't like PJs."

"It's my fucking bed, Jude!" Aeron shouts, rising from his seat at the dining table, his glare focused on me. His laptop sits on the glass tabletop, his phone placed next to it, but it's the way his cheeks flush that really captures my attention. Interesting that my Nightingale has already ensnared him. I enjoy seeing him ruffled.

"You could have joined us, brother. I don't mind," I tell him reasonably, my grin growing wider as his left eye twitches. Dismissing him, I turn and head towards the kitchen area, thinking about something to make for her to eat. "Eggs are too messy, something that I can feed her, I think..." I say aloud, opening the fridge and looking at the contents.

"What are you doing?" Aeron asks me, coming up behind me, annoyance still clear in his tone.

"Do you think chicken ramen? Or maybe some Bellinis?" I question, turning back to see the perplexed look on his face, and chuckling. "No, you're right, we need something we can feed her bite-sized pieces of so she has to wrap her lips around my fingers."

"What the fuck are you talking about, Jude?" He leans over and slams the fridge door shut with enough force to rattle the bottles inside. I don't jump though, nothing much frightens me anymore, not since June. I briefly wonder where the others are, then dismiss them as I look at my brother.

"Nightingale needs feeding, brother mine. You said we need to take care of her," I remind him, trying to think of something to give her.

"So you decided you were going to feed her in my fucking bed?" he asks, and I can practically see the grinding of his teeth. It makes me smile. I knew he liked her, he wouldn't be this annoyed if he didn't.

"Well, she can't exactly get up right now, can she, silly?" I chuckle, then click my fingers as the perfect idea springs to mind. "Pancakes!" I shout, opening the fridge and grabbing out the milk, then pushing past my older brother to grab the other ingredients. He stumbles back, and I just know that he's glaring at me. The thought makes me cackle softly under my breath.

"You're going to feed her fucking pancakes? In. My. Bed?" he growls, and it's just too funny that I can so easily wind him up, thoughts of the mess we might make fucking with his OCD. I hope he explodes.

"Yep," I reply, mixing the batter and heating the pan on the stove.

"With all the trimmings; maple syrup, Nutella, golden syrup, strawberries..." I trail off, thinking about the other combinations. I bet my Nightingale has a sweet tooth.

I glance over to Aeron, biting my lips to keep my laugh from spilling out. He looks ready to burst, his face all flushed, and I swear the vein in his head is throbbing triple time.

"And how, pray tell, are you going to feed her pancakes covered in syrup in my fucking bed without making a mess?" His voice is deadly calm, his body statue still, both signs any normal person would take to run the fuck away. Luckily, I'm far from normal.

"Easy," I answer, pouring some of the batter into the hot pan to create the first pancake. "I'll make sure any drips land on my cock so she can lick them off with her delightful tongue."

I flip the pancake, grinning like a loon at the growl behind me before catching it in the pan and placing it back on the hob, then stepping away towards the cupboard to grab a plate.

"Oh, for fuck sake, Jude! Point that shit away from me!" Aeron grunts out, and I look down to see I'm standing to rigid attention. The thought of my Nightingale wrapping those red lips around my shaft was enough to make it hard as granite.

"You could always help me out here, bro," I suggest, looking up at him with a tilt of my lips to see what he makes of my baiting. His upper lip curls and I let loose a chuckle.

"I'm not into that incest shit, Jude," he sneers.

"No kink-shaming, Aeron. It's not friendly," I chastise, placing the cooked pancake onto the plate and pouring another measure of batter into the hot pan. "And anyway, I don't really see the difference if we're both fucking her at the same time. Especially if we're in that delicious pussy of hers together," I muse aloud, my dick bobbing at the thought. A hand grabs me and spins me around, and I can feel my teeth show as my smile widens.

"No one is fucking her," he seethes, panting hard, which just makes me smile wider.

"Sure thing, *boss*," I reply, poking him with my still-hard cock, and he leaps back. He doesn't give a shit if I walk around naked, but I guess he draws the line at me touching him with my dick. And they say I have issues.

I hum the "Bare Necessities" as I assemble my Nightingale's pancakes, adding chopped strawberries and lots of syrup.

"I fucking mean it, Jude. No attachments to this one. Remember, she's a Soldier. Remember what they took from us." His voice is hard and unyielding.

I pause on my way past him, sweet tendrils of black rage swirling inside me like smoke from a gun barrel.

"I remember every fucking day, brother," I reply, my voice sharp like my flip knife.

His hand lands on my shoulder, squeezing gently as we share our pain. The pain of June's death was like an infected wound, seeping pus and blood. Taking a deep breath, I shake my head, as if that'll help rid me of the sticky feeling of rage that lives within my soul.

Without saying another thing, I step away from him, taking my Nightingale her food. Something about her makes me want to take care of her, to treasure her like the beautiful bird that she is. I don't care that she's my enemy and that her shit of a father is responsible for the other half of me dying five years ago, but I will break her. It's all that I'm good for now, after all.

Ironic that I called her broken when she's far more complete than I'll ever be.

CHAPTER FOUR

"BAD BOYS" BY AZEE

LARK

I drag myself up and shuffle towards the bathroom to pee and clean up a little after that wake-up call. *Jesus*. That boy is fucking trouble, mark my words, but fuck if I don't want to buy what he's selling, even if we're sworn enemies.

Keep your head on straight, Lark! It's fine to get a few kicks, but remember, the goal is to escape this shithole.

By the time Jude returns—still gloriously naked and sporting another massive erection—I'm half propped up in bed and wondering why my back doesn't hurt as much as it did yesterday and why I don't feel quite as shit.

"Nightingale, you moved," he pouts, and the sweet aroma of pancakes makes my mouth water. He strolls towards me like a jungle cat, the dead madness shining clear in his ocean eyes, and don't ask me how something can look dead and mad at once. He just pulls off that kind of vibe.

"I needed to piss," I inform him primly, his maniacal grin going wider at my crude words.

"Careful, Nightingale, talk like that will only turn me on," he replies, climbing onto the bed next to me and setting the plate between us.

"You into water sports, devil boy?" I query, reaching for the plate, only to yelp when he slaps my hand away.

"I'm into a lot of things, Nightingale." His voice drops, and I notice his shaft getting harder as I watch, my mouth watering now for an entirely different reason. My tongue darts out to lick my lips, and I wonder why these guys have affected me like this when all the others before them just leave me feeling numb.

"Why can't you people get my name right, huh?" I ask, deflecting the tension and unease which sticks to me like sweat on a breezeless summer's day, my skin tight and itchy. "It's Lark. A nightingale is a different type of bird."

"Ah," he starts, picking up an already cut piece of pancake and letting the syrup drip down his fingers. I track the moving liquid, my core tightening. *Fuck's sake.* "But I'm going to make you sing like a nightingale, my little songbird. Just as soon as you're healed." He holds out the piece of pancake, hovering it just above my lips. A shiver cascades down my body, my nipples peaking at his words. I can't tell whether I'm more scared or...excited?

A drop of sticky, golden yumminess falls onto my breast, my eyes darting down to watch its path as I swallow his words with a lump in my throat. I believe him; you don't get far in the life I'm in without hearing Jude Taylor's name whispered with terror and fear. It's just a case of whether I'm strong enough to hold out.

"Eat up, precious," he insists, and I swing my gaze back up to his, taking a final deep inhale as I open my mouth and let him place the morsel on my tongue. The sweet taste has my eyelids drifting closed, a low moan falling from my lips as strawberry and sugar fills my mouth. I gasp when a warm tongue laps at my breast, and I open my eyes, looking down to see Jude licking the syrup off. "Fucking delicious," he mumbles, straightening up and picking up another piece in his still-dripping fingers. "More." I follow his instruction, and soon we're both sticky and panting as the heat between us flares, the room feeling like a sauna. Jude looks at me, a frown marring his brow. "Aeron said that I'm not allowed to fuck you," he tells me with another very cute pout.

"You always do what he says?" I ask, a hint of challenge in my tone. His face hardens, and my heart beats wildly as I get a glimpse at the Tailor boy who strikes fear in grown-ass men's hearts.

"No," he says, setting the plate on the side table and crawling over to me on his hands and knees until he's hovering above me, his thick, pierced shaft millimeters away from where I want it. "But I will not play with you yet, Nightingale," he whispers, nuzzling the side of my neck, a full body shudder making my skin pebble. "Not until you're tied up and bleeding. Then I might."

He gives me one last lick, pushes up, and walks from the room, hard-on and all.

What the actual fuck have I got myself into?

I fall asleep not long after that, even with Jude's ominous words caressing my ears. My dreams are filled with dark-haired boys making me bleed and come in equal measure, and I wake up with feverish skin and a sharp ache between my thighs.

I half gasp, half moan when a cool soothingness flows across my back, bringing me to consciousness and when I crane my neck, I see mismatched eyes staring intently at my exposed body. I take a sharp inhale, my body frozen as I watch his face cast in the gentle, yellow glow of the lamp beside me, his skin glossy and the color of my favorite caramel hot chocolate. It must be dark again. The curtains are closed, and I can't see any light filtering round the edges. Saying that, what the fuck do I know? Aeron might just have fantastic fucking blackout blinds.

I remain still, a hiss of pain whistling through my teeth when he passes a really fucking sore spot, probably one of the deeper lashes, and suddenly I'm trapped in this beautiful monster's intense gaze. I'm fascinated by them, the sharp, pale blue in contrast to the deep jade green.

"I'm sorry if I hurt you," he tells me, his voice a delicious purr that leaves my toes curling. He has the hint of an accent, Middle Eastern perhaps, that makes his tone caress like smoke from the finest marijuana.

"That's okay," I reply in a breathy whisper, cursing the Tailors and their porn star genetics. I'm not sure why I'm trying to reassure him. It was his gang who tortured me, after all, and Jude has made no bones about the fact that at least he plans to hurt me again. "What's your name then, handsome?"

There's a slight twitch of his lips, the barest of smiles, but it's gone in the next blink.

"Tarl."

And fuck me seven ways' til Sunday. The way his name slips from his lips is fucking sinful. It winds around me in a sinuous whisper, heating my skin and slicking my core. *Why the fuck am I panting for these men?* My captors? I mean, I know I'm a horny bitch, but I never get this worked up. Must be Stockholm Syndrome. Though I guess normally it's less of a choice, which is always a mood killer. We learn to deal with the hand we're given or some shit.

"You been drugging me up, Tarl?" I ask, my voice repeating his name in a brush of sound, elongating the syllable. A slight clench of his jaw and a flaring of nostrils is my only sign that maybe, just maybe, he likes his name on my lips.

"Just to take the edge off, pretty bird," he murmurs after a moment, again with that fractional tilt of his lips on his face.

"The good shit, yeah? I don't want no second-rate narcotics," I sass back, kind of grateful that he has been giving me something to help with the pain. I know, how fucked up is my life when I'm grateful to my captors for giving me drugs to ease the pain they created? It's more than my father has ever done, that's for fucking sure.

I earn another mouth twitch, and I'd pump my fist if it wouldn't hurt so damn much. I feel that Tarl gives out smiles as rarely as a teenage boy finding your clit.

"Only the best for our pretty little bird," he tells me, stepping back and gathering up bits of bloody cotton wool and placing them in a plastic bag before snapping off latex gloves, the sound sharp in the quiet room.

"Our bird?" I repeat with an eyebrow raised and a tilt to my own lips. He turns that intense gaze back to me, laughter dancing in the depths of his eyes.

"You belong to the Tailor boys now, beautiful," he informs me, stepping up to where my head is and crouching down, his face level with mine. "All of this pretty flesh is ours to play with. Worship. Destroy. To do with as we please."

A tremble takes over my entire body, and as with Jude, I don't know if it's from terror...or sweet anticipation.

The next week passes much the same, Jude feeding me whilst Tarl tends to my wounds. Apparently, I'm not allowed a shower—Dr Tarl's orders—so Jude takes one for the team and gives me a sponge bed bath, mostly leaving the bed wet and the place between my legs dripping and not with just water.

He refuses to ease the ache he creates there, and I don't see Knox at all. Jude laughs and tells me that Aeron is punishing Knox with blue balls after sinking balls deep inside me when he was meant to be collecting me. *Fucking cuntblocker.*

I don't see the stoic leader of their band of cunt teases at all during the next seven days. Well, apart from one night when I wake up from another of my usual nightmares, panting and the pillow damp with tears that I refuse to let escape when I'm awake. I'm shaking all over. I haven't had a dream this bad since being in Aeron's bed. In the basement, sure, but ever since I landed in this bed, my dreams have been filled with pleasant demons with dark hair, sexy smiles, and mismatched or ocean eyes.

Still gasping, I push up to sit on the bed, untangling my legs from the damp, sweat-soaked sheets, and come to a complete standstill as I lock gazes with devil man Aeron himself. My chest heaves as we stare at each other in the faint light of dawn, the weak sunshine filtering around the edges of his curtains.

"Who hurts you in your dreams, Dove?" he asks, his voice a violent whisper. The skin around my nipples puckers with the sound. Yep, I'm still naked. Jude laughed when I asked for clothes. *Fucking pervert.*

"Too many men to keep track of," I answer truthfully, bringing my knees up to my chest and wrapping my arms around them. I ignore the sharp tug on my back, the bite of pain somehow a comfort. The lashes are still healing, though they've mostly closed up now. I don't know what makes me answer him so truthfully. After all, he's going to be one of those men before my time here is done.

I swear the skin around his eyes tightens, but it's hard to tell as he's wreathed in shadows. They cling to him like spectators, perhaps the ghosts of all those he's killed before.

"You're safe here," he replies after a time, his husky voice smoky and smooth, like velvet from the pillow that smothers you to death.

"For how long?" I question, not expecting an answer, just stating a simple truth.

"Go back to sleep, Dove," he instructs quietly, and we both know that my time of healing is drawing to a close.

I've had men tell me what to do my whole shitty life, so perhaps that's why I obey him and settle back down. Or maybe it's that my chest feels less tight knowing that he's there, watching, scaring away all the monsters that try to claim me in the dark. Stupid fucking thought, I know. He's the biggest monster I've met so far. You can tell by the deadened look in his deep blue eyes that he tries so desperately to hide.

I sleep peacefully for the rest of the early hours, waking up to bright sunshine and Jude bringing me eggs and bacon for breakfast. He makes me eat off of his chiseled abs, drowning them in maple syrup, and once I'm done, he pours the sticky, dark syrup onto my pussy and indulges in some breakfast of his own, finally easing the ache that he's been building over the past few days.

Best fucking way to wake up ever.

CHAPTER FIVE

"SCARS" BY BOY EPIC

KNOX

Fucking Aeron, grumpy motherfucker. You stick your dick in one prisoner and get stuck with all the worst fucking jobs, not allowed to even see the alluring bird.

Fuck, what was I meant to do? I'm a hot-blooded male, after all.

In the chilled fall air, I rub my hands together, my stomach rumbling as I skulk in the shadows opposite a bar owned by the Dead Soldiers. I'm waiting for two of their guys to come out. I think about the way Lark looked at me last night, like I was her favorite snack, and well, I'd defy any man to ignore that invitation. Shit, even cold man Aeron couldn't keep his eyes off her, hoarding her in his room like a miserly dragon. *Fucking asshole.*

God, that woman. Even in her pain, she was hotter than the fucking sun. Maybe more so because of her agony, her warm blood running as hot as the inside of her pussy that gripped my dick in a chokehold. Just the thought of her naked body wrapped around me has me semi-hard, the cool air around me not so cold anymore.

Movement across the street has me snapping out of my daydream as two gangbangers get into their muscle car and drive away. I make a note of the time, cursing out Aeron for making me miss lunch as I stomp through the trees and back to my matte black, Indian Scout.

I give her an appreciative smile, running my palm across her pristine paintwork before swinging my leg over and lifting the kick-stand with my foot. Pausing, the image of an auburn-haired beauty draped across my lap riding me flashes across my vision, making my dick go fully hard in my black jeans.

Fucking hell, I've got it bad for that chick, my little bird.

With a self-deprecating laugh, I gun the throttle and get out of there like a bat out of hell, wondering if Aeron will allow me to see the fiery-haired beauty anytime soon.

✂

S talking into the warehouse, I stall as Jude comes sauntering down the stairs, wearing purple fucking velvet pants and looking too fucking pleased with himself. My eyes narrow. He catches me watching him, gives me a wink, and then strolls over to the sink and grabs a cloth. Strolling over to him, I shed my leather jacket and drape it over the back of a dining chair, my forehead wrinkling as he begins to clean his abs.

"What the fuck you doing?" I ask, grabbing a glass from the cupboard and going over to the fridge to get out the juice, and hopefully something to eat. I wouldn't bother with the glass, just to fuck with Aeron, but he's angry enough with me as it is. *Jealous bastard.*

"Nightingale missed a spot when she was licking off her lunch,"

Jude tells me matter-of-factly, missing the fact that I'm rooted to the fucking spot, mouth agape as I stare at him.

"What did you just say?" I ask through clenched teeth, my fingers tightening on the carton, the sound of the plastic popping loud and sharp in the silence of the room. He looks up at me with that unnerving deep blue gaze of his, though I could swear it's less, well, dead than it was before Lark arrived.

"I made Nightingale lunch, and then she ate it off me," he informs me before throwing the cloth into the sink which admittedly makes my lips twitch upwards as that's the kind of shit that drives Aeron wild. "Do you want to eat lunch off me too, Knox baby?" he asks, stalking towards me and running a hand down my torso. I feel his touch through my T-shirt, and my breath catches in my chest. I swear he's been trying to get into my pants for years, even while I was dating June, so it's not unexpected, but it's getting harder to deny my...curiosity.

"Fuck off," I reply on a forced laugh, tension easing from my shoulders at his comically wounded look. I pour myself a glass of OJ, then put the carton back in the fridge. "You and Tarl can keep your dick play, thanks."

"But you have such a beautiful cock," he whines while pouting, and I can't tell if he's serious or not. Probably is, knowing Jude, though when he would have seen it is anyone's guess.

"Is my cock not beautiful enough for you?" Tarl asks, his tone firm, and like the good little sub Jude is, he saunters over to him and palms Tarl's dick over his jeans. Tarl stands there, his stare fixed on me as Jude fawns over him. It's not unfriendly, more challenging if I had to guess, but he didn't earn the name The Inquisitor for being easy to read.

"You have a wonderful weapon, babe," Jude coos, then looks over his shoulder at me, batting those long lashes of his. "But don't tell me you wouldn't want to have a little fun with Knox's purple-headed pork sword?"

Juice sputters over the countertop as I choke at Jude's description of my dick.

"Fucking hell, Jude," I rasp, thumping my chest as I try to breathe, tasting orange in my fucking lungs.

Tarl's mismatched eyes meet mine as he stares at me, his gaze slowly perusing my body before coming back up to my face, my fist dropping away to my side. I let him look his fill. I don't give a shit if he or anyone else wants to check me out, regardless of their gender, but while I don't care if he wants to suck my dick, I don't want to return the favor.

Tarl just shrugs as if to say your loss, then grabs the back of Jude's head, tangling his fingers in the other man's hair, and pulling his lips into a heated kiss. I watch as Jude melts into Tarl, giving over to him completely, just like the way Lark gave into me, sinking into my caresses.

"You taste like her scent," Tarl murmurs, loud enough for me to hear, and a slight rumble sounds in the back of my throat. Looks like Aeron isn't the only jealous bastard around here.

Jude giggles, like honest to fuck giggles, and I swear, somewhere, a newborn is crying at the sound. "Aeron said I couldn't fuck her like Knox did," he replies, my lips flattening as heat flushes through me. "But he said nothing about licking."

"Enough," I growl, attempting to loosen my tightened jaw.

"If only you'd let me help with those big ole, blue balls of yours." Jude sighs like I'm a fucking naughty child, and I swear to fuck that I take a step forward, ready to punch that smirk off his pretty boy face. Maybe my little bird would like him less with a broken nose.

"Dad just called," Aeron declares, storming into the room like a fucking thundercloud, tucking his phone into his suit jacket pocket. He completely misses the tension rolling off of me, but his lips tighten when he notices the damp cloth in the sink. *Fucking jackass.* "He wants progress with our pretty captive. We start tonight."

And just like a bucket of ice-cold water being thrown over me, all jealousy washes away to be replaced with something uncomfortable, like a lump in your throat. I glance over to Jude and Tarl and see them staring at Aeron, their faces blank, though Jude has an excited gleam in his eyes.

"I won't beat her," I grit out in the quiet room, and three sets of eyes swing my way, but I don't back down. "I don't hurt women or children," I state, my chin lifted as I stare at Aeron. I'm usually the one that goes in first with fists flying, breaking bones and faces until our captives talk to end the pain, or Tarl steps in, but not this time.

"One taste and her gash is making you soft, Knox?" Aeron questions, one dark brow lifted, but the fucker knows he won't get a rise from me, and I know that he's not asking any of us to hurt her like that. We may be gangbangers, but even we have lines we refuse to cross.

I stay silent, holding his icy stare until he lets out a sigh, pinching the bridge of his nose.

"I have other ways to make the canary sing," he tells us as he looks back up, and a shiver runs through me at the sparkle in his blue orbs. I'd be lying if I said I didn't feel a matching rush in my own limbs. We may have lines, but we're still fucked-up bastards, and there's something intoxicating about making that beautiful woman submit to us.

The doorbell rings and Jude claps with a squeal as he rushes over to answer it. The rest of us look at him with matching frowns, but my eyebrows soon go up into my hairline when he wheels in his latest purchase.

"Let the fun begin," he declares with a manic gleam in his eyes, practically hopping from foot to foot, and the fucked-up man that I am, my lips lift into a grin as I contemplate all the ways that we will make my little bird tell us her secrets.

I just know that she will sing beautifully.

✂

"PANIC ROOM - ACOUSTIC" BY AU/RA

LARK

Gazing out of the window in Aeron's bedroom at the night sky, the lights of the city below replace the stars that are all but hidden above. I chuckle to myself whilst imagining the stars falling from the sky and landing here, their glorious, celestial light being gobbled up by the sin and depravity that lurks in Whetstone, Colorado.

The door opens behind me, but I don't turn around, knowing that the day of reckoning has finally arrived. I'm healed enough to be broken again.

Heat engulfs my back, the intoxicating mix of clean cotton, amber, sandalwood, and vanilla smell of Aeron Taylor wrapping around me and ensnaring my senses. Strong, warm hands alight on my naked shoulders and a shudder runs through my whole body at his featherlight touch.

I've just released a lust-filled sigh when a warm, minty breath caresses my cheek moments before lips brush my ear and my nipples pebble to hardened nubs.

"Time to go, Dove." His voice is dark and unemotional, and yet it seeps into me and devastates me all the same. I swallow painfully, like I've tried to eat too much in one go, and give a small nod, turning around, his hands falling from my shoulders. He doesn't step back, doesn't move at all, his face limned in the city lights behind me as he stands so close that I can feel the brush of his suit jacket. He takes me in, his eyes devouring my nakedness; from my puckered nipples to my hot pussy. One of his hands reaches out, his fingers trailing along the side of my face, his own expression remaining hard and unyielding. "I'd be lying if I said that I won't enjoy hurting you, Dove," he confesses softly, his thumb running along my bottom lip.

"I'd be lying if I said that I won't enjoy it," I reply, his nostrils flaring at my words.

My chest rises and falls rapidly, my skin tingling at his nearness, his touch confusing me. I shouldn't want him, and yet there's something about him that makes me feel alive, and not in a state of suspended death like I have been for the past ten years.

We stand there, Aeron looking at me like he wants to devour my very essence. It wouldn't be much of a feast for him, shriveled and tainted as it is, but a part of me—a large fucking part, if I'm being totally honest—wants him too. I want him to take all of my ruin and make it his own.

"Come on," he murmurs after a time, his hand falling from my face and shocking the absolute shit out of me by tangling it with my own, leading me out of the room.

"Do I get any clothes?" I ask, trying to calm my racing heart as we head down the mezzanine level towards some metal stairs. It's the first time I've left the room, and I try to absorb my surroundings as much as possible.

It's a warehouse conversion by the looks of it with lots of metal beams and exposed brickwork. I find comfort in its openness. Its space.

"Not until you earn them," Aeron answers in that same monotone voice, not letting go of my hand as he leads me down the stairs and back to that fucking basement door.

My steps falter then, and I hate myself for showing even that small glimpse of fear. I grew up in the Dead Soldiers with my sadist father. I shouldn't be afraid of anything anymore, but yeah, I guess heading back into a torture chamber is not on my list of Friday night fun things to do.

Aeron steadies me with his other hand on my waist, his face filling my vision, and suddenly I'm drowning in his ocean eyes. He holds me captive, his hand on my body tightening marginally, my breath catching at the move.

In another mind-blowing gesture, he leans down and brushes his lips over mine in the ghost of a kiss. My breath completely stills in my chest as my eyes automatically close. I hold immobile as his soft lips feather over mine, and whilst my brain curses me out for not fighting like a fucking banshee, my cunt seems to be in charge as it pulses and holds us still for him.

"Ready, Dove?" he asks softly, his lips again brushing mine in a whisper.

"Yes." I sigh, hearing the lie in my shaking voice. Of course I'm not fucking ready. What kind of mentalist would be ready for torture?

"Good girl," he says back in a soft, dark tone, and fuck me seven ways, that praise does things to my core that it shouldn't.

After a beat, he steps back and turns towards the door again, taking my hand once more as he leads me towards it. Opening the door, he takes us through it, and my skin instantly prickles with a mixture of the cold and the dank, coppery smell that hits my nose.

Heart pounding, we make our way down the steps, my feet quickly becoming chilled on the freezing concrete. My fingers involuntarily tighten in Aeron's, but he doesn't complain or let go as we reach the bottom. Instead, he leads me to a room that will definitely haunt my nightmares for years to come.

The nondescript door opens when we approach, and I'm surprised to see the soft flicker of candlelight in the room where my back was ripped to shreds, my fingernails torn off, and my skin branded with the Tailors' insignia.

"Good evening, Nightingale," Jude coos, skipping right up to me, grabbing my head in his palms, and slamming his lips onto mine.

I'm so worked up and all over the fucking place that I don't think, just react, as I melt into the kiss, a deep, pussy-melting groan sounding low in his throat as I step into him, one hand still clutching

Aeron's as the other comes to rest on Jude's bare chest. My naked breasts press against his hot body, the heat of him warming my chilled one. He claims my mouth as his, branding me as effectively as those other gangbangers did with their burning metal, and I fucking love it.

I've never enjoyed being kissed, mostly because someone forcing slug-like lips onto mine whilst they take what is not theirs kind of turns a girl off, you know?

But Jude's kiss is like him, full of fun and madness. I want to die here, with his lips on mine. *Fuck, Lark! Snap the fuck out of it!*

He pulls away with a shit-eating grin and reaches down to adjust his very obvious hard-on in his purple velvet pants.

"Missed you, Nightingale," he says, then practically bounces on his bare toes. "I bought you a gift."

He steps aside and all the warmth he just gave me drains from my body, leaving me quivering as I try to make sense of what's in front of me. My eyes trace over the hard, sparkling panes of glass and gold filigree that make up a...coffin.

"A coffin?" I whisper, rooted to the spot as Jude bounces over to it and whips out a fucking handkerchief to polish the glass.

"Isn't it beautiful?" he asks reverently, his eyes shining in the candlelight. Dripping candles surround the coffin, some on tall holders, some in old wine bottles, and some just on the floor, wax pooling underneath them. "Come see, I had it engraved for you."

Aeron tugs my hand, and I realize with a start that he didn't let go the whole time Jude kissed me. Stumbling, my feet follow his lead, and as we approach the coffin—*my* fucking coffin—I see that the glass on the top is etched in swirling script.

Nightingale.

Icy dread shivers down my spine.

"I'm not getting into a fucking coffin," I snap out, my voice shaking as my body trembles.

"You don't like it?" Jude questions, his brow furrowed and low like I've just refused a wonderful gift.

"It's a fucking coffin!" I shout, flinging out my arm to indicate the glass box. "How am I meant to even breathe in there?"

"It's actually quite clever," Jude answers, ignoring my outburst and pointing to the filigree decoration. "There are air holes all along here. I had it made especially for you, Nightingale."

"You're fucking crazy," I say, tugging my hand free of Aeron's and stepping back, immediately hitting a hard body behind me. Firm hands wrap around my biceps and try as I might, I just can't break free.

I won't go into that fucking box.

"Calm down, Little Bird," Knox's deep voice sounds in my ear as the man himself pushes me towards the coffin, Aeron opening the lid.

"Fucking traitor cunt!" I seethe, my bare feet slipping on the cold floor as he pushes me closer. "You didn't deserve my pussy."

"I know, Little Bird," he mumbles back, but I barely notice his broken tone as I flail and try to get out of his grip. It's fucking useless, he's too strong and I'm too fucking weak. The story of my shitty life.

"I could give her something to calm her down," Tarl's soft voice suggests, and my head whips around to see him step forward with a fucking syringe.

"No!" I shout, fear coating my tongue as I immediately cease my struggles. I don't want to go into the coffin, but I want to be drugged even less. I can't lose control like that. Not again. Never again. "I—I'll go."

Tears prick my eyes, but I blink furiously, refusing to let them fall as I take one shaking step and then another until I'm standing in front of the coffin. My coffin.

"H—" I start, swallowing hard. "How do I get in?" I ask, looking inside at the white silk lining the base and a small, silk pillow at the head end. It really is a beautiful object, you know, if it wasn't a coffin meant for me. My hands tremble at my sides, and I bite my lip hard, tasting the coppery tang of my blood when I break the skin.

"Here," Knox whispers softly in my ear, then he turns me to the side and sweeps me off my feet like a fairytale princess. Only, instead of whisking me away to my happily ever after, he lowers me into a glass coffin. I would laugh, as didn't Snow White end up in one of those? *Look at me being a regular Disney princess. Jesus.*

He lowers me down onto the silk, and at least it's soft against my skin, cradling my body in its embrace as he pulls his arms away. They all come to stand around me, Aeron and Jude on one side, Tarl and Knox on the other, staring down with intense gazes.

"So fucking beautiful, Nightingale," Jude purrs, his tone worshipping as his eyes glide along my body.

My heart still thrashes, but not with just fear, and I feel so confused my skin itches. I'm terrified, tears pricking my eyes, but my body flushes with heat at his praise. Fucking hell, I've never wanted to please a man before, but these guys leave me craving the nuggets that they keep dropping.

Jude reaches over me, grasping the lid and pulling it closed on silent hinges, and my pulse picks up, my palms sweating as it swings shut. I watch as they each take a golden padlock and lock me in. My breath fogs the glass above my face, obscuring my view of their handsome, cruel faces.

"Don't break the glass, Dove," Aeron tells me, giving a nod to the others and suddenly the room gets darker as they begin to snuff each candle out. My head turns, eyes frantically watching as Jude pinches each flame between his fingers with a sigh of pleasure. "It's safety glass, so won't shatter anyway," Aeron continues, and I look back up at him in the dim lighting.

"Please," I beg, unable to stop my plea from falling from my trembling lips. "Please don't leave me in the dark, Aeron."

He stares back at me with no emotion on his face, and I know that my begging is falling on deaf ears.

"Goodnight, Dove," he hums just as the last candle blinks out, and I'm left in complete and absolute darkness.

CHAPTER SIX

TARL

I sit back in my chair, swirling the amber liquid as I watch the others, amusement tickling my lips and pulling them upward.

Jude is practically bouncing off the walls with excitement, the evidence of his arousal at having our bird trapped in her glass coffin clearly outlined in his velvet pants. Knox seems the least happy, his own glass of whiskey clenched tightly in his fingers, his elbows resting on his knees as he stares into the glass. Perhaps he is seeking answers, or maybe absolution. Aeron, well, our unflappable leader looks cool as the proverbial cucumber. To anyone outside of our group anyway, but his jaw is tight and his nostrils flared, which lets me know he's not as unaffected as he's trying to present. *Interesting.*

"Sit the fuck down, Jude," he snarls at his brother, the words cracking across the room like a whip. My lips tilt upwards further at his command. "And you can stop fucking smirking, *Inquisitor*."

My smile drops, the name that I've earned myself grating on my skin for the first time since it was bestowed on me many years ago. I've only myself to blame I suppose. My penchant for using methods favored by the Spanish Inquisition back in the sixteenth century to extract any information we need is legendary. My eyelids narrow when Aeron's own lips twitch upwards.

"Just ignore the grumpy bastard, babe," Jude purrs, depositing himself on my lap and wrapping his arms around my neck, my drink spilling onto my hand. I raise an eyebrow at him, my chastisement clear. "His blue balls are giving him trouble, and only a certain Dove can warm them up," he continues, letting go of my neck and raising my hand to his mouth.

Not looking away from my mismatched eyes, he licks and sucks the alcohol from my hand and fingers, using his other hand to steal my glass and then down the rest of my drink. He doesn't swallow, just leans in and places his lips against my own.

Still staring into his beautiful, ocean-colored eyes, I part my lips, letting the shot flow into my mouth, warmed by his own. The slight burn of the whiskey is a welcome reminder of the blood that continues to run through my veins. My dick hardens in my slacks, imagining another set of soft lips against my own, her body pliable and aching for me.

"You feel it with her too, don't you?" Jude murmurs against my lips, pulling away, still holding my gaze.

I don't answer, admitting my curiosity about the bird in our basement feels like an admission of weakness somehow, but he sees through my omission, the grin spreading his plump lips telling me that like Aeron, I too cannot hide what I feel for her.

"On your knees," I order, my voice gruff and my cock as hard as fucking steel in my trousers.

"Yes, sir," Jude replies, slipping from my lap and grabbing my shirt as he does, tearing the buttons off as he rips it open.

"Brat," I comment without heat, exhaling loudly a minute later as he nips and kisses my abs, paying special attention to my Tailor's tattoo just over my hip. Fuck, he's so good at the foreplay, knowing just how to wind me tighter, leaving me desperate for him.

I watch as he undoes my belt, the sound of the metal clasp loud in the quiet room.

"For fuck's sake! Can you not fuck in the living room?" Aeron spits out, and I lift my gaze to lock on his eyes, so similar yet so different from his brother's.

"He's not fucking me, just choking on my dick a little," I reply, my voice groaning at the end as Jude makes a truth of my words and swallows me whole in one go proving that he is indeed a pro.

I hold his older brother's stare with hooded eyes as Jude goes to town on my cock, paying close attention to the Prince Albert piercing at the tip. My hand tangles in Jude's midnight hair, holding him in place as I bury my shaft to the hilt down his throat. He relaxes like the psycho that he is as I continue to cut off his air supply, still staring into Aeron's eyes. There's anger in their blue depths. There's always a banked rage, but I can see heat there too. Dirty bastard is getting horny over his brother giving me a blowie.

"Jude can do you next, if you like?" I suggest in a breathy voice, feeling my release inch closer at the idea. I never said I wasn't a sick bastard too. Jude's vision must be spotting by now, but I feel his lips lift at my comment. He likes to bait his brother just as much as the rest of us.

"Fuck off," Aeron snarls, slamming his glass down hard enough to shatter, the pieces skittering across the polished wood floor, before storming out of the room. I don't miss the hard length in his own pants, or that he heads to the basement door.

I finally let Jude up to breathe, and he gasps down air, chuckling before sucking me down again as he works my base with a corkscrew motion that he knows drives me wild.

"You two have a fucking death wish," Knox says, shaking his head as he adjusts himself, setting his glass aside.

"Don't let us stop you from taking care of yourself," I groan out, my head falling back as I let the waves of ecstasy that Jude's mouth is causing flow over me.

A few moments of the slurping and sucking sounds that Jude's making fills the space before I hear a mumbled, "fuck it," and I crack my eyes open to see Knox pulling out his impressive length and gripping it in a tight fist.

I buck my hips at the sight, appreciating the erotic image as he watches us, pumping his hand up and down his hard dick.

My hand tightens in Jude's hair, my hips thrusting forward as I pour my release down his throat and he swallows every damn drop like he's desperate for it. My chest heaves and he doesn't let up, licking and sucking until I chuckle and push him away. It's just too damn much.

Sitting back on his heels with a smug as fuck grin, I see his own climax glistening on his beautiful, chiselled stomach, his dick softening in his lap.

"Oh, fuck!" Knox grunts out, and we both look over to see hot cum spurt out of his tip, covering his abs and chest, his T-shirt raised. It's a beautiful sight, the pleasure on his face is almost enough to make me hard again.

"Want me to clean you up, big boy?" Jude asks, licking his freshly fucked lips. Knox huffs out a laugh, his own closed lids lifting as a sexy, satisfied smile graces his lips.

"What is your obsession with my dick?"

"It's just so big and pretty," Jude pouts, then faces me fully and bats his lashes. "Variety is the spice of life, after all."

"Brat," I tell him again, leaning forward and placing a kiss on his puffy mouth, loving that my taste lingers there.

Knox just laughs again—cocky fucker—before getting up.

"I'm going to go clean up," he tells us, heading to the stairs that lead up to our rooms.

"Nightingale will get him to share the cock love," Jude says aloud, getting up himself and cracking his neck. "You coming to bed?" He looks down at me, and I shake my head. "Suit yourself," he replies with a shrug, turning around and heading upstairs too.

I wait for a long time in the darkened room, my eyes locked on the door to the basement, but Aeron doesn't emerge. Eventually, I give up, going to bed in the small hours with dreams of a small, beautiful bird of paradise trapped in a glass cage.

✂

"PANIC ATTACK" BY LIZA ANNE

LARK

I lose track of time, lying in the darkness with just my monsters to keep me company, caressing my soul with their vile fingers. There's something about being in a coffin, a glass coffin with my name on it —well, my new nickname anyway—that allows my demons freer access. I drift between realities, losing myself in the dark nightmares of my past.

The day my mother was murdered by Tailor pigs plagues me, and I'm transported back to the time when I lost more than a beloved parent. My innocence was taken then too, I was forever fucking changed and discovered firsthand the demons that men possess and unleash on the unsuspecting.

A whimper escapes my lips, the sound bouncing back off the glass and sending me further into my spiraling thoughts.

Like a reel from a movie, all the times my father used my body as a reward for his gang members flashes in my mind's eye in brilliant technicolor. I can't stop them, the feel of unwanted hands and cocks ghosting over my body until I'm trembling and sweaty all over.

"Please," I beg in a broken whisper, my fists clenching in the soft silk at my sides as my panic takes root and spots dance in my vision. "Please leave me alone."

I don't know why I bother, my pleas have always fallen on deaf ears before. My heart pounds and tears leak down the sides of my face as I see more men, all taking what was never freely given.

"Breathe, Dove," a deep voice murmurs near my head, and I turn to stare out of the glass, but it's too dark and I can't see.

"I–I—" I start, gasping for breath. "C–can't."

Silence greets my ears, just my rasping as air saws in and out of my straining lungs.

"In, Dove," the voice orders a moment later, the tone firm and enough to penetrate the panic fluttering at the edges of my vision. "And out. That's all it is. Follow me."

I hear him—for it's definitely a man—taking a deep inhale, and my chest automatically follows, sweet air rushing into my starved lungs. We continue to breathe together, the black dots receding the more oxygen I take in.

"That's it, Dove. Good girl," he praises, and I startle, my body twitching as I realize that it's Aeron who coaxed me out of my panic attack.

Once I can speak, I ask him, "How did you know what to do?" My voice is shaky as fuck, but at least I can talk, so props to me. I don't expect an answer, surely the whole point of putting me in here is to fuck with my mind. Which begs the question of why he's down here in the first place.

"Jude used to get panic attacks after June..." He trails off at the mention of June, and it takes a second for my brain to make the connection. When I do, my whole body goes ice-cold.

"June Taylor, Jude's twin and your—"

"Little sister," he interrupts in a tight voice, and my mouth snaps shut as tears prick my eyes. I never knew June, but we were the same age and I realized how easily it could have been me who was shot down. How much I wanted it to be me when I heard, just so that the horror of my existence would stop. "After the Soldiers gunned her down right in front of Jude, he would have night terrors and regular panic attacks. So I learnt how to bring him back," he tells me, his words clipped, and although I know he's trying to hide it, I can hear the pain in his rough voice.

"Are you going to kill me, Aeron?" I ask quietly, my heart pounding painfully in my chest as I await his answer. Unlike years ago, I'm not ready to die just yet. Not until I've got my brother Rook out from my sperm donor's clutches.

Aeron doesn't answer for so long that I think he won't, but when he does I jump a little at the sound of his voice.

"Not yet, Dove," he says into the darkness, his tone hard and unforgiving. "But maybe one day."

"Fair enough," I reply with a bravado that I'm not sure I feel all that well anymore. Panic flutters in my stomach like cannibal moths at the thought that these boys have already started breaking me down, unlike their predecessors. "Just let me know so that I can inform my fans in good time. Can't disappoint them."

"Your fans?" he questions, and I smirk even though I know he can't see it.

"Look up 'Daddy's Little Angel' on OnlyFans," I tell him, my handle making me smile wider. Gotta love irony, given that I'm saving the money I earn from the body that my *father* gave away for free, to escape him and take his only son and heir too. Thank fuck I scheduled content to go out way in advance, though that'll run out soon.

My grin becomes Cheshire Cat proportions wide when I hear a rumble from the clearly grumpy devil in the room.

"You'll be shutting that shit down when we let you out of that coffin," he informs me, and a bark of laughter peels from my chest.

"Sure, Devil Man. You gonna replace the decent income I get from people watching me flick the bean?" I sass back, my cheeks hurting with my smirk as another growl sounds out. "How about I give you guys a discount code as a gesture of goodwill? Between enemies?"

Hands slap down on the glass, and I fucking twitch so hard that I bang my head. *Motherfucker!*

"You will shut that down and delete any evidence of you 'flicking the bean' as you so eloquently put it," Aeron snarls, and although I can't make out his face in the pitch-black room, his tone tells me he's pissed as all hell. "I won't have anyone else viewing what belongs to me."

My brows raise at that, and I just can't help myself poking the bear, or the devil as that's more apropos of the man before me.

"Awww, Aeron baby. I knew you cared," I coo, laughing when the sound that comes from his chest is as loud as thunder and just as hard. My thighs clench with the noise, wetness inching down them from my aching cunt.

"Get some sleep, Dove. You'll need it for what we have planned for tomorrow," he tells me, his voice back to that cold, unfeeling tone that he seems to have perfected.

He doesn't speak again, but I don't hear the door so I assume he stays with me which is all kinds of head fuckery. Why lock me in a glass coffin in the pitch-black only to keep me company so I'm not as scared? There's a comfort in knowing that he's here with me though, his presence filling me with a calmness that I definitely shouldn't fucking feel around the son and heir of a rival gang.

Confused thoughts swirl around my head, and I wonder if I'll ever get to sleep. Eventually, I do, my dreams full of being chased in the sunshine by four dark figures, and rather than a feeling of terror, I'm laughing and desperate to be caught.

CHAPTER SEVEN

"FALLING TOO" BY VEDA GAIL

LARK

I awake to four shadows surrounding my coffin—*yep, that sounds fucked even in my mind*—and soft candlelight flickering off the walls. Their faces are covered in shadows, the candles clearly behind them, yet I know that it's the Tailor boys instinctively. Yeah, I will not read into that too much right now.

"Wakey, wakey, beautiful Nightingale," Jude's voice floats to me as the shadows move to one side of me and I hear the click of padlocks, the lid unlocking.

A rush of warm air caresses my naked skin, and I realize with a jolt that the room is warm, which explains the lack of shivering on my part. I wiggle my toes as I sit up, stretching my arms upwards and twisting my torso.

"Shit," Knox hisses, but I catch it and give him a wink.

"I bet you're remembering what it felt like to be balls deep inside me, aren't you Daddy?" I ask in a purr, and he rubs a hand over his face. If he wasn't reliving the scene that lives rent-free in my head before, he is now if the way his jeans have strained over his crotch is any sign. *My work here is done.*

"Naughty, Nightingale," Jude tsks, and I can just about make out his teeth gleaming in a feral grin. He reaches inside the coffin, encouraging me to wrap my arms around his neck and scooping me up in his firm grip, bridal style. "Now I'm all hard imagining being balls deep inside you," he whispers against my ear with a nuzzle to my neck, and my nipples pebble. "Or balls deep in Knox while he's buried in that sweet cunt."

Fuck. Me.

My pussy clamps violently at that visual, and Jude nips my neck as my thighs twitch.

"Your cock is going nowhere near my ass," Knox growls out, and Jude just laughs.

"He's living in denial," he tells me conspiratorially as he turns around and carries me from the room into the brightly-lit corridor.

I squint, wincing as pain shoots through my eyeballs at the sudden light.

"Fucker," I grumble as he takes unhurried steps forward, another chuckle vibrating in his chest. His bare chest that I can't help but snuggle into, breathing in his sunshine and popping candy scent. Don't ask me what that smells like, it's just delicious and fun, and the best kind of trouble.

"I thought you might need a piss, and unless you want to use a bucket?" he questions, pausing in his steps, and I crack a lid to glare at him. "Okay, Nightingale, no piss buckets." He chortles again, and I find my lips pulling upwards of their own accord.

"Jude!" I hear Aeron bellow down the corridor, and I suspect Jude wasn't supposed to bring me away from the basement. "Bring her back!"

"See the trouble I get in for you, my Nightingale?" Jude asks as he picks up speed, jogging up the stairs and bouncing me in his arms.

My bladder protests at the jostling, but I can't help grinning as we run away from Aeron.

"I feel you like trouble," I reply and another infectious laugh leaves his plump lips, which I really want to kiss, when we reach the top of the stairs. He darts across the vast living space to the other stairs.

"Damn right I do," he answers. I hear movement at the top of the basement stairs and look over Jude's shoulder to see a red-faced, fuming Aeron glaring at us and rushing to catch up.

"Shit, he's gaining on us," I mock-whisper, laughing as Jude practically sprints down the hallway, and barges into a room to the left. He slams the door behind us and somehow engages some complicated-looking locks all while still holding me tight in his muscular arms.

"Not fucking funny, Jude!" Aeron snarls on the other side of the closed door, pounding the wood so hard that it rattles in the frame.

"You had her all night, brother," Jude replies cockily, barely out of breath from our flight across the building. "Learn to share."

I choke on my saliva at that comment and almost fucking piss myself for real.

"Toilet," I squeak between gasps, and Jude turns around, heading to a door on the other side of the vast bedroom.

I catch little more than a glimpse of a room in bright rainbow colors before he's taking me into his en-suite and carefully sitting me down on the toilet. He steps away, but just far enough to lean his fine ass on the sink countertop opposite, his inked-up arms crossed over his equally tattooed chest.

"Pervert," I murmur as I take a piss, the need too desperate to ignore any longer. A long sigh of pleasure leaves my lips as I empty my bladder, having had to hold it for god knows how long.

"Next time you moan like that, it'll be around my hard dick, Nightingale," Jude promises darkly, and I look up from wiping myself to arch a brow at him.

"Promises, promises, Devil Boy," I tease, stepping up and

flushing the chain, then walk over to where he's leaning to wash up. He doesn't move—fucking shitwad—so I have to reach around him to wash my hands.

Glancing up under my lashes, I watch as his head turns towards me, his eyes dark like the deepest depths of the ocean as he looks over my naked form. I've never been ashamed of my body, regardless of how men have used it in the past, so I let him look his fill as I do the same to him.

Fuck, he's gorgeous. His muscles ripple under all the ink and scars, his Adonis belt, aka cum gutters, begging to be filled with my release. Unfortunately, his black and white checkered pants hide what I know is a dick that would make saints weep and plead to wrap their holy mouths around.

"Nightingale..." he murmurs in a pained voice. "Aeron is going to fucking kill me."

"Why?" I ask, finally looking back up and drowning in the lust burning in his eyes.

"Because of this," he tells me, suddenly moving so that he's pinning me against the counter, pressing his pants-clad hardness against my lower stomach, the fabric rough against my skin. Damn, if only I were slightly taller, it would reach where I currently crave him.

Moving achingly slowly, he glides his palm up my naked side, the heat from his touch sending pulsing waves all across my skin. His fingers reach my breast, my peaked nipple desperate for his touch.

"Jude," I gasp as he toys and plays with the bud, my skin tingling under his caress. I know I shouldn't be enjoying this, he locked me in a glass fucking coffin all night, but I want him. I want him so badly that my teeth ache with the need to have him inside me.

A sharp, tugging pain has me flinching, and I snap my head down to see that he's placed a nipple clamp over my sensitive peak. Several delicate, gold chains dangle from the clamp attached to me, and there are two more clamps swinging from them.

I watch enraptured as he repeats the move on my other side,

playing with my nipple and causing a keen full of need to fall from my lips before placing the clamp over it, tightening it until I let out a hissing groan.

"It won't hurt for long, Nightingale," he whispers in a throaty voice, yanking on the chains that connect the clamps and making my breath hiss again.

"What's the other clamp for?" I ask, my voice fifty shades of husky as my fingers flex at my sides. I know damn well what the third clamp is for, I just want him to say it.

Slowly, Jude sinks to his knees with such a sexy smile that I could almost come right then and there.

"That's the part that'll get me in trouble," he says, voice soft, his hot breath brushing against my wet folds. I shiver, the clamps on my nipples feeling tighter suddenly.

He leans in, and my head falls back with a groan as his mouth clamps down on my clit, sucking hard. I cry out as a fierce orgasm rips through me. No build-up. No warning. Just sheer, painful bliss. My nailless fingers claw at the stone countertop behind me as the pleasure becomes almost too much, Jude's tongue caressing me until I'm fucking twitching and shuddering, begging him to stop.

Another shriek leaves my lips when he places the clamp on my pulsing clit.

"Fuck!" I shout, so sensitive that it's painful.

"So fucking delicious, Nightingale," he murmurs, kissing my sweaty thigh before standing up, his lips glistening with my release. "Fucking exquisite."

He leans down, capturing my lips with his own, and I groan loudly when I taste my cum on his tongue. He kisses me like he ate me, all hard and demanding like he can't get enough. I kiss him back just as fiercely, my hands tangling in his soft hair and pulling him closer. A moan falls from my lips into his mouth when my nipples brush his chest, the clamps providing an incredible pressure.

Capturing his lower lip in my teeth, I bite down hard until copper fills my mouth and Jude gives a low, sexy growl, thrusting his hips and poking me with his member that's still trapped in his pants. Just as I reach out to grab it, desperate to feel his silky length in my hand, there's a fucking explosion and the door to the bedroom flies into the room. I jump hard, my heart thudding in my chest.

"Busted," Jude murmurs, placing his forehead against mine.

I laugh, the sound dying in my throat as I spot Aeron walking into the room with measured steps, his suit pristine.

"Evening, Devil Man," I sass him, and he just raises a single brow.

"You didn't need to blow the door off, asshole," Jude comments, turning around and blocking me from view. "Especially as I dressed our bird up so prettily for you."

Like a fucking showman at a circus, he steps aside, taking my hand and pulling me forward to show me off to Aeron. I spot Knox and Tarl in the bedroom too, both taking deep inhales as they spot me.

"Fucking hell," Aeron rasps, and my gaze swings back to him, a fissure of pleasure running through me at his hooded eyes. He rubs a hand over his face, and I know that I've broken him a little in that moment. My lips tug upwards in a sultry smirk.

As his hand moves from his face, his expression resumes its usual coldness and I know that the heir to the Tailors is back. Stepping forward, he takes my hand from Jude's.

"Time to go back downstairs and start singing, Dove."

"DEVILISH" BY CHASE ATLANTIC

AERON

Fucking Jude.

I'm rock-fucking-solid in my slacks as I pull our little Dove behind me, back towards the basement. The image of the gold chains dangling from her breasts and down to her sweet pussy is burned into my retinas, and I don't dare look at her. If I do, I'll be dragging her to my room and fucking her until we both pass out.

As much as I crave that release, we have a job to do, and a pretty pussy can't get in the way. We've delayed long enough.

I hear a feminine gasp as we descend the stairs to the basement; I turned the air con all the way up, and I bet her nipples are as solid as my dick. Plus the clamps teasing her tight buds will be making her feel every degree that the room lacks.

Shit, I should not be thinking about her nipples.

She stalls as we enter the room with her coffin in it, which has been pushed to the side to make room for a toy I bought just for her.

Turning around, I give her a smirk as she takes in the piece of furniture currently dominating the room.

"Do you know what this is called?" I ask, keeping hold of her hand and drinking in her reaction. Her eyes are wide and her lips parted. Her tongue darts out to lick the lower one, and I have to clench my jaw almost to the breaking point to stop the groan wanting to escape from me.

"A St Andrew's Cross," she whispers, her chest rising and falling with quick panting breaths. Fuck me. She's just as turned on as I am about strapping her to it. I can practically smell her arousal and can see it seeping down her thighs that keep clenching.

"Good girl," I praise, bringing up my free hand to stroke her cheek and turning her hooded gaze to mine. "Here's how this is going to go. We'll be tying you to the cross, and if you're a good girl and tell us what we need to know, then you can come."

Her nostrils flare, and a challenge clears her vision as her eyes narrow.

"And if I don't talk?"

I smirk, my hand dropping from her cheek, my fingers teasing the delicate chains hanging between her lush breasts.

"Then you don't come and get punished."

I yank the chain, not hard enough to pull the clamps off but enough to make her squeak. Using the chain and letting go of her hand, I pull her towards the cross. She follows, although the gleam in her emerald eyes tells me that this is the most cooperative she's going to be. Good. I hope she fights every damn second. My cock weeps at the thought, no doubt staining my pants but I just don't give a fuck right now.

Switching our positions, I force her to walk backwards until her spine hits the cross. She glares at me, but I just smile back, all teeth, as I stroke my hand down her arm, watching as goosebumps pebble her creamy skin. Grasping her wrist, I bring it up to one end of the cross.

"Knox," I call out and feel him come up beside me. He opens the leather cuff, strapping it around her slender wrist. I repeat the move, holding her stare as we pull her upwards so that she's on her tiptoes.

I kick her legs further apart so he can strap her ankles next and my hand skims her waist, no longer able to fight the pull she has on me. So leaning in more, I run my nose up her beautiful neck, inhaling her summery cherry blossom scent and committing it to memory.

"I would tie you up with ropes instead of the cuffs, but we're short on time so perhaps next time," I whisper in her ear, my fingers digging into her soft flesh ever so slightly.

I take a step back before I lose control completely, and then regret it as I run my eyes over her at our mercy, strapped up and waiting for our attention.

"Fuck me," Knox breathes out and adjusts himself.

"She's fucking perfect," my brother states hungrily from my other side.

"A goddess," Tarl murmurs next to him, and that makes me snap my head away from the sight before me. I stare at him but he doesn't take his eyes off the Dove, eating her up with his gaze.

If he's taken with her, we have no hope.

"Tarl, blindfold her," I command, and he turns those mismatched eyes onto me, one brow raised. I say nothing else, asserting my leadership over him. After a few moments, he just gives a slight nod, steps towards her, and pulls a length of red silk from his pants pocket.

I smirk, knowing that he'd have one on him. Our proclivities all run to having our lovers tied up and at a disadvantage.

"No highs for me today, Mr. Sandman?" she asks him in her sexy, husky voice. A bark of deep laughter sounds from his throat, and it's enough to make both brows hit my hairline.

"Only the kind between your creamy thighs, pretty bird," he purrs back, sliding the silk over her eyes and cutting off her gaze. "If you're a good girl that is."

A small whimper leaves her throat as he ties the knot behind her head. Perfect. Jude steps forward, but I place a hand across his chest, halting him.

"You've had your turn." I scowl at him, and he pouts in return, but like a shit, he shrugs and grins. "And Tarl is our resident interrogator, so he gets to start."

"Don't trust your control, brother?" Jude teases, and my jaw clenches once again.

"Fuck off," I snap. "Tarl, make sure she doesn't come."

"Fuck you, Devil Man," Lark snarls, her voice a little raspy as Tarl runs his palms down her sides and around her breasts but ignores her nipples completely. She thrusts her chest forward as much as the restraints allow, begging for his attention.

"Later, Dove," I coo, watching unblinkingly as his lips press delicate kisses up her neck. "For now, tell us where Dead Soldiers HQ is."

It is the one thing that has irritated my father for years, not knowing where their base of operations is. How a gang as big as theirs has kept it a secret is actually quite impressive. Annoying but impressive.

"Suck my clit, asshole," she replies, moaning as Tarl sucks a spot on her neck. Her thighs try to clench, but the cross stops them, so she'll get no friction unless we give it to her. A heavy exhale sighs out of my nose at the slickness that coats her inner thighs.

"I will, if you're a good little bird," I counter, enjoying this game far too much. "I'll ask again, although I don't enjoy repeating myself, Dove. Where does that cunt of a father of yours lay his ugly head?"

"At least we agree on that," she gasps as Tarl moves to the side of her breast and begins sucking. He likes to leave his mark, as we all do in different ways.

"Agree on what, Dove?" I question, curious as to what she meant.

"That my sperm donor is a cunt," she tells me through gritted teeth when Tarl gets to work on her other breast, still avoiding her nipples.

"So why protect him? Why not tell us what we want to know?"

"Who says it's him I'm protecting?" she responds, and suddenly her reluctance makes sense.

"Rook," I murmur, understanding dawning like the proverbial light bulb. "You're protecting your brother."

She doesn't respond, just moans again when Tarl moves back up to her neck, biting as he goes. Her entire body jerks with each nip, and the slickness inching down her inner thighs tells me just how much she likes a little pain.

Shaking my head to clear the lust haze, I consider her for a moment and think about what I'd do to protect Jude. Shit. Still, I can't give up.

"Knox, perhaps you can help persuade her to sing?" I suggest, watching her body tense as Knox strides towards her, then drops to his knees in front of her.

I chuckle, knowing that he thoroughly approves of this type of torture for our little bird. I don't think we'll get anything from her, not unless I can guarantee her brother's safety, which I'm not sure I can.

But I've never failed to extract what I want from our prisoners before, and I'm not about to start now.

CHAPTER EIGHT

"STOCKHOLM SYNDROME" BY SOFIA KARLBERG

LARK

Hours fucking pass, their hands and tongues bringing me to the brink of sweet release, only to stop and leave me sweating, fucking aching, and on the edge of madness. It's a new sensation for me, being desperate for a man's touch. I'm so used to it being forced upon me, that desire on my part was never a requirement, which was lucky as it was never there.

Shit, this is worse than the whipping, the branding, and fingernail pulling, and that shit was bad. Blue ovaries is not a state I want to be in, but still, I don't sing for them. I don't tell them anything of use. My brother's safety is worth more than a few orgasms.

Aeron sighs, and I can hear the frustration that is no doubt all over his face. His brow is probably furrowed and his jaw clenched tight. Good. Boy needs to learn disappointment.

"Knox, Tarl," he snaps out, and it's my turn to sigh as cool air kisses my heated skin when they step away. I'm still blindfolded, which only made the torture worse as I couldn't see what they were about to do, only feel it. Every swipe of their tongues, every press of their lips, and nip of their teeth. "Let's see if a night spent on the cross will loosen her tongue."

"I need a piss," I croak out, voice strained and raspy. The cold air in the basement does little to ease my discomfort.

Fingers pull the silk away from my eyes, and I blink in the sudden brightness of the room. When I can finally focus, ocean eyes fill my vision, a hand cupping my cheek. The look in his eyes is soft, almost proud, as a small smile tickles his lips.

"I've got you, Nightingale," Jude whispers, and removing his palm from my face he finally takes off the clamps on my nipples and clit. A deep moan leaves my lips as he removes them, the blood rushing back into my buds with an almost orgasmic pleasure. A small sound lets me know that he drops the jewelry to the concrete floor, his beautiful, hypnotic eyes hold my focus making it impossible to look away.

Swooping down, he picks up a metal jug and places it between my legs underneath my pussy. My cheeks burn as the realization of what he expects washes over me, and my eyes widen as I look back up to him. He steps closer, the heat of his bare, scarred and inked-up chest pressing against my naked torso.

"You did so well today, beautiful Nightingale," he coos, his free hand coming back up to my cheek, his thumb stroking my hot flesh. "Not spilling your secrets."

"W–what?" I ask, the urge to pee fading under a blanket of confusion.

"Jude," I hear Aeron admonish in a growl, but Jude ignores him.

"Such a beautiful bird," he compliments. Tears sting my eyes, and I have to swallow past the lump in my throat. "It's time to let go, love. I won't let you make a mess." The tinkling sound of my piss hitting metal is loud in the quiet room, and my shoulders try to cave as I do as he says and let go, unable to hold on any longer. My cheeks burn with shame. "Such a good girl," he tells me in a soothing voice, leaning in and flicking his tongue over the wetness on my cheek. "That's it, just let go."

I take it back. This humiliation is far worse than anything that's happened to me so far. Having him hold a literal pot for me to piss in, all while his soft words and touch make me preen at the praise he's giving, it's the most embarrassing thing I've had to endure in a long time. It's almost too much, and I can feel my posture trying to sag in my binds, a painful lump in my throat.

Finally, the stream ends, and I would hang my head if Jude wasn't holding it up. I can't look at him, or the others, my gaze dropping to a point on the floor across the room.

"You finished, Nightingale?" Jude questions gently.

"Yes," I answer, my voice small.

He doesn't move away, but I see in my peripheral vision that he hands the jug to Tarl, who passes him a white flannel. Sweat glistens on my brow as Jude swipes the warm cloth over my pussy, cleaning me up.

I feel movement on my other side, and turn to see Knox standing there holding a plate of chopped fruit and what smells and looks like French toast, cut into small, bite-sized pieces.

"Oh, for fuck's sake!" Aeron exclaims, and I glance at him, his usually neat hair disheveled.

"Fuck off, Aeron," Knox snarls back, stepping closer until the heat of his naked chest warms my side. I take a moment to study it, the way his muscles ripple and his six-pack clearly defined, all helping me to forget my previous embarrassment. The ink on his arms spreads across his chest in a stunning mix of images that flow into each other. Religious iconography surrounded by script and moths with skulls on their bodies. Flowers are mixed in, and I'm sure there's a tree of life in the melee. "Like what you see, Little Bird?"

I snap my head back up to look into his teasing, hazel eyes, his dirty-blond hair flopping into one eye. He's so close that I can smell myself on him, my scent clinging to his dark brown stubble. My core pulses again, naughty pussy.

He holds up his hand, a square of the soft toast in his fingers. "I thought you might be hungry."

My stomach chooses that moment to growl loudly, and he gives a sexy, masculine chuckle, bringing the morsel to my lips. I hold his stare as I open them, letting him place the bite on my tongue and giving his fingers a small lick as he withdraws them. A deep moan leaves my closed lips as the buttery flavor explodes in my mouth, and his eyes darken, his pupils widening and threatening to swallow the hazel whole.

"Shit, this wasn't just torture for you, Little Bird," he groans, his hand raking through his messy locks. I dart a look down at his jeans to see the fabric straining at the crotch. A smirk tugs at my lips. Good. I'm glad it fucking affected him too.

"More," I demand, opening my lips once more, and he quirks a brow, holding the next piece just out of reach. "Please, Daddy."

"Good girl," he praises, and it's a gargantuan effort not to let my toes curl. Fuck, I did not see that kink coming.

We spend the next few minutes with Knox feeding me, Jude still pushed up against my other side, like he can't bear to be parted from my skin. I'm not going to lie, the warmth both men exude pressed so closely to me is delicious, and I soon find my eyes growing heavy with a wave of exhaustion.

"Our beautiful bird is sleepy," Jude comments, taking away the straw from my lips that I was using to drink the juice they gave me. "Time for sleep, little one."

"I don't enjoy sleeping alone," I say without thought, and like, what the fuck was that?! I've always slept alone and loved it. I could never sleep if one of my father's goons tried to snuggle after using me.

"I know, precious one," Jude whispers, nuzzling the spot just behind my ear. "I'm sure Aeron will come and keep you company later," he whispers so quietly that I'm sure no one else hears him.

My eyes find the man in question, noticing that his hair looks back to its normal neatness, his suit pristine. His eyes, however, are a messy mix of emotions as he watches me back. I just wish I knew what he was thinking, what he was feeling, and they call me fucking broken. One look in his eyes right now shows me just how shattered his soul is.

"Time to go," Aeron announces, and Jude heaves a heavy sigh against me, his breath feathering my hair.

"See you tomorrow, Nightingale," he murmurs, placing a soft kiss against my lips.

My vision fills with Knox as he takes Jude's place in front of me.

"See you in my dreams, beautiful," he tells me with a grin that must make angels come undone. Leaning in, he, too, kisses my lips softly, swiping his tongue over the seam before withdrawing and walking his admittedly fine ass away.

Tarl stands before me next, his mismatched eyes taking me in, assessing. If the heat in his eyes is anything to go by, he doesn't find me wanting.

"Such a pretty, pretty bird," he states, stepping closer and trailing his long fingers down the side of my neck, over my collarbone, and down the side of my breast. He leans in, his soft, full lips brushing mine in a ghost of a kiss and I taste my musk on him for the briefest of moments. Fucking cunt tease. "Sweet dreams, my bird of paradise."

He steps away then, walking towards the door, and suddenly I'm all alone with Aeron staring at me from across the room. It's not so far that I can't feel his dark energy seep into my skin though, clawing its way to my bones.

"You gonna give me a goodnight kiss too, Devil Man?" I sass, a spike of satisfaction flaring in my belly when his jaw grinds.

"Goodnight, Dove," he says, his tone hard.

Then I'm plunged into darkness again as he shuts off the lights.

Dick.

✂

"FUCKED UP" BY BAHARI

AERON

A couple of hours later, once the others have gone to bed, I give in to the pull that's drawing me back down to that fucking basement, and the bird trapped down there. Although, perhaps a siren would be a better creature for her. My sudden obsession to be near her is inexplicable.

The room is cool, the frigid air wafting over me as I step inside the room and shut the door silently behind me. No light filters in, but I know where she is. Her damaged soul calls to me in the darkness, guiding my bare feet in the right direction.

"I know you're there, Devil Man," she says, her voice a whisper against my naked chest. I don't answer, just step closer until I can feel her chilled skin pressed to my body and the shiver as she basks in my body heat. "I can't sleep," she confesses, a sigh brushing my clavicle.

My hand reaches out of its own accord, landing on her shoulder, and rather than flinch, she sighs again, like she was desperate for the contact. My dick jerks in my sweats at that. At her craving for me, even against her better judgment. I trace upwards, my fingertips gliding up the side of her neck until I can cup her face in my palm. She leans into the touch, rubbing her face in a way that makes my dead heart pound painfully.

"What are you doing to me, little Dove?" I murmur, stepping even closer, her lithe body pressed up against mine, shivers dancing across my skin with more than just the contact of her cold skin.

"The same thing that you're doing to me, Devil Man," she

answers, her voice a breathy rasp that makes my cock solidify fully in my pants.

"Then we'll get lost together for a while," I tell her, ghosting my lips over hers, inhaling the sharp breath she releases until my lungs are filled with her.

I place a light kiss on her cheek, her neck, and the top of her breast, relishing the soft noises she makes, the scent of her arousal making my nostrils flare. I love the way I can feel the heat as her skin flushes, all because of my touch.

"Aeron," she moans, pulling against her bonds, and Jesus fucking Christ that's a sound I want to hear more often. "Please, Aeron. Please, I need you so fucking bad it hurts." Her voice catches at the end, her plea hardening my dick further until it becomes painful.

The need to taste her becomes overwhelming. Watching the guys take turns lapping at her sweet pussy all fucking day gave me a desperate thirst for her juices on my tongue, but my dick needs to feel her right fucking now.

"Will you scream my name if I let you come?" I question against her breast, my voice a deep, husky sound. She gives a full-body shudder that I feel across my own rapidly heating skin.

"Yes, sir," she answers, trying to jerk her hips closer to me.

Fuck, hearing her call me sir leaves me panting like a fucking dog. God, she's worked her siren magic on me and I'm helpless against her. Straightening up, I press closer into her until our bodies touch from chest to groin. Pulling my hard length from my sweats, I angle it down and press it against her clit.

We both groan at the feel of her wetness coating my tip, lubing me up. With slow, steady movements, I slide my hand up and down my shaft, hitting her swollen nub on every downward stroke.

"Fuck, Aeron," she gasps, her hips thrusting forward. "That feels so fucking good."

My hand tightens around my cock, my motions speeding up. I've given up on my tightly-leashed control, and I just fucking feel her surrounding me. My other hand comes up to wrap around her neck, feeling her pounding pulse underneath my fingertips.

"Aeron!" she cries, wetness soaking my hand and cock as she comes hard all over me. Fuck, I know she's beautiful when she climaxes, remembering how she looked when Knox fucked her up against her cell wall, and feeling her come now, my shaft soaked with her release, turns me into a beast.

Sparks shoot up my spine at the feel of her tied up and dripping all over my dick, my hand furious as I pump harder and faster. I tighten the grip around her throat, feeling every gasp and cry as she bucks underneath me.

"That's it, Dove, come for me again, baby," I growl out, my balls drawing up as my own climax threatens to sweep over me.

"Shit, Aeron!"

Her whole body goes rigid, more wetness coating my dick as she comes a second time. This time I follow her, painting the outside of her pussy with ropes of hot cum. I regret not lighting a candle so I could see her glisten with my release.

I feel as though I'm on fire, my nerves alight as I squeeze her throat and just let fucking go. A low groan sounds in my chest, and I can feel her struggling to breathe, which makes more cum leak out of my dick. I wish I could see her covered in my seed; I bet she looks fucking glorious.

What follows is something I've not experienced in so long that I'd wondered if it ever existed. Peace flows over me, relaxing my grip on my dick and her throat as I sink into her soft body, my sweaty forehead resting against hers.

"Dove..." I start, not knowing what I intend to say, lost for words for once.

"I know," she murmurs back, turning her head to place a kiss on my jaw as her breaths pant out of her heaving chest. She mewls when I place my cum-covered hand over her pussy, needing to feel her inner warmth.

"I still need to get that intel from you," I tell her, hating that I'm going to have to up my game, and perhaps even hurt her. I have to give my father something soon, or he'll come back and hurt her more. The thought leaves a sour taste in my mouth, the idea of anyone hurting her making me want to gnash my teeth like a fucking rabid dog.

"I know," she answers again, pressing her lips against mine.

We stay that way for a time as I taste the resignation in her words, and I wait until her body sags in her binds, her even breathing letting me know that she's finally fallen asleep.

Carefully stepping away, I place my dick back in my sweats, still covered in her release. I have no urge to wash it off, wanting to keep her on me for as long as possible, the need to have this small part of her overriding my usual OCD tendencies. Walking over to the door, I slide down the wall beside it to sit on the floor and face my Dove.

I don't sleep, just wait there while watching over her, wondering what the fuck I'm going to do next.

CHAPTER NINE

"SMOTHER ME" BY KELASKA

LARK

"Little, naughty Nightingale…" a low voice filters through my mind, infiltrating my dream.

Wisps of darkness loosen their grip, but I don't feel the usual heart-stopping terror that accompanies most of my nightmares. Instead, it's like a warm caress, a parting kiss.

"Wake up, beautiful," another voice cajoles, and I find my eyelids fluttering open, bright hazel eyes laughing back at me. "Good morning, sleeping beauty."

"Argh. I need a piss," I grumble, my voice low and husky. My nose wrinkles as I feel the dried evidence of Aeron's visit last night, but when I look around, I can see that he's not down here. "And a shower."

"Anything else, princess?" Knox asks, his plush lips pulled up in a smirk. Dammit. He's too fucking good-looking this early in the morning.

"Yeah. Some coffee, some food, oh, and my fucking freedom would be nice," I deadpan, smiling sweetly at him. His brows dip, and the skin around his eyes tightens. I could swear that guilt flashes across his eyes, darkening their brightness.

"The last one I can't help with," he tells me, reaching up to loosen the clasps on my wrists as Jude bends down to unfasten my ankles. I take a huge inhale of Knox's scent; a mix of motor oil, cloves, and leather, and I have to forcibly stop my eyes from rolling back into my head at how fucking delicious it is. "But the others we can fulfill."

"What?" I question, a little dazed and yes, maybe a smidge dick-struck. His smile widens when he sees my confusion, undoing the final clasp and catching me when I tumble forward.

"Let's get you upstairs, Little Bird," he says with a chuckle before sweeping me up into his arms.

"Hey! No fair!" Jude complains, following closely behind as Knox strides from the room, heading towards the basement stairs. "I wanted to carry her!"

Despite my better judgment, my lips tilt. He looks edible this morning; his brightly-colored Hawaiian shirt is open, showcasing his muscled torso, ink, scars and all. He's paired it with some hot pink chinos and rainbow sparkly DM's that I secretly yearn for.

"You get to touch her for the rest of the day, so quit your bitching," Knox says, and I straighten in his arms.

"Why? What's happening today?" I ask, a mixture of excitement and trepidation causing butterflies to explode in my stomach.

"Naughty, Nightingale," Jude chides, darting in front of Knox who curses, and bopping me on the nose. "That would ruin the surprise."

We head up the stairs, emerging in the main living area which is empty. I chew my lips as I look around, not examining the sudden heaviness in my body too closely when I can't see Aeron or Tarl.

"Don't worry, Little Bird," Knox murmurs, continuing across the floor to the other set of stairs that leads to the mezzanine level. "They'll be back later. They're just taking care of something."

"Like kidnapping another innocent girl?"

His steps falter, and my body moves with a great sigh as he exhales like the weight of the world is on his shoulders. Or maybe I'm just super heavy.

"In some ways, I wish things were different," he confesses, pausing at the bottom step and looking me straight in the eye. "But, I can't say that I'm sorry about you being here. Because I'm not."

"Me neither," Jude adds, coming up next to us. He strokes some of my hair away from my face, his ocean-blue eyes fixed on me and his face soft as if he's at peace after a long, lonely battle. "You were always meant to be ours, Nightingale."

My heart pounds, and I swallow hard, looking from one set of eyes to another, seeing the truth of their conviction in their depths.

"Do you always break the things that belong to you?" I whisper, hardly daring to breathe as I wait for their answer.

"Yes." They speak in unison, and a shiver runs along my skin. I can see that truth clearly too.

"There's nothing more to break," I tell them, pushing down the memories of the past few years that threaten to surface. The leering faces. The grasping hands.

"Then we shall mend you first, my broken bird," Jude coos, placing a soft kiss on my temple. "And maybe you can mend us too."

He steps away, striding upstairs with his feline grace, leaving me speechless and gaping like a fish. *Did he suggest that I have power here?*

"Come on, beautiful," Knox says, carrying me up the stairs after Jude. "Let's get you cleaned up and ready for the day."

My head spins around these guys. They talk about breaking me, and then in the next sentence, they're taking care of me.

And the worst part?

Both make my heart race, my nipples tighten, and my core ache to be filled by each of them.

Maybe I'm more broken than I thought.

⚘

They leave me to wash alone, Jude saying that he needs to prepare for what is coming. My heart thuds with both excitement and apprehension, my mind unable to admit that I might look forward to his attentions, whatever they may entail.

I know that regardless, I won't be divulging anything until I get an assurance of Rook's and my safety. It's why I held out when the other Tailor cunts had me. My brother is the most important person in the world to me, and we need to get out of this life. Out of this Hell.

I luxuriate in the huge shower, letting the hot spray wash away the evidence of Aeron's visit last night. That boy gives me the most whiplash of them all. One minute cold, and the next burning so hot that he feels like lava against my skin.

They all make me forget myself, especially Aeron when he looks at me like I'm his destruction, and possibly his salvation too. I find myself falling into their darkness more and more by the day. Craving it like the oxygen filling my lungs.

Shaking my head, I try to remember my goal; get out of here and run as far from the Soldiers and Tailors as possible. I'll leave the fucking country if I need to, taking my brother away from all the ruin that awaits us and the pain that this cursed city dishes up on the daily.

"Grubs up, Little Bird," Knox drawls, and I look up with water clinging to my lashes to find him leaning in the doorway, enormous arms folded across his chest. He's wearing his usual white T-shirt, fitted jeans, and boots, and looks fucking edible as he stares at me with heat in his hazel eyes.

"Perv much?" I sass, stepping out of the shower. His eyes track the droplets that fall down my skin, and the shiver that cascades over me has absolutely nothing to do with the temperature in the room.

"I like to admire the pretty things that I own," he replies in a deep voice, stalking towards me like a lion who has spotted his mate. I gulp, the sound audible, and his smirk widens.

"You can't own a person, Knox," I tell him, but my voice is a breathy whisper, not even convincing to my own ears.

"Sure you can, princess."

I'm frozen as he approaches, not stopping him as he stands right in front of me. He's so close that my hardened nipples brush his shirt, and I have to crane my neck to look him in the face. *Tall, sexy bastard.*

His large hand comes up, his fingers grasping my chin and tilting my head back further until my neck is strained at an awkward angle.

"I own every fucking inch of you, Little Bird," he murmurs, dipping his head and licking the side of my throat, drinking the droplets of water from my skin. His other hand lands on my breast, grabbing it hard, and I gasp at the sharp pain.

"These gorgeous tits are mine." He squeezes again, his fingers letting go and leaving an ache behind them as they skate down my side. "This fucking stunning body is mine." His fingers dig into my hip hard enough to bruise, and I whimper at the roughness of his touch. At the possession. "And this sweet cunt?" he asks, and I hold my breath, waiting for his next move. "That's mine too. And you're going to show Daddy just how much it belongs to him, aren't you?" A small squeak leaves my lips as he strokes my folds, and I watch the moment he discovers how wet I am for him, his grin turning feral. "Such a good little fuck toy. So wet for Daddy," he breathes out, shoving two fingers inside my heat with no warning.

A cry leaves my parted lips, and I don't know if it's more pleasure than pain. All I know is that I don't want him to stop doing what I'm praying he's about to do.

"Who owns this pussy, fuck toy?" he growls, his fingers buried to the knuckle but not giving me any friction. His other hand reaches up, fingers tangling and tightening in my hair, and water drips down my still-healing back from where he's squeezing it out.

"Please," I beg, my hands gripping his shirt as tears gather in the corners of my eyes as I plead for something that I never wanted before, but was forced upon me regardless. Only this time I want it. Desperately.

"Who owns this cunt?"

I bite my lip, my eyelids fluttering closed as I admit out loud what I don't want to acknowledge in my mind.

"You do."

"I do, what?" he probes further, and a rush of anger has my eyes snapping open and my lips pulling back to bare my teeth at him.

"You own my cunt, Daddy," I snarl, my nostrils flaring.

"Yes, I fucking do."

Suddenly, his fingers leave me empty, and I howl with rage at being left so unsatisfied. Before I can curse him out, he spins me around, using his grip on my hair, and pushes me forward. My arms fly out in front of me, my hands grabbing hold of the sink, and I watch in the mirror as he kicks my legs further apart.

Not letting go of my hair, his free hand fumbles around his crotch, and I hear the clink of his belt being undone. The sound makes my heart thud in my chest, my limbs trembling with the anticipation of having Knox's beautiful cock inside me again.

"Eyes on mine, fuck toy," he barks, yanking my head up, and I hiss at the strain on my hair. I look back up into the reflection of his heated gaze. He gives me no build-up, holding my stare as he forces himself inside me with one punishing thrust. I scream, the pain of his intrusion sharp and leaving me breathless. "You want Daddy to fuck you hard and fast, don't you, Little Bird?" he questions, his own chest heaving. His muscles are strained, coiled like a snake about to strike.

"Yes," I answer through gritted teeth, wiggling as my body adjusts to his impressive size. Many men have fucked me, but none have even come close to his length.

"Yes, what?"

"Fuck me hard, please, Daddy!" I beg, tired of his denial, and watch as he smirks at me through the mirror in front of us.

"Such a good little fuck toy," he coos, his hand stroking the globe of my ass. "But still a little wilful." I watch as, in a blur of motion, his hand lifts and then comes slamming down hard on my behind. A yelp tears from my lips, the area burning as he soothes it with his palm, tears stinging my eyes. "Shhhhh," he whispers, moving his hips so that he rubs a spot deep inside me that leaves me groaning and sends tingles racing across my body. My eyes close as I lose myself to the rhythm of our bodies, letting the waves of pleasure flow across my skin, making it feel as though an electric current runs over it.

Thwack!

My eyes jolt open as another shout sounds from my throat, my ass cheek burning under his palm. I groan again as he keeps moving his hips; the pain heightening the pleasure in a way that I didn't know I needed.

"You like it when Daddy spanks you, fuck toy?" Knox asks, his voice sounding strained and several octaves lower than normal. His grip tightens in my hair once more, and even that hurt only adds to the waves of ecstasy that I'm experiencing.

My heavy-lidded eyes find him in the mirror, his pupils blown as he watches my reactions.

"Yes, Daddy."

A growl that makes wetness seep between my thighs sounds in his throat, and I pant as he picks up the pace, fucking me like he promised. Hard and fast. My fingers dig into the porcelain, my breaths sawing out of my chest with every hard thrust. He watches me in the mirror, watching the way my tits swing with each move he makes.

Thwack!

This one barely registers on the pain scale, but the way it jostles his dick inside me, the sting of it, sets me alight. I can feel myself climbing higher, reaching for my pinnacle.

"Fuck, Little Bird," he groans, his voice strained and gravelly. "You clamp around me like a vacuum when I smack your ass."

Thwack!

This time I feel my inner walls clenching around his hard length. We both moan, my eyelids threatening to flutter closed with the heady sensations this man is creating inside me.

Movement in the mirror catches my eye, and they widen when I see Jude standing there, his own dick palmed in a tight fist as he watches us with bedroom eyes.

"You like it when he watches me fuck the ever-loving shit out of you, fuck toy?" Knox whispers, and I find him in the mirror, also watching Jude. His pace doesn't slow down, instead, it picks up until the sound of our bodies slapping together is obscenely loud and echoing in the tiled room.

"Yes, Daddy," I gasp, my body tightening with my impending orgasm. "Fuck, yes!"

Thwack!

The hit sends me spiraling down into oblivion, my climax tearing through me with a furious energy that leaves me unable to breathe. I keep my eyes open as I come, watching as I buck and writhe in Knox's grip. His fingers dig into my hip to hold me as he fucks me even harder, chasing his own release.

I watch through star-struck eyes as Jude groans, ropes of cum spurting out of the end of his shaft and covering his hand. The sight triggers another orgasm out of me, and I pant as my body is on fire once more, the pleasure almost too much.

With a growling roar, Knox thrusts so deep that I scream, holding me in place as he finds his own climax inside of me. We stay locked together; me watching the blissful agony that fills his face as he empties his load.

After some moments, a deep, contented sigh brushes past his

lips, and his grip loosens as his closed lids open and his bright eyes stare into mine.

"You are so fucking beautiful, Little Bird," he says, his voice breathless and satisfied sounding. I know the feeling, my throat feels raw yet my body feels like liquid. Using his hold on my hair, he pulls me upright until our bodies are pressing together, his arm wrapping around my torso possessively. "What are you doing to me, princess?"

I wish I could answer his question because maybe it would tell me what they are doing to me. This was never part of the plan, to fall for my captors, but here I am, doing just that.

We hold each other's stare in the mirror, neither of us able to answer the riddle that has become our connection. He sighs, and his soft cock slips from between my pussy lips. I cringe when his seed slips down my inner thighs.

"Looks like I'll need another shower," I say, and he chuckles, the vibrations of his laughter making me shudder.

"Allow me," Jude says, and I look up to find his reflection walking toward us, his own lips lifted in post-orgasm satisfaction.

Knox turns us, keeping his hold on me and my hair until we're side on to the mirror, and I watch as Jude sinks to his knees in front of me. My legs are still spread wide, mine and Knox's combined releases painting the inside of my thighs, slick in the light.

"Hmmmm," Jude hums, and I stare at him entranced as his head dips, his tongue darting out in anticipation.

"Juuuuude..." I groan when his hot tongue traces a path up my inner thigh, my skin tightening once more with the teasing pleasure that he's offering.

"So fucking delicious," he murmurs, repeating the move on the other thigh as Knox holds me tightly against him. I gasp when his shaft hardens again, his cock trapped between my thighs. Jude chuckles. "This just keeps getting better."

My brow dips, wondering what he's referring to when Knox gives a deep growl of pleasure in my ear, his arm like a vice around me.

"Jude—" he warns, but he doesn't move and I glance into the mirror to see Jude's tongue lapping at the tip of Knox.

Fuck. Me.

All thoughts fly from my mind when, in the next second, Jude buries his face in between my thighs, his tongue licking my slit hard. I cry out, one hand flying up into Knox's hair as the other tangles in Jude's.

"Oh God," I gasp, unable to stop grinding my hips into Jude's face. He grunts and moans, making the same noises that someone might make when they're eating their favorite dish.

Jude's tongue leaves my cunt for a moment, affording me a reprieve from the overwhelming pleasure, only for Knox to keen in a low, deep tone, his grip tightening around me and his teeth sinking into my neck. The pain adds to the sensations running riot throughout my body, and coupled with the knowledge that Jude is sucking Knox's dick in between my thighs has wetness slicking my core even more.

"Fuck, Jude!" Knox exclaims, his hips thrusting forward and pushing my clit into Jude's nose.

I've no fucking idea how the guy is even breathing right now, but I don't want him to stop. I can feel my release fluttering around the edges of my vision, and my nails dig into their heads, urging them to keep going.

I know when Jude releases Knox, as the latter's body goes limp against me and his mouth returns to my neck to suck and nibble. I hiss out a breath when Jude's tongue resumes its assault on my cunt, his fingers, on one hand, digging into my thigh to pull me closer. The other is between my legs, and by the way his fist keeps brushing my opening, and that Knox's hips are moving in that age-old rhythm, I know that Jude's hand is wrapped around Knox's cock.

It doesn't take much more to make my release scream through me; a nip to my clit seals the deal, and I come, squirting all over Jude's face with a strangled cry. I ride out my orgasm, the waves of pleasure dragging me under repeatedly as he keeps licking until I'm a shuddering, hot mess.

Finally, he lets me go, the noise of him sucking Knox's dick loud over my panting breaths. Knox stiffens, moaning as his hips thrust against mine. He holds me close as, with a roar, he snaps his hips forward, and the sound of Jude swallowing Knox's climax has me almost orgasming again.

I look down through barely open eyes to see Jude sit back on his heels with a satisfied look on his face, his chin glistening. Unable to resist, I tug him up by his hair and slam my lips onto his. I moan as a combination of my sweet musk and Knox's salty release bursts on my tongue, my tongue invading Jude's mouth and savoring the taste.

His head is ripped away, a whine leaving my lips only to turn to a groan when Knox copies my move and kisses Jude over my shoulder. It's a kiss full of domination, Knox's hand over my own in a bruising grip in Jude's dark locks as he eats his face very similarly to what Jude just did to my pussy.

Jesus fucking Christ.

They break apart, both gasping and with such intensity in their eyes that it hurts to look at them.

After a few moments, Jude swings his gaze to mine, his palm coming up to cup my cheek in a gesture so tender that tears sting my eyes.

"I knew you'd be the one to bring us together, Nightingale."

My mouth opens then closes again as he places a gentle kiss on my swollen lips before he turns and saunters towards the door.

"Your breakfast is waiting downstairs for you, broken bird. It won't be as delicious as the one I just had, but it's still pretty tasty if I say so myself."

Well, how's a girl to say no to that?

CHAPTER TEN

"DEMONS" BY JACOB LEE

KNOX

We leave our Little Bird to have another shower, Jude didn't exactly clean her up. I glance over at the guy, my eyes narrowing at his smug as fuck grin as he studies me back.

"Fuck off," I grumble, my cheeks heating at the memory of those lips around my cock, his tongue lapping at me like a fucking popsicle.

"You want me..." he sings, sauntering closer to where I'm sitting at the kitchen island. "You want to suck me..."

"Fuck. Off. Jude."

But there's no heat behind my words as he stops, just out of arm's reach, in front of me. I can't deny that I didn't enjoy him giving me head. If I'm being honest, it was the best damn blowie I've had in a long fucking time. Possibly even the best ever when I consider my bird's warm heat covering me too.

"You want to fuck me..." he adds, his voice lower than before and husky. Damn, it's like the floodgates have opened and I get a visual of bending him over this counter and fucking him hard and viciously. "I'd be so good for you, Daddy."

Jesus.

He steps closer, trailing a finger down my T-shirt-covered chest. My cock twitches in my jeans like it hasn't just had two mind-blowing releases in the last hour.

"You're playing with fire, pretty Jude," I mumble, frozen as his head dips, his lips a hair's breadth away from mine.

"Good thing I like to get burnt," he whispers, the touch of his lips on mine making my breath catch. I can smell our combined climaxes on his breath. *How have I resisted him all these years?* Oh yeah, I'm not usually into dudes. I'm about ready to pounce on him when I hear footsteps on the metal stairs. "Next time, Daddy." Jude licks my lips in a lightning-fast move, then dances away towards the stairs to meet our naked bird at the bottom step. I'm left in a daze, blinking like a fucking twat at his departure, and her delectable body being on show just adds to the jumble my mind is currently in. "Your break-fast awaits, Nightingale!" Jude declares, and I shake my head of the lust fog he created to see him ushering her towards the table. She glances back over her shoulder, her cheeks flushing when she catches my stare.

On the immense table, there's a single place setting; a bowl and a glass full of fresh juice set on it.

"What is it?" she asks, and her rich voice makes my balls ache, along with the center of my chest.

"Handmade granola, coconut yogurt, and local honey. Plus freshly squeezed orange juice. Full of vitamins, and I've added some seeds and nuts to the granola for some protein. Gotta keep your strength up," Jude tells her, pulling her chair out and pushing it in just like a perfect gentleman. *Fucking schmoozer.*

"Strength for what?" she asks warily, picking up the glass of juice and taking a large gulp. The ice tinkles in the glass, and I watch as she licks her lips after setting the glass down. Twitch goes my clearly insatiable cock again.

"For playtime, silly," Jude chides, taking the seat next to her and grabbing the spoon before she can. He dips it into the bowl, collecting yogurt, granola, and honey, then brings it to her lips. "Open up, buttercup."

She holds his intense stare as she obeys, and fucking hell, I can feel pre-cum leaking out of my tip at her compliance.

"Yuuummmm," she mumbles around her mouthful, Jude chuckling as he fills the spoon once more. I watch captivated as he feeds her until the bowl and glass are completely empty. She sits back with a contented sigh; her stomach a little rounded with fullness. "That was delicious, thank you," she says, and I see a moment of hesitation on her face before she darts forward and places a light kiss on his cheek. He freezes.

"What was that for?" he asks, looking as dumbstruck as I felt earlier when he licked my lips. I get why. Affection is not something that we've experienced much of around here.

"No one has made food for me in a long time," she answers, tucking a strand of deep mahogany hair behind her ear. "Well, not since Mom..." she trails off, and I can't help the tightness I feel at my center.

She means not since the Tailors murdered her mom. God, if she ever discovered exactly who pulled the trigger...

"You are most welcome, Nightingale," Jude replies, taking her hand in his and kissing it. "Time to go downstairs."

"Will it hurt?" she asks him, biting her lower lip in a way that has a growl sounding in my chest. Her wide eyes swing to find mine, and I'm not surprised to see heat mixed in with trepidation, her lids lowered slightly.

"A little," I tell her, rising from my seat and stalking towards her. "But you like pain, don't you, Little Bird?"

"Yes, Daddy." No hesitation, her words just come out as she tells me her secret desires. My cock is rock-solid in my jeans, and I see her eyes dart down, her pink tongue flicking out to lick her lower lip.

"Let's get started before Aeron comes back and rips us a new one," I say, locking down my desire to fuck her senseless again, losing myself in her sweet cunt, and maybe Jude's hot mouth. The comment about our group leader is more for Jude, although I'm looking at our bird, holding my hand for her to take.

"He's gonna be so mad that you fucked her again." Jude cackles, his smile infectious. A grin splits my face at the thought of Aeron losing his shit.

Our Little Bird doesn't protest as I lead her back to the basement, and I have to wonder if she's coming to accept her place here. Her fate with us. Because no matter what Aeron or his father, our true boss, says, I'm not letting her go. She's tied to us now, and after today, our ownership will be even more clear.

She takes a deep inhale when we cross the threshold into the room we've been using this whole time. Our torture room. Though I notice Aeron has made sure it's clean for her, not something we usually bother with until the job is done. Her coffin is still against the wall, as is the St Andrew's Cross. Sitting in the middle of the room is a black leather tattoo chair, laid flat so it's like a bed.

"What is that for?" she asks, inquisitive eyes tracking Jude as he walks over to the chair. He opens one drawer on the black metal set that is next to it, taking out a pair of black latex gloves.

"It's time to make sure everyone knows who you belong to, Nightingale," he tells her, picking up his wireless tattoo pen. A low hum sounds in the room when he switches it on before he settles down in the leather stool and pats the chair.

I tug her hand, and she follows with only brief resistance.

"Not gonna put up a fight, princess?" I question, wrapping my hands around her waist and hoisting her up onto the chair. She hisses when the cool leather hits her bare ass, but soon swings her legs up and lies down.

"No," she answers, her brow furrowing. "Although, I don't understand how this will make me talk?"

I look to Jude, who just shrugs, switching the pen off and picking up a Sharpie. He likes to work freehand, drawing the design in pen, and then going over it with ink. All of us have his artwork decorating our bodies. We're his breathing canvases.

"It's not," he says, and she turns that beautiful gaze onto him. My mouth pinches and my throat constricts at me not having her attention anymore. "Although you'd be surprised at what people say when you're tattooing their bodies."

I'm always impressed with how his chaotic mind settles when he's drawing and when he's inking designs on another person's skin. His attention to detail is mind-blowing. I watch as he covers her entire torso in a series of delicate chains. He starts by circling her neck with ropes of them, dripping with jewel-like shapes that dip down between her beautiful breasts and morph into a stunningly intricate mandala, more chains following the curve of her underbust. A chain drops down the center of her stomach, splitting and spreading out over her hips with more swooping over her upper thighs. She gasps when his pen draws a series of complex mandalas over her pelvic bone; the design coming down to just above her delicious cunt.

She tries to tilt her head down, to see what he's drawn, but he snaps his head up and tsks at her.

"No peeping until it's finished, Nightingale," he chides, adding a finishing flourish to one of the intricate designs. Smirking, I pull out a red, silk blindfold that I stashed in my back pocket earlier, holding it out in front of her eyes.

"Spoilsports," she grumbles, allowing me to wrap the cloth around her head and cutting off her vision. She settles back down again without complaint once I've tied it securely. I chuckle as I take in her disgruntled pout.

"If you're a good girl and lie still for him, I'll help take the pain away when it gets too much," I tell her, smoothing my hand over her messy hair. It's a riot of reds; from the brightest orange of sunset to the darkest red of maple leaves in the fall and soft as silk. She nods, her lips parting when the hum of the gun starts up. I watch as her body tenses up, waiting for that first swipe of the needle. I can see when it happens in the way that her jaw clenches and the skin around her mouth tightens. "Such a beautiful bird," I whisper, stroking her damp hair again as she takes the pain and makes no noise. I guess this is small compared to what the others did to her. Her nails are still missing, and a flash of anger burns through me whenever I catch sight of the red tips of her fingers or the raw destruction of her back.

Her heaved sigh brings me back to the present, and I look down to find her facing me as Jude tattoos her collarbone and across her upper chest. Fuck, even I know that hurts, but she barely reacts, just the occasional baring of teeth.

"I always wanted a tattoo," she tells me, taking a deep inhale when he hits a spot close to the bone.

"Yeah?" I stroke her hair again, unable to help myself. There's something about the way her body relaxes in contentment when I do it that's becoming addictive.

"Yeah, but Rufus wouldn't let me. Some bullshit about 'women shouldn't have tattoos. It's not ladylike'." She lowers her voice in a terrible imitation of her pops, and both Jude and I scoff at his outdated views.

"What tattoo would you have chosen?" I ask, and I see Jude perk up, his eyes not leaving her body, even as his spine straightens a little.

"Birds. Flying free," she answers straight away with no hesitation. A pang of something sharp stabs me in the solar plexus, and I can't fucking breathe for a second. We may treat her like a pampered pet, but she's just as trapped here now as she was with Adam Taylor and his men, and her father and the Dead Soldiers before us. This is her prison.

"Why flying free?" Jude questions and I jolt to think that she wanted to be free long before she came here.

"I've spent my whole life being trapped in one prison or another. For once, I'd like to feel the wind in my wings."

I look away from her and see Jude paused in his work, his hand hovering over her skin as he swallows roughly. I glance back at our Little Bird to see her fists clenched, but I feel that it's the past that's causing her distress rather than the pain from her new ink.

The saying goes that if you love something, let it go. If it comes back, it's yours. If it doesn't, it never was.

But that's bullshit. I think that if you love something, you keep it close.

If you don't, someone will come and steal it away.

CHAPTER ELEVEN

"BIG BAD WOLF" BY ROSES & REVOLUTIONS

TARL

I step back, the sound of the tooth hitting the metal dish loud in the vast, windowless warehouse Aeron and I are in. The man in front of us gurgles, the ruby-red of blood dribbling down his chin. He can't move his head to spit it out and can't move his body as he's strapped on a metal gurney that's tilted up to allow me access to do my bloody work.

"You've already squealed like a fucking pig, Soldier scum," Aeron says, the sleeves of his shirt rolled up, his jacket laid carefully out of range on the table containing my tools. "So why not give us something useful and we can ease up a little, huh?"

"Fuck you, Tailor brat!" the pig—a foot soldier, I believe, by the lack of chevrons on his person. The Soldiers like to ink their rank onto their skin, using the US Armed Forces insignia. Typical that they'd send a grunt to spy on us, they don't give a shit about their members and new recruits need to prove themselves somehow.

"No thanks," Aeron replies, giving me a nod and I delve back in, grabbing another molar with my pliers and bracing my boot against the gurney. The pig tries to bite down, but my grip on his jaw keeps his mouth open, preventing that nonsense, and so with a lot of tugging and a cry of pain from him, I wrench another tooth out to add to my collection.

Just think of me as the tooth fairy. Only, without the wings.

Clink it goes as it lands with the other three in my dish. I'll clean them off later, maybe I'll make Jude a necklace, or a pair of cufflinks. So many options for a creative person like myself.

"Anything else to say?" Aeron asks after our pig stops squealing.

"Yeah, I hear your mom screamed like a whore when the Soldiers each took their turn!"

Oh. Shit.

Aeron goes deadly still, and I can barely see him breathe as he stares at our victim, who most definitely will be a Dead Soldier before long. Just not how he'd hoped.

Heather Taylor's kidnap and rape started this war between the Tailors and Dead Soldiers over a decade ago. It was the catalyst for what has been ten long years of bloodshed and pain, the tit-for-tat cycle we can't seem to get out of. First Heather, then Lark's mom was shot, dying in Lark's arms on her twelfth birthday. They shot June two years after that, Jude unable to stop the blood flowing as she bled out before him, and now we have Lark, the Soldiers' Darling as they call her, on account of her being Rufus Jackson's, the leader of the Dead Soldiers, daughter.

"Tarl. The Cradle."

A fissure of excitement runs through me at Aeron's words. I haven't had a play with this toy for a while, and admittedly it's one of my favorites. Dropping the pliers in the dish, I wipe my hands on my butcher's apron, then grab the gurney, releasing the brakes and wheeling it over to where my beautifully restored Judas Cradle sits.

It's an original, used by the inquisitors from the sixteenth century, and the dark wood gleams. It's a beautiful design, simplistic really, but it definitely gets them talking. Well, screaming. A wooden pyramid sits atop four wooden legs, and it stands about ten feet tall. I added a metal tip to the pyramid top, all the better for penetration.

Dangling above it is a metal hoop that's attached to ropes hanging from the ceiling. I lower the hoop to prepare for attaching it around his waist.

"What the fuck is that?" he croaks, more blood dripping down his chin.

"Boys," I order, ignoring his question as two of our loyal Tailors come forward from the shadows to unstrap our spy from the gurney. He tries to fight, but the hours that he's already spent in our care have left him weak and missing a lot of blood. They quickly over-whelm him, binding his wrists behind his back and attaching them to another pulley hanging from the ceiling.

They hold him still while I clamp the hoop around his waist, locking it with a padlock that makes a satisfying snick. I can see the fine tremble in his limbs as he wonders what's going to happen next, and my heart pounds as the phantom sounds of the Cradle's previous victims fill my ears.

I walk back over to the pulley that attaches to his waist hoop, and sharply tug, hoisting him up into the air. He shouts, and even Aeron cracks a small smile at his fear permeating the room.

Our guys help to get him into position, legs either side of the pyramid, the tip pressing into his asshole. I always strip our victims before starting, which saves time later on and means I don't have to pause whilst torturing them. Preparation is key after all. They secure the metal cuffs around his ankles; the boys taking the ropes coming off each and tugging slightly.

"What the fuck is this?!" he screams as they pull him down by his ankles just enough so that the metal penetrates his anal sphincter.

"Have you ever heard of the saying 'rip him a new one'?" I ask him conversationally, and his eyes go wide at the sound of my voice.

It's the first time I've spoken, and if my reputation has preceded me, he knows that to hear my voice is akin to signing his death warrant.

He shakes as the meaning of what I'm saying becomes all too clear.

"Now, you can still avoid having your asshole widened further. So perhaps you'll answer our questions?" Aeron interjects, and my smile widens when I watch our little pig's face grow hard.

"Go to Hell!" he howls, and I can't help the crazed laugh that tumbles from my lips. I fucking love it when they refuse.

"Time for a brief history lesson," I tell him, tying off the rope that attaches to the hoop around his waist so that there's enough slack for us to lower him as much as we like. "Back in the sixteenth century, the Spanish Inquisition invented some of—in my opinion—the best methods of torture the world has ever seen." I walk towards him, stroking my hand down the smooth wood when I reach the Cradle. "The Judas Cradle was one such invention, and the beauty of it is that we can have you on here for hours, days even. Widening you bit by bit until you're ripped apart from the asshole up."

The dripping sound and sharp ammonia scent lets me know that he's pissed himself, and I tear my hand away just before any touches me. My nose wrinkles as I stalk away to stand next to Aeron. I give our guys a nod, and they tug hard, impaling him further as the point slips inside of his back passage easily. I did him a favor and oiled it up earlier.

His scream is like music to my ears, and my dick twitches in my pants when I hear a feminine echo, imagining our pretty bird impaled on my hardness. Maybe even Jude's alongside mine, stretching her and stuffing her with our cocks.

"I'll talk! Please! I'll tell you anything!"

The shout has me blinking away my fantasy, and I focus to see blood now dripping down my beautiful Cradle. He's sweating, shaking, and sobbing like a baby. I walk over to the pulley, pulling him up so that he's no longer impaled by the pyramid. A wounded noise leaves his lips as he dangles there.

Aeron walks up to him, looking up at the blubbering mess of a human.

"Where is the Soldiers' HQ?"

"I–I don't know," the man stutters, snot running down his face to mix with the blood from his mouth. "They don't tell you until you make Corporal."

Aeron growls at that.

"Then what fucking use are you to me?" he snarls, glancing over to me and giving a nod before turning his back. I pull the rope, making our piggy squeal.

"W–wait!" he shouts, and I pause. "They sent me to find out where you're keeping her!"

Aeron and I both freeze at this, Aeron slowly turning around.

"Who?"

"The S–Soldier's Darling! The Bossman wants her back. She's how he keeps the others in line, and things are getting messy now she's been gone so long."

My blood boils at his words, at the implied meaning, and my knuckles whiten with how hard I'm clenching my fist around the rope.

"What do you mean, 'keeps the others in line'?" Aeron asks, his voice deadly and cutting. He has that stillness again, like a snake about to strike. Like me, he needs to have his suspicions confirmed.

"W–when they've done a good job, a–as a reward, they get a night with The Darling. To do whatever they like," the dead man stutters, eyes flicking from Aeron's face to my own. He'll find no comfort from either of us.

"Who gets her?" I ask, and his head whips over to me. I barely recognise my voice, it's full of a darkness that rarely gets to see the light of day.

"A–as s–soon as you g–graduate to Corporal. I–it's part of the celebrations. A–all the Corporals that graduate that night get a go." His words stutter out more as the blackness of rage descends upon me. The Dead Soldiers are not a small gang and they're constantly gaining new members with the lure of drugs, easy money, and presumably free pussy. Our bird's unwilling pussy it seems.

With a calmness that belies the ire swirling in Aeron's eyes, he walks over to my table of tools, placing his hands on the surface. His chest heaves once, twice, and on the third time, he lifts the whole thing and throws it against the wall. Metal tools and instruments go flying, the noise loud and echoing in the vast space.

Chest heaving, he turns back around, smoothing his hair with hands that have a fine tremor which most people would miss, but not me. He stares straight at me and gives a single jerk of his head.

"Split him in half."

"My pleasure," I reply, meaning it as I loosen the rope and let go, our pig falling back onto the cradle's point hard.

He screams loud enough that I can hear his throat tearing, but this time it does nothing to excite me, the feminine echoes in my head now full of pain as my little bird is violated over and over again by men who will soon die for daring to touch her.

His screams become the plaintive cry of a wounded animal as our men heave his legs down, blood and bits of his insides sliding down the wood as they rip him apart.

I make a vow, watching this pig die horrifically, unmoved by the gory sight before me. Every Soldier who has dared touch our bird will die a bloody death, begging for mercy that I will not show them.

Looking over to Aeron, I can see the same promise of violence in his tumultuous eyes. The same lack of mercy. Their deaths already written in his stormy, ocean eyes.

Until this point, our Pretty Bird may have been alone, but now she has demons on her side. Ready to go to war and avenge all who have wronged her.

For she is ours, and no one else will ever touch her again.

CHAPTER TWELVE

LARK

The hours flow past in waves of pain and numbness. They allow me slight breaks to go to the toilet or to feed me lunch but am not allowed to take the blindfold off, so I have no fucking clue what the design on my skin is. Knox stays by my side, at least it feels like he does, his body heat flowing into me as he strokes my hair and places a straw between my lips to give me sips of sweet energy drinks.

Jude is pretty silent the whole time, and I find myself opening up to them both, just as Jude predicted. Tales from my childhood, before Mom was murdered, fill the silence, and I find myself smiling as I recall them, the action feeling a little foreign on my face. Everything that has happened to me in the years that have passed since her death has left me with little to smile about. I am regaling an especially funny story of the time that Mom snuck Rook and I to the

Grand Lake beach and Rook got his head stuck in a bucket when a loud crash has me sitting up with a shriek.

"Bro! What the fuck!" Jude shouts, and my hand flies to my blindfold, ready to tear it off and see what is going on.

"Don't you dare fucking touch that, Dove." Aeron's cold voice lashes over me, and my traitorous body responds by coating my lower lips in wetness even as my heart races. I carefully and slowly lower my hand back to my lap.

"You could have ruined it!" Jude seethes, and I've never heard him so angry before, the sound of his fury like that of hundreds of ant bites.

"Stand aside, Knox," Aeron orders, and I realize Knox must be in front of me, protecting me. My brows furrow as I wait for Knox to do as he's bidden. "Don't fucking test me right now. Move. Aside."

A rush of cool air hits my front a moment later, and I can feel my whole body stiffen, awaiting Aeron's wrath. My nostrils flare with annoyance that I can't fucking see anything, but I daren't anger him further, my hands clenching into fists in my lap, and I'm practically biting my tongue to hold in any harsh words that want to escape.

I jump when fingertips brush my cheek, my inhale sharp as they run down the side of my neck, then along the sore, freshly-inked skin across my chest.

"How long?" Aeron whispers, and I shake my head slightly as I try to work out what he's asking.

"How long what, Devil Man?" I murmur back, something keeping me from making my voice any louder, fear making my stomach knot.

"How long has your father been letting his men rape you?"

I flinch back, my heart racing as my whole body trembles. Phantom hands try to grasp me, and I have to concentrate hard on not hyperventilating, his words tearing at my insides. I struggle to push the memories back into their tiny box and lock it tight.

"What are you fucking talking about?" Jude asks, his voice soft and hollow sounding.

"Answer the question, Dove," Aeron commands, and I'm so thrown by my sordid home situation finally coming to light, of them discovering just how damaged I am, that I answer.

"Since the day after my twelfth birthday. The day after..."

"We killed your mom," Aeron supplies in a tone completely devoid of emotion, and I nod. His hand turns to a fist against my collarbone, pressing into the stinging flesh, and I brace myself for the blow, but it comes in a different, more confusing and devastating form as he speaks again.

"No man will ever touch you without your consent again, Dove. That is a fucking promise."

"And we will tear apart every man who has dared to touch you," Tarl adds, his voice close, and I startle at the darkness which laces his tone. It reminds me of being trapped in the cell a few doors down, full of hopeless despair.

"How can you promise that?" I question them, my voice small and frightened sounding. I fucking hate it. A sigh escapes my lips when a palm cups my cheek, and a forehead presses against mine. The scent of clean cotton, vanilla, and sandalwood tells me it's Aeron.

"Because we are the motherfucking Tailors, and no one touches or hurts, what belongs to us."

I'm left speechless as he presses a light kiss to my lips, and then cool air hits me once more as his body heat no longer reaches me. His steps sound across the floor, followed by his light tread up the stairs.

"Lie back down, Nightingale," Jude softly orders, and a large hand—Knox's, I think by the callouses—helps me to lie back, grasping my elbow.

Tears sting my eyes, forcing their way past my closed lids and soaking into the silky fabric, and I can't seem to swallow past the lump in my throat.

"It's okay, Little Bird," Knox soothes, taking my hand in his and interlacing our fingers. "You will never be alone again. We'll always be here to protect you."

A sob escapes past my lips, and once that's out, I can't seem to stop the flood of grief that washes over me like a waterfall. I grip Knox's hand tightly as I let it all pour out of me for the first time since that awful day.

My mother had just died, shot down at my twelfth birthday party when she'd taken Rook and I to the local diner to get burgers and milk-shakes. Not much of a party, but enough for me as we got so few happy times, always under the thumb of my tyrannical cunt of a father. We were just leaving, and I remember the loud sound of a car backfiring, only my mom fell forward onto the asphalt, red spreading in a puddle around her.

I held her as she died, begging for help, but they came too late, and I watched as the light left her eyes, her mumbled words of love faint. I was numb as my sperm donor drove us home, unsurprised when he locked me in my room. Her death was my fault. After all, we wouldn't have been at the diner if it wasn't for my birthday.

They left me alone in my blood-soaked grief for twenty-four hours, not even allowing me a shower to wash the stain of my sin off. I remember the feeling of relief when the lock clicked, my door swinging open. But no angel stepped in, instead my father's second-in-command, Sherman. A man I'd known since birth.

Only, he didn't look at me like someone looks at a child. The devil was in his eyes as he told me I had myself to blame, that what he was about to do was just punishment for what I did to my mother.

I come out of the memory screaming as hands pin me down, desperate voices calling my name, but they can't reach me, and all I see is Sherman's leering grin as he forces his way inside of my unwilling child's body, feeling the agonizing pain of being torn apart by his twisted desires.

"Little Bird! Lark! Calm down, baby, please!" Knox's face appears, only to be taken over by one of the Soldier's faces.

Then another.

And another.

They keep coming, filling me with their lust and depravity until I truly am the broken bird that Jude accused me of being when we first met.

"I'm so sorry, Pretty Bird," Tarl's deep melody reaches my ears right before I feel a sharp pain in my neck a second later.

Then nothing but blissful darkness.

I open my eyes, the black of my blissfully dreamless sleep fading to be replaced with the light of predawn that fills the room. It's a struggle to get them to open fully, like great weights are trying to pull them back down.

"'It was the lark, the herald of the morn,
No nightingale,'"

I look to the side to find Jude lying beside me, his chest bare, all of his beautiful ink and tattoos on display. He reaches out a hand, pushing sweat-slicked hair away from my face as he leans down and brushes our foreheads together.

"Did you just quote a line from Romeo and Juliet?" I ask him, my voice hoarse and scratchy, as if I've been screaming for hours.

"I'm not just a pretty face, Nightingale," he murmurs against my lips, rubbing our noses together. "And it's one of the great romances. Plus, it seemed fitting."

"But it's so sad," I say, swallowing past the sudden lump in my throat. "They die, Baby Devil. All because they fall in love, and their families hate each other."

"I told you it was fitting, Nightingale."

"Are you telling me you're in love with me, Jude?"

My heart races and my blood thrums in my veins as I wait for his answer. He takes my hand in his, pressing it to his exposed chest, all the while keeping our foreheads touching.

"It hurts here whenever I'm apart from you," he confesses in a whisper, and I can feel the thud of his heart as it pounds against my palm. "I feel rage here in my soul when I think about anyone hurting you." He moves our hands down to his diaphragm, to the place that's often associated with someone's soul. Next, he moves them up to his temple. "It feels calmer here whenever you are near. You chase the darkness away, Nightingale. Now tell me, is that love?"

My breath stutters as I think of his words and I open my mouth several times, only to close it again. I blame the fogginess that lingers in my brain for the truth that comes spilling out.

"I've never wanted—no, craved anyone, as much as I crave you. All of you. I should fear you, but I'm not scared. I feel safe for the first time in ten years and have had nights unplagued by fucking demons. For what happened to Mom, I should hate you all, but I don't. I can't."

His body quivers, his hand tightening around my own which is still against his temple. He brings them between us, moving his head back so that he can kiss each of my knuckles.

"Whenever I hear a gunshot, I go back to that day. To holding the other half of me as she died in my arms," he confesses in a strained tone, his ocean eyes swirling like a stormy sea.

His image wavers as warm wetness spills onto my cheeks, leaving a trail of anguish.

"Me too," I choke out, gripping his hand like it's the only thing keeping me afloat. "My childhood ended the day she died. I often wondered if she kept them away up until then."

"I'm so sorry, Nightingale," he whispers, his neck corded and throat working. "So fucking sorry."

I take a shuddering inhale.

"Me too, Jude. Me too."

CHAPTER THIRTEEN

"MR. SANDMAN" BY SMYL

JUDE

I watch as our beautiful, broken Nightingale falls back asleep, Tarl's drugs doing their job and giving her some rest. Wrapping her in my arms, I pull her tightly until our bodies press so closely together that not even a sliver of air is between us.

It's funny really, in a fucked up kind of way, anyway. We have a lot in common; both losing our mothers to violence. I mean, Mom isn't dead, just holed up in a nice, cushy mental health facility on the west coast with top-notch security. The Soldiers fucked her up, literally, but it wasn't until the murder of my sister that she broke completely. She couldn't cope with the loss of a child, kept talking to June like she was still there, and wouldn't let anyone touch her room back home.

It was six months later, the second time that we found her in the bath with slit wrists, that Pops admitted she needed help, so sent her to Mount Pleasant. She seems to get along well there, Aeron and I are due for a visit as we try to go once a month just to check in on her. Perhaps we could take Nightingale this time.

Light fills the room as the door cracks open, and I look up to find my brother standing in the doorway.

"Family meeting, Dad's on the phone," he says, his voice low as his eyes trace over Nightingale in my bed.

My stomach drops, just like when you're on a rollercoaster but not nearly as fun.

"Shit," I mumble, carefully untangling myself from our broken bird. Getting up and out of bed, I bend back down and tuck the blankets around her. She doesn't stir, her breaths even and deep as she sleeps on.

I hesitate, something pulling me back down, and I press the lightest of kisses on her temple, eliciting a sigh from those sweet lips of hers.

"Come on," Aeron mutters from next to me, and a smile lifts my lips when I straighten up, only for him to lean down and kiss her too. She's definitely ours to keep.

We leave our sleeping beauty, quietly closing the door behind us —a brand new one that I had a couple of our members put in after Aeron blew the last one off. Still worth it for a taste of my Nightingale's sweet nectar.

"So, what does the old man want?" I ask as we make our way down the stairs, and Aeron gives me this look that tells me I just asked a stupid fucking question. "Alright, don't get your balls in a twist. I'm guessing it's something about Nightingale?"

"I imagine so," he answers as we reach the bottom of the stairs, heading towards a door off the main living area that leads to our office. My chest tightens as he confirms my suspicions.

I hear Pops' deep voice as I open the door, his laugh warming me as it always has since I was a child.

Unlike my Nightingale, our father always showed us love and affection. Yes, he was hard on us sometimes, but family is very important to him, always has been. As he likes to remind us, we are his legacy, the future, and he wants us to be men that can hold our heads up and defend our home.

"Hey, pops," I say as I spot him on the enormous TV screen mounted on the wall. He's in a lavish hotel suite in the Middle East somewhere, if the modern yet tribal decor behind him is any sign.

Adam Taylor is who I will be in thirty years. If I need to know what I'll look like when I'm in my fifties, I just need to look at my Pops and there's my answer. He has thick, dark hair, longer on top and slicked back–that's currently covered by some sort of patterned head cloth–and deep blue eyes that have a darkness in their depths that only comes from gang life. Overall, pretty fucking handsome.

"Jude!" he exclaims, the lines around his eyes prominent as he grins at me. "How are you, my boy?" There's an edge of concern in his tone as he checks me over, no doubt trying to see if there are any fresh scars on my bare torso. He knows my need for pain when my emotions run high, and although he hasn't pushed me to seek medical help, I know that he worries.

"I'm fine, old man," I tease, and his grin grows wider.

"Careful, boy, I can still whoop your ass!"

"A little hard to do from all the way...where are you exactly?"

"Just outside of Dubai, boy, and you won't believe the Arabian stock they have here. Absolutely fucking stunning!" His eyes are gleaming as he speaks on his most favorite topic; horses.

"So you'll be bringing some back then, Adam?" Tarl asks, his own passion for the creatures rivaling that of my father's. He's especially excited at the prospect of some being brought back from his home-land, his mismatched eyes gleaming and sparkling as he waits for Pops to answer. I'm surprised that Pops didn't take him with on this trip. He usually would, but maybe it's because it's so close to Tarl's homeland or Tarl asked to stay here to help deal with our little Nightingale.

"I may be in talks with Prince Faisal," he tells my lover, both their eyes twinkling at the thought of new Arab thoroughbreds in the stables. "And on that topic, I need you boys to go down to the stables and check everything is set for race day. You'll also need to be there, top hats and tails, on the day as I'm going to be extending my stay a little."

"Yes, sir," we all say in unison, and he chuckles.

"Stand down, soldiers." He laughs, his face becoming serious and more like the face he shows to the rest of the world. "On that subject, how is our little Soldier doing? Has she broken yet?"

We all go still, and it's taking all my concentration not to blurt out how fucking strong our Nightingale is. How beautiful and fierce she is. How much I want to hold her as we break her and then help put her back together again.

"We're trying an alternative approach," Aeron says, his back ramrod straight. "Hopefully, by getting her to trust us, she'll tell us what we need to know. We've already discovered that she hates her father, so I know we can exploit that somehow."

"Good work, son," Pops replies with respect shining in his eyes as he gives Aeron a nod. I want to sink a kitchen knife into Aeron's left testicle for exposing our Nightingale like that. Even if it is to the man that I look up to most in the entire world.

Aeron returns the nod, but I notice his hands clench into tight fists at his sides, his jaw tight too. Looks like he didn't want to spill that tidbit either.

"Well, boys, that's all for now, I think. I got your report on the foot soldier that was spying. Shame he divulged nothing of use," Pops muses, and I look between Tarl and Aeron.

Tarl gives a minute shake of his head, confirming that they didn't tell my father about our bird being the Soldier's Darling. Even the thought of that raises my temperature, and I count slowly back from ten to keep my cool and not fly off the handle like I did when they told Knox and I exactly what they discovered. We still need to clean up the living area after Knox went apeshit and smashed everything he could get his hands on.

"Goodbye, father," Aeron says, bringing my mind back to the room.

A chorus of farewells follow, my Pops giving us his own before disconnecting the call.

"She needs a break," Knox says quietly into the silence.

"I know," Aeron replies, scrubbing a palm over his face in a rare show of emotion. "And don't think I don't know that you fucked her again, Knox."

They both glare at each other, their war as old as, well, as old as my sister's rotting corpse. We all know that Aeron blames Knox for her death, she was sneaking out to meet him the night it happened, and even though I'd followed her to see what she was up to, I couldn't do a fucking thing to stop her fate. Suddenly, heat flushes through my body, my pulse speeding.

"Enough!" I shout, and they all whip their heads towards me. "Stop fucking fighting! What happened to June wasn't anyone in this room's fault. So, just stop. Please." Both their faces soften, all the anger draining out of them at my plea. "I propose we take Nightingale to the horses, and then she can be my date to the races."

"Seconded. Though, she'll be *our* date," Tarl states, sauntering over to me and placing a kiss on my lips, and the red haze drains out of me. "I can smell her scent on you, Brat. Like a warm summer's day and sweet cherry blossoms."

"She does smell like that, doesn't she?" I exclaim excitedly. It's been bugging me not being able to describe her sweetness.

"I also vote in favor," Knox says, and Tarl and I look over at him and beam.

"Thank you, Daddy."

I see Tarl raise a brow from the corner of my eye, and I can't help the way my grin widens at Knox's blush.

"Oh, for fuck's sake! Will you all stop fucking my brother!" Aeron throws his hands up, and a bark of laughter escapes my lips at how emotional he's been lately. I knew Nightingale was going to be good for us.

"You could always join in, bro. I'm sure Nightingale would like that too. She could be the filling in a Tailor brother sandwich!"

"Jesus fucking Christ, Jude." Aeron sighs, rubbing his face again. "I will not fuck you. End. Of."

"But you wouldn't object to sharing pussy space with Nightingale?" I press, unable to help to tease him. Although, that would be hot as fuck. Both of us squashed in that tight cunt of hers, rubbing up against each other's dicks.

His jaw ticks and that's when I know I've got him.

"Back to the matter at hand," Aeron says through clenched teeth, instead of answering. It's okay, I know that it's a yes. A firm one if the way his slacks are straining at the crotch is any indication. "Let her rest today, then tomorrow we'll take her to the stables."

"And the races?" I ask, waiting with bated breath.

"And the races."

Looks like I'll need to go *My Fair Lady* on Nightingale's ass.

CHAPTER FOURTEEN

"MIDAS" BY SKOTT

LARK

The next time I wake up, I find the other ocean-eyed brother staring at me, his eyes soft like the calm, cool depths as he watches me from the end of Jude's bed.

"Good morning, Dove."

"Uh, morning?" It comes out more of a question than a greeting. I'm not used to this gentle politeness.

"Don't look so fucking confused," he huffs, and my lips tilt up in a half grin. There's the asshole that we know and love. *Wait! Not love, I meant like. Definitely like.* "Time to get ready. We're going out."

"What?" I sit bolt upright, uncaring that the sheet pools in my lap, and his eyes rake over my exposed tits with molten, passionate fire making the blue glimmer.

"You know I don't enjoy repeating myself," he says, voice an octave lower than it was before. He looks back up at my face, although it appears like it takes some effort to tear his gaze away from my body. "We're all going out today, and you'll be coming with us. Here."

He lifts a pile of clothes, and I just stare dumbstruck.

"You're giving me clothes? And taking me out?"

"Well, as much as I'd like you to remain naked, it's not appropriate outside the house. Plus, no one gets to see what belongs to us," he tells me, his eyes darting back down to my nipples, which harden under his continued stare.

I stay still for a moment, trying to work out what all this means, what the new angle is, my hands wringing the sheet pooled in my lap. He sighs.

"Look, Dove, we just thought that you needed a break and some fresh air." He gets up from his place at the foot of the bed, still holding the pile of clothes, and walks around to my side.

He extends his arm, holding his free hand out, and waits for me to take it.

I pause for a moment, still unsure what price I will pay for this kindness. Nothing in life is free, I know that more than most.

With a huff, I decide that I'm not some wilting flower to cower over a pile of fucking clothes, and I really want to get out of this house, spacious as it is. So I throw back the sheet and reach for his hand.

A zing of electricity zaps up from my fingers as I make contact, and I'm sure he feels the same way when his eyes widen briefly. I can't deny the flash of satisfaction when those deep blue eyes of his travel down my naked body.

"Jude left you some ointment for your new ink," he says in that deep voice which always makes my core clamp. I register his words, gasping before releasing his hand and rushing over to the full-length mirror on the front of Jude's closet.

"Jesus," I whisper, taking in the admittedly stunning design of delicate chains that cover my body. They dip across my upper chest, dropping between my breasts and swooping underneath them, only to drop again and cover my hips and upper thighs. There are intricate mandalas at the center of my underbust and just above my pussy. What, perhaps, is most surprising is several small birds that hold the chains up, draping them across my body. "He gave me my birds."

I watch as Aeron comes up behind me, his body warmth seeping into my back as he steps closer, one hand coming around to trace the outline of a swallow on my collarbone. My skin shivers at the touch, my nipples hardening to points.

"He said something about 'not all chains keep you from flying'," he tells me, and tears rush to my eyes. That shouldn't touch me, they tattooed fucking chains all over my body to declare their ownership for fuck's sake, but maybe Jude is right. Maybe, by becoming theirs, I'm freer than I have been before?

Taking a deep inhale, not ready to face that clusterfuck of a mind fuck, I turn so that I'm pressed up to Aeron, my breasts touching his shirt, my palms coming up to rest on his pecs. They flex under my touch and I'm almost wild with curiosity to see what he looks like with no clothes on. Is he inked up? Knox mentioned Jude has marked them all.

"Thank you for the clothes, Devil Man," I whisper, needing to get rid of some of this vulnerability that's coating my insides and making my throat tight.

Leaning in further, I ghost my lips over his, unable to stop the small moan that leaves my mouth at the softness of them.

"Dove," he warns, his lips moving against mine, and I quiver at the sensation, needing more.

I run my tongue along the seam, dipping inside his hot mouth to lick inside. With a groan that has my thighs clenching, he tangles one hand in my hair and the soft sound of the clothes falling to the floor reaches my ears moments before his other hand grabs my hips as he yanks me closer. I whimper as he thrusts his tongue into my mouth, completely dominating the kiss, but I don't care. He tastes like darkness and sin, like the things that you should run away from, but also, it's a little like coming home on a frozen winter's night to find a roaring fire and a cup of hot cocoa waiting.

"Aeron," I whine as he releases my mouth, angling my head to run lips, tongue, and teeth down my neck. "Please."

"Please what, Dove?" he growls, delving back to suck a spot on my throat that has wetness seeping down my inner thighs.

And I know that it's probably all kinds of fucked up given what happened yesterday with my past rearing its ugly head, but I need the release that only these guys seem to be able to give me.

"Please make me come, sir."

He snarls, his entire body going taut as his mouth leaves my throat.

"You make me fucking wild," he accuses, using his grip to back me towards the bed.

He shoves me hard, and I land on my back with an oomph, my eyes wide and my chest heaving with fucking need. I get just enough time to note his rumpled appearance and then he's pouncing, growling as he pushes my thighs open and buries his head in between them.

"Fuuuuck," I groan out long and low as he destroys me with his wicked tongue, and the noises that he makes as he holds me open are criminal.

The strokes of his tongue make me feel feral and wanton, my body writhing as I simultaneously try to move away and get closer. The pleasure is almost painful, my teeth clenching against the sudden onslaught of electricity that zaps across my skin.

"I fucking knew that you'd taste like heaven," he pauses, swiping a finger through my folds, my hips bucking at the tease.

"You gonna keep chatting, Devil Man? Or are you going to make me come?"

His head snaps up, his eyes narrowed in a glare as his whole body freezes.

Oh. Shit.

"You are in no position to make demands, Dove," he tells me, voice deep and deadly. It doesn't matter that the lower part of his mouth and chin are slick with my juices. Aeron Taylor can be one scary motherfucker when he wants to, and right now, my body trembles in fear and pleasure. "Now, for your disobedience, you won't come until I tell you to, understood?"

"And what will you do if I do come?"

He smirks, the smile sharp enough to cut.

"I'll edge you until it's time to leave, stroke myself to completion all over your face, and then make you walk out of here covered in my cum and desperate for a release that no one will give you until you've learned your lesson."

Fuck me.

I lick my suddenly dry lips.

"I'll be good."

"There's my perfect little doll," he praises, and something about the names that these boys give me when we're getting down and dirty makes my core quiver in anticipation. With more control than he had a moment ago, he lowers his face again, studying my pussy. "Such a pretty pink pussy, Dove. So ripe for us to taste."

An obscene noise falls from my lips as he does just that, tasting me with slow, firm strokes of his tongue as if he's licking his favorite ice cream. I get lost in the pleasure, the fire that makes my nerves tingle slowly building up to an inferno until I'm sweating and panting.

"Please, please, please," I beg, clenching my fists into the comforter to hold back the wave that is threatening to take me under.

"Not yet, little doll," Aeron coos, the feel of his breath as he speaks over my swollen cunt making me grit my teeth with the need to hold back my release. "I want to feel you strangle my cock as you come."

I blink my eyes open to see him stand up, slowly loosening his tie. He places one knee on the bed, reaching over my panting body as he holds the silk out over my eyes. Wordlessly, I lift my head, allowing him to slip the fabric around and bind it so I can no longer see.

"Good girl," he whispers over my mouth, and my tongue flicks out to taste myself on his lips. "Now I want you to feel me completely as I consume you."

><

"DADDY" BY SAKIMA, YLXR

AERON

I watch as her chest hitches with her sharp inhale, and pulling away, I can see the moment when she can't feel me over her anymore, her body moving towards my heat. A part of my inner beast likes that, that her body wants me so badly.

"Hands above your head, sweet Dove," I order, my rock-hard dick twitching when she immediately obeys, raising her arms.

Fuck yes. This is how I want her. Blindfolded and at my mercy. Little does she know that she's the one with all the power here, my cock weeping with the need to feel her around it, my balls aching to empty themselves into her warm heat.

Her body tenses, waiting for me as I unbutton my shirt, letting it drop to the floor of my brother's room. They're all downstairs, waiting, and my lips tilt with the thought that soon they'll be hearing her scream my name.

She twitches at the clink of my belt buckle, her chest rising and falling faster when the dull thud of my pants hitting the carpet sound around us. I grip my dick, squeezing the base hard and shivering at the intense sensation that rolls over me.

"Who do you belong to, Dove?" I question, kneeling between her still-splayed thighs. Her pussy glints in the morning light, and I have to bite my lip to stop the growl that wants to leave them from escaping.

"Y–you," she replies, swallowing, and this time I can't hold back the purr that rumbles in my chest.

"That's right, Dove," I tell her, leaning over her delectable body and lining myself up with her dripping entrance. "You belong to the Tailor boys now. You're fucking ours."

I surge forward, and the cry of pleasure that falls from her lips sends a zing of pleasure straight to my balls, filling me with liquid fucking fire at how tightly she grips me.

"Fuck, Aeron. You're so big," she gasps, her legs coming up and thighs trying to clench together to stop me from going any deeper.

"And you're going to take every fucking inch like a good little doll, aren't you?" I snarl, my palms gliding up her arms to clasp our hands together, keeping them above her head.

"Y–yes, sir." Her thighs open again, and she gasps when I surge forward more, smashing our pelvises together until I'm fully seated to the hilt.

"Such a good fuck doll," I praise in a gravelly voice, feeling wetness coat my dick as the words soothe her. I've never cared to praise a woman before, but she responds so well to it that I find myself unable to stop. I move my hips, and my teeth clench at how fucking good she feels wrapped around me. So warm, and wet, and fucking tight. I won't last long at this rate. "I'm going to fuck this delicious pussy so hard that you'll be feeling me inside you for weeks," I growl into her ear, and she whimpers as I pick up the pace, thrusting hard and fast into her tight channel. God, it feels fucking incredible, and I can't help but run my tongue up the column of her neck to lick at the sweat that drips down it. Fucking delicious.

"Aeron–god–fuck–that feels so fucking good!"

Her moans spur me on, my body demanding that I fuck her brutally. Letting go of her hands and growling out for her to keep them there, I push up onto my knees and grab her ass, hauling her up so I can go deeper.

We both groan at the new angle, and I can feel her tightening around me, choking my dick just like I told her to.

Such a good fucking girl.

"That's it, Dove, come for your master," I grit out, one hand digging into her hip as the other makes its way to her swollen clit. The noise our bodies make as they slam together is fucking music to my ears, and her cries only grow louder when I strum the bundle of nerves nestled at the apex of her thighs.

Her whole body stiffens, and it takes all my strength to hold her as she bucks wildly, her inner walls gripping me so tightly that it's a monumental effort not to come inside her right now.

I hold off—barely—watching as every stroke of my cock sends her spiraling into the depths of shuddering ecstasy. Her mouth is open on a silent scream as she comes, and she's so fucking beautiful that it takes my breath away.

Unable to hold back any longer, I pull out, grunting in satisfaction when she squirts all over me as I hit a sweet spot on the way out. Shit, that was fucking hot.

Letting her legs drop to the bed, her whole body lax and pliant, I move so that I brace my knees either side of her glorious tits. She lifts the blindfold up to look up at me as I stroke myself; her eyes go wide when she catches the glint of silver at my tip.

"No wonder that felt so fucking good," she breathes out, licking her lips as I furiously pump my dick.

Knox may like to fill her up to bursting with his cum—he has a breeding kink after all—but I want to cover her in my seed. I want everyone to know that I have marked her as mine and that she belongs to me, even after she's washed it off.

"Open wide, Dove," I hiss out, and the sight of her pink tongue sticking out in readiness for my load undoes me.

With a deep growl, my dick pulses, hot cum shooting out and covering her tongue, lips, and chin. Fuck, some even lands on her cheek and in her hair, and it's enough to have more spurting out of my tip.

When I've finally finished marking her, I slump, knowing that my weight is probably crushing her but unable to give a fuck. Covering her pussy back in the basement was exquisite, even if I couldn't see it, but it's nothing compared to seeing her entire face glistening with my release.

"Can't. Breathe," she rasps out, and heaving a sigh, I roll off, landing on my back on the bed next to her, staring up at the ceiling while I get my breath back, my chest heaving. "Jesus, Aeron."

I chuckle, the sound surprising even to my ears, and I look over to see her gazing at me, eyes wide and those lush lips parted, cum dripping down her chin and the side of her face.

She's fucking breathtaking.

Something tightens in my chest, my tarnished soul telling me she's finally ours now. Ours to cherish. Ours to destroy.

Reaching out, I gather a drop of cum on my thumb, taking it to her lips and pushing the digit inside. She laps at it greedily, and a rumble of satisfaction sounds in my chest.

"Much as I love this look on you, Dove..." I sigh, withdrawing my thumb and watching a string of her saliva cling to the tip. My dick fucking twitches at the sight, like we haven't just exploded with the best orgasm to date. "You need to shower and get ready."

"Okay."

Leaning over, I place a soft kiss on her lips, tasting the saltiness of my release. Reluctantly, I curl up and get off the bed, swooping to pick up my discarded clothes, but not bothering to put them on as I head towards the door.

"Aeron?" I pause, my fingers wrapped around the handle as I turn back to look at her. She's standing now, looking freshly fucked and fucking glorious, her hair a mass of tumbling red waves. My grip on the handle tightens. "Thank you," she says, biting her lip and looking at me, her light blue eyes sparkling with uncertainty. They dart down to my left pec, to the Tailors' shears tattooed there that look like they're cutting into my skin, before she brings them back up to my face. "For the clothes, and, well…"

Something fights within me, a part of me recognizing how fucked up it is for her to thank us for giving her clothes. She should have them by rights, but another part relishes having that power over her, knowing that she is under my control.

"You're welcome, Dove."

Then I turn away from the siren behind me and open the door to find Jude smirking on the other side.

"You had a cuntcuddle without me, bro," he pouts, crossing his arms over his bare chest. I blink, noting that there are no recent scars, and the tension that I always hold in my shoulders drops when I see the lack of them. I hate that my brother needs to cut himself to help when things get too much, it's why I encouraged him to learn how to tattoo and why I was one of the first he inked up. He has a fresh tattoo though. A lark right above his fucking heart. His lips tilt upwards when he sees the direction of my glare. "Next time."

Stepping to the side, he allows me to pass, and I turn to see him saunter to the waiting beauty still standing there, looking too fucking tempting covered in cum.

My jaw drops as he tilts her head to the side, and licks up the side of her cheek, clearing the cum that was dripping down it. Specifically, *my* cum that was dripping down it.

Shaking my head, I turn away from the sight of my brother licking up my release like it's his favorite dessert and stalk towards my bedroom and the shower that'll wash off her sweet, intoxicating scent.

It won't help clear away the grip she has on my soul though. No, that's hers, hook, line, and sinker.

CHAPTER FIFTEEN

"MONSTERS - ACOUSTIC VERSION" BY RUELLE

LARK

After Jude lapped up his brother's cum off my face—*which shouldn't be as fucking hot as it is*—he swatted my ass and told me to get into the shower so that, and I quote, 'my fine ass would be ready to do some riding of something other than Tailor cock'.

Fucking twisted bastard.

Getting out of the shower, and after brushing my teeth with the spare brush that Tarl gave me, I head into the bedroom to find it unoccupied. I can't help but breathe a sigh of relief at being alone for a moment.

The Tailor boys consume me when they're around, and I lose sight of who I am and what I'm doing here. All I want is their touch, their fucking approval, and I've not wanted a man's approval since my father gave me away to his best friend the day after my twelfth birthday.

But I want theirs, and it leaves me all kinds of confused and messed up. Not to mention the unease that coils in my stomach at the thought of my task here.

Picking up the ointment that Jude left me, I head over to the full-length mirror and swipe some over the sore and raised skin, the calming scent of lavender washing over me. I study the design as I work, having to admit that it is beautiful, even if he's chained me up.

And what the fuck did he mean by 'not all chains keep you from flying'?

Fucked if I know.

Sighing, I set the pot down and head over to the bed where my clothes are neatly laid out. Jude must have picked them up after Aeron dropped them earlier before he rocked my fucking world.

There's a henley-style, short-sleeved shirt in a delicate pink shade, and what looks like tight leggings, only they have extra pieces of thicker fabric along the inside of the legs. There's also a set of lacy lingerie in dusky pink, and I breathe a sigh of relief at the soft lace bralette instead of an actual bra. My back is still healing, the fresh skin that now covers the lashes a little sore, my new tattoo adding to the pain.

Picking up the underwear first, I slip the panties on and can't help turning to admire the way the lace shorts make my ass look peachy. The bralette goes on next, and even this small amount of fabric feels strange after so long without clothes.

Once I'm fully dressed, I walk over to look at myself in the mirror, turning round to see that the leggings hug my ass like a second skin.

"How the fuck did they know my size?" I whisper, looking over my reflection to confirm that everything fits me to perfection.

"We know everything about your body, Pretty Bird," a deep, melodic voice says from the doorway and I jump at the sound.

"Fucking hell, Tarl. You scared the shit out of me!"

"Such a dirty little mouth," he says, his tone husky as he stalks into the room towards me. He moves like a jungle cat, all feline grace and coiled danger. His mismatched eyes bore into me, and I wish I could read the emotion in their depths. "If we had more time, I would fill it."

I swallow hard, my new panties effectively ruined with dampness. I might as well not fucking bother.

"Where are we going?" I ask, blinking when he takes my hand and leads me to the desk which sits against one wall. It's covered in pages of artwork, more tacked onto the wall behind it, spreading out like a spill of ink. Apt given that this is Jude's room after all.

Placing his hands on my shoulders, he gently pushes down until my ass hits the leather stool that sits in front of the desk, and then swivels me around until I'm facing the stunning artwork.

My heart hammers in my chest as I wait for his next move, jerking slightly when I feel a brush being pulled through my wet hair.

"Calm down, *Azizam*. It's just a brush," he soothes, the smooth cadence of his voice relaxing my bunched shoulders. I'm just not used to soft touches, but something tells me that these Tailor boys are going to make me get used to the feel of them. I do just that, my limbs loosening as I get lost in the rhythm of the strokes as he guides the brush through my hair. It hits me when I remember my mom used to do this, brush my hair, and my vision blurs, the artwork before me bleeding as my heart aches.

I frown when he stops, and then an embarrassing moan escapes my lips when his firm fingers dig into my scalp, massaging some sweet-smelling product in and chasing the lingering sadness away.

"That feels amazing, Tarl," I groan on an exhale as he hits an especially sore spot.

After a few minutes, his hands leave my head to be replaced by the brush once more. I study the art before me, seeing Jude's signature expressive style all over it, the lines like my tattoo. The designs are hauntingly beautiful; moths with skulls on their bodies, little girls with the shadows of monsters, and faceless women with stars for hair.

Tarl's fingers suddenly grip my hair, and I gawp when I realize that he's braiding it.

"Where on earth did you learn how to braid hair, Tarl?"

He chuckles.

"I was not born here, Little Bird," he tells me, and his voice reminds me of a time when storytellers wove magic in the air with their tales. "Adam Taylor found me on the streets of Tehran, the capital city of Iran, homeless and without parents. He took pity on me, and bought me back here, to live with, and serve his son." He reaches to the end of my braid, then uses a hair tie at his wrist to tie it off. It's light pink, the same color as my shirt. "But before I became homeless, I had sisters, and I would help my mother to braid their hair."

He swivels the stool around, and I gaze up into his eyes; one the blue of a summer sky and the other the green of a sage plant.

"What happened to them? Your sisters? Your family?"

His whole face changes, going hard and shuttered, and the pain that he's not quick enough to hide brightens his eyes, making the colors pulse.

"They were killed."

He goes to turn away, but I reach for his wrist, holding it as the brush dangles from his hand. Turning back, he looks down at me, his expression a blankness that screams of loss.

"Then we have something in common."

His chest rises and his whole face softens before his other hand comes up to stroke my cheek.

"I wish it was something other than the death of loved ones, Pretty Bird," he tells me, and there's no hint of a lie in his tone. He means it, and it leaves my stomach churning with uncertainty about how we reached this point between us. Are we still enemies? "Let's go."

He removes his hand from my cheek, holding it out for me to

take, and ignoring the confusion that wraps around me. I take it, letting him lead me from the room and down the stairs.

When did I start to trust the Tailor boys?

The guys usher me into an enormous truck, all black and monstrous-looking, and I have to basically climb into the back like a mountain goat. It takes about forty minutes to get to our destination, and I press my face to the blacked-out back window, drinking in the way the cityscape turns into countryside. It's so green, and with the mountains in the distance and the summer sunshine bathing the landscape with its glow, I'm awestruck by its majesty.

"Never left the city before?" Jude asks, his hand massaging the back of my neck, sending tingles racing across my skin and threatening to distract me from my staring. I briefly turn my head to look into his deep blue eyes, but there's no teasing there, his softened voice and raised brows letting me know he means no offense.

"Mom took Rook and I to the Grand Lake beach once, maybe twice when we could sneak away, like the time I told you about," I tell him, remembering the feel of the sand between my toes and the sound of the waves lapping at the shore. I mean, it wasn't the sea or anything, but as a kid, it always amazed me, the vast body of water that was Grand Lake. I suck in my lower lip, remembering the punishment she received at the hands of my father both times upon our return. After the second time, I begged not to go again.

"Why the frown, Nightingale?"

Blinking, I see his eyes once more, the blue not dissimilar to the bruises that decorated Mom's skin so often. Too fucking often.

"Rufus punished her for taking us away. Any time we did something fun, she'd be beaten and be limping for days afterwards," I tell him, watching as his eyes narrow, his brows drawing down.

"Your father is a wicked man, Nightingale."

"I know."

We spend the rest of the trip in silence, lost in our own thoughts. I straighten in my seat when we pass through a large, wooden archway, a sign that reads 'Tailor Stables' hanging above it.

"Stables?" I turn to look at the guys, my eyes wide and my pulse fast as I practically bounce in my seat. I've always loved animals and always wanted a pet, but obviously was never allowed one.

"That's right, Dove," Aeron says from the front passenger seat, turning around to face me. "These are Tailor-owned stables. One of my father's passion projects." His chin is high, his shoulders back as pride gleams in his eyes.

"Also helps to clean all the dirty money," Knox adds with a chuckle from the driver's seat, and Aeron gives him a glare.

"Just tell her all of our business, Knox."

"Who exactly am I going to spill your dark secrets to, Devil Man?" I interject, my eyebrow arched in amused contempt, before they can start an argument. Bloody men will fight over anything, though I suspect there is something more going on as there's a crackle of tension between Aeron and Knox that never quite goes away.

Aeron concedes my point with a sharp nod just as we pull up in front of a vast, white stable block with what looks like a fucking mansion at one end. I knew the Tailors were rich, but they must have a hell of a lot of dirty money to launder if they can afford this kind of setup.

As soon as we pull to a stop, Aeron exits the car, an older man with a mustache and a fucking cowboy hat strolling over to greet him. Knox appears at my door, opening it from the outside because the fuckers engaged the child lock so that I wouldn't try to escape. Although, Jude got pretty excited at the idea of hunting me down if I did try anything, and even Tarl had a banked heat in his eyes at the idea. *Fucking sick bastards.*

Knox holds his hand out and rolling my eyes, I take it, letting him help me out of the car, my new knee-length boots molding to my feet as I stand on them. The others exit the car, and I just stand there breathing in the fresh, sweetly-scented air. My nose crinkles when the pungent smell of horseshit hits me.

"Don't worry, Little Bird." Knox laughs, letting go of my hand to sling an arm over my shoulder. His motor oil, cloves, and cedarwood scent completely overpowers any other smell, and like a dickhead, I lean in closer, taking a deep inhale. "You get used to the smell of shit around here."

"I should already be used to it then, hanging around you guys for so long," I sass back, and his whole body goes rigid before he chuckles darkly.

"Oh, Little Bird. You just poked the wrong bear." I gulp, glancing upward to see the look of sheer, debauched pleasure on his handsome face. "Tell me, how's your cardio?"

Before I can answer, knowing that his question relates to a future punishment that I may even enjoy, Aeron beckons us over. He quirks a brow at Knox, who just mumbles that he'll explain later. Aeron accepts this, clearly trusting that if it was important, Knox would tell him straight away. I feel a twinge in my solar plexus, wondering what it would feel like to have someone so close like that.

"Jim, this is Dove," Aeron says by way of an introduction, and I can't help the eye roll at his use of my nickname.

"Lark," I state, trying to step out of Knox's grip, but he just tightens it. *Dick.* "Nice to meet you."

"A pleasure to meet you too, ma'am," Jim replies. His deep voice has a Southern twang to it and I find my lips pulling up at his clear charm. Aeron scowls at me. *Possessive bastard.*

"We're going to show Dove around," Aeron tells the man. "And then take her for a ride."

"Wait, what?" I ask, my body freezing. I look down at my legs and realization hits me. They're not leggings, they're fucking jodhpurs.

"Come, Little Bird," Knox coos, completely ignoring my slight freak-out about having to get on top of a fucking horse. "You can ride with me."

"She's riding with me," Aeron interrupts, and once again, Knox goes still, his stare deadly and focused on the leader of this little crew. Jesus, those boys definitely have some kind of baggage together.

"I'll ride with you, Knox baby," Jude teases, and Knox jolts when a smack lands on his ass. I giggle, quickly covering my mouth when Knox glares down at me.

"This way, Nightingale," Jude singsongs, grabbing my hand and pulling me from Knox and away from all that nonsense.

I laugh again, jogging to keep up with him as we head toward the first stable door, the top half open. A gray head pokes out, and I pause at the beauty of the animal before me. Jude continues to lead me to the animal, grabbing a packet of mints out of his blood-red jeans pocket and offering one up to the horse, who nickers and immediately gobbles it up.

Tentatively, I reach a hand out, having to stretch it upwards to let the animal take a sniff. *You do that with dogs, so horses can't be too different, right?* Warm breath tickles my palm, then I gasp in delighted surprise when the animal presses its soft nose into my hand.

"She likes you," Jude whispers, reaching up to stroke his own hand down her muzzle. "She's Mom's."

"What's her name?" I ask, my voice soft like his so that I don't scare the beauty before me.

"Bluebell, but we all call her Blue."

I take a soft inhale, dreading asking the next question. I know what happened to their mother. How, sanctioned by my sperm donor, members of the Dead Soldiers attacked and abused Heather Taylor, leaving her bleeding outside the Taylor family home. Apparently, Adam Taylor had undercut my father stealing business or something.

Why is it always the innocents that get caught in the crossfire?

"Where is your mom, Jude?" I question, watching how the skin around his eyes tightens, his hand halting in its movements.

"Mount Pleasant Care Facility," he answers just as I see the others come up behind us. Ignoring them, and the scowl on Aeron's beautiful face, I place my hand over his, both of us resting them atop Blue's nose.

"I'm sorry that they hurt your mom, Jude."

"Apologies don't do shit, Dove," Aeron sneers, and I flinch at the venom in his tone. Poor Blue shakes her head and whickers, clearly sensing my distress, our hands falling away from her.

"Will you come with us to visit her, Nightingale?" Jude asks, his voice full of sorrow as he ignores Aeron's comment, lacing our fingers together.

"If you want me to, I'd like that," I tell him, following his lead and dismissing the angry Tailor behind us. Jude beams, one of his completely carefree smiles that sends my stomach fluttering and which I'm slowly becoming addicted to.

"For fuck's sake! Want to show her all our safe houses next? Or maybe share our bank details?" Aeron fumes and I drop Jude's hand, turning to face his brother and then taking a step until I'm standing before him, not cowering before his anger.

He stands taller, trying to intimidate me with his size and the power of his body. It doesn't work. Men have been using their bodies against me for years, I've learned to be unafraid.

"Why are you so scared of me, Aeron?" I ask softly, my eyes bouncing between his, and his glare narrows, his body practically vibrating with tension.

"I'm not scared of you, Dove." He scoffs, his upper lip curling. It should make him unattractive, but it doesn't. "Dead Soldiers are lying, conniving, scheming cunts, and you are a Dead fucking Soldier."

As if on instinct, I reach my hand out, slowly like I just did with Blue, and cup his smooth cheek. His eyes widen a fraction, his chest heaving so that it brushes against mine.

"I'm not here to hurt you, Aeron."

Lie.

My gut twists for a moment, my chest tightening with the untruth that spills from my lips.

"How can I trust that? Our families have been at war for so long, Dove. We're fucking enemies," he confesses, his voice quiet, and the sounds around us fade as he brings his forehead down to mine, my eyes closing with the contact. "And why is it so fucking hard to remember that when you touch me?"

"I don't know."

Truth.

My breath sighs out of me, my whole body relaxing at his nearness. Slowly, his lips meet mine in a kiss that brings tears to my eyes with its gentleness. Out of all of them, Aeron is the one that undoes me so completely. He makes me wish things were different. That we could just be together like this always.

But, there is a bigger picture here, so much more at stake than my broken heart, so reluctantly, I pull away.

"Let's show you the rest of the stables, and you can meet Samson," Aeron says, lacing our fingers together and taking a step back, my hand tingling as it falls from his cheek.

"Samson?"

"He's my stallion," Aeron tells me, a boyish grin titling his lips upwards and making him fucking devastatingly handsome. "And has sired many winning Tailor horses." Pride shines in his voice, his smile wide as he leads me over to another stable.

I jump when a kick rattles the half door, gasping when the head of a stunning, pitch-black horse pokes through.

"Steady, boy," Aeron coos, letting go of my hand and reaching out to grasp the stallion's head. "That's no way to greet a lady."

I snort at the same time that Samson does, and Aeron looks over at me with a raised brow.

"Perhaps you should practice what you preach, Devil Man," I sass, taking slow steps closer to the magnificent beast and his horse.

"Hold your hand out, Dove. Let him sniff you," Aeron commands, and there should be nothing sexual about his words, but somehow, my core still clenches anyway. *Jesus.*

With butterflies fluttering in my stomach, I reach up, letting Samson smell my hand just like I did with Blue, and when he seems to make no objection, I place it on his soft nose, marveling at the silky, black hair beneath my palm.

"He just needs a soft touch sometimes is all," Aeron murmurs, and I can feel his stare on me, burning like the glare of the midday sun.

"I'll keep that in mind."

CHAPTER SIXTEEN

"CAN'T HELP FALLING IN LOVE - DARK" BY TOMMEE PROFITT, BROOKE

LARK

We spend the rest of the day looking around the stables, and they're fucking vast. There must be over fifty horses here, all thoroughbred and winning racehorses, probably worth a fucking fortune, but as we've established, the Tailors are as rich as King Midas himself. After a few hours, they take me to where four horses are saddled out in the yard. Samson is there, snorting and pulling his head, as his groom—*look at me getting all fancy with the correct terms*—tries to calm him down. Spoiler alert; it's not working and I swear the groom has to dodge a vicious kick to the nuts several times.

Three other equally beautiful horses wait, and I watch in awe as Tarl, Knox, and Jude all walk over to them, stroking the animals' necks and then swinging up onto their backs with an ease that is as sexy as it is unfair. I swear I fall over standing still half the time, yet these guys just mount horses as if they've been born in the saddle.

Jesus.

I can see why all those damsels let the highwaymen rip off their bodices. There is something criminally sexy about these guys on horses, controlling them with strong thighs and firm hands. Especially in their tight, black jodhpurs, henleys, and tall, black riding boots.

Aeron tugs my hand, pulling me towards the snorting, pawing, black beast which is his horse. *Go figures his would be a bit of a bastard. Like owner like horse, right?*

"Uh, I think I might just sit this one out," I say, my voice only slightly trembling as I look up at just how fucking high this animal is.

"Not a chance," Aeron replies, a smirk on his beautiful lips. He untangles our fingers, then grabs my hips and turns me to face the saddle, Samson having calmed down now that Aeron is near. Running his palm down my left arm, he takes the back of my hand in his and wraps my fingers around the front of the saddle. "One hand here." My heart thuds in my chest, my core tightening with a mixture of trepidation and arousal as he repeats the same move with my right hand, placing it in the back of the saddle. The leather cracks as I grasp it. "Other hand, here." His large palms come to cup my waist, squeezing lightly before sliding down my hips, and then he trails them down my left thigh, pausing at my knee. "Bend your leg at the knee so that it sticks out behind you." Fucking hell, I'm panting, my skin is tingling along the path that he took, and even though I'm wearing clothes, I felt every fucking caress. Taking a deep inhale, I do as he commands, deciding that it's probably not worth the argument. *He said earlier that he'd be with me, so what's the worst that can happen?*

"Now what?"

Slowly, he grabs just under my knee and around my booted ankle, and I swear by all that is fucking unholy, I'm about to pass out with how wound up I feel. I'm literally panting for his touch on my naked skin.

"Now, I give you a boost up, and you swing your leg over. Understand?" His voice is a deep rumble against my ear, and the feel of his breath tickling the shell of my ear has me shuddering.

"Yes, sir," I reply, my tone a little sassy, and hella husky, and he full-on growls behind me, the sound vibrating straight to my aching clit.

I yelp as he suddenly throws me into the air, just remembering to swing my leg over and land with a not-so-graceful thump on poor Samson's back.

Of course that pisses off the stallion—*like owner like horse, remember?*—and he huffs, stamping his feet. Thank fuck he doesn't rear up as I scramble to sit up, otherwise, I'd be flat on my ass. My heart pounds regardless, and I swallow thickly when I see how far away the ground is.

"Graceful, Dove. Real elegant." Aeron scoffs, placing his foot into the stirrup.

"Fuck off," I grumble back and just catch the flare of his eyes as he fucking effortlessly swings himself up behind me, just like the others did.

Samson skitters again, pawing the ground, and I only make a small squeak this time as I grab for the front of the saddle, the pommel I think they said it was called.

"Shhhh," Aeron soothes the stallion before lifting me up to settle more in his lap. At least I think it's the horse that he's trying to calm down, even if his hands run down my thighs. I shiver when I feel his solid legs beneath mine, the leather of the saddle pressing into the front of my pelvis not unpleasantly.

He takes the reins from the groom, leaning forward so that his mouth is against my ear.

"Lean back into me, Dove. Hold on to the front of the saddle like a good girl."

It shouldn't turn me on, it really shouldn't.

But damn, I'm only fucking human, and my panties grow damp as he clicks his tongue and we move. I can feel the blood as it rushes around my body, my heart freezing then pounding when I look around at the others.

I'm on a fucking horse!

I can't stop my lips from tugging up in a wide grin when several minutes later, Aeron clicks again and we move faster. Yeah, I probably look like a sack of fucking potatoes being thrown around up here but I don't give a shit. It's exhilarating, the wind rushing past me and being so high up I can finally breathe.

"Enjoying yourself, Dove?" Aeron asks, and I can hear the smile in his voice. I wish I could see it. I bet it's devastating.

"It's...it's unlike anything I've ever experienced before," I gush, my cheeks heating at showing so much to him. I should be more careful, we are enemies after all, but right now, I've no fucks left to give.

"Ready to go faster?"

"Ye—" I don't get to finish, the rest of the word cut off in a cry of delight when we launch forward, Samson's hooves eating up the grass beneath us.

My breath comes faster as we sail through the landscape, and tears form in my eyes at the sheer beauty of feeling so free for the first time in my life. I let them track down my cheeks, not wanting to let go to wipe them away, and uncaring if the others see my joy if they catch up.

We slow down as we approach a wooded area, a worn path running through it. My chest heaves as we come to a stop, Aeron's own torso moving mine with his rapid breaths. The others draw up alongside us, all looking even more gorgeous with their windswept hair and sparkling eyes. The braid that Tarl wove into my hair seems to have held up, much to my surprise.

"Get down, Dove," Aeron whispers into my ear, and it takes a moment for his words to sink in.

"W—what?"

Letting go of the reins, he lifts me up, forcing me to let go as he swings my leg over Samson's neck and unceremoniously drops me to a crumpled heap at the horses' hooves. Fumbling, I get up, brushing off loose leaves and dirt from my grazed palms, wincing when blood wells in the scratches.

I glare at Aeron; the others forming a semicircle around me, matching smirks on their faces as they stare down at me from the height of their horses' backs. I'm reminded of those damsels from the bodice rippers, and I can say that, although my heart thuds painfully in my chest, my nipples are also hard as fucking diamonds.

"What the fuck was that for?" I snarl, glaring at each of them, settling on the leader of their fucking merry band of assholes.

"You were told earlier that we would punish you for your rudeness," he replies, waiting for when my eyes go wide, flitting over to Knox. "This is your punishment, Dove."

"W–what is my punishment, exactly?" I stutter, wanting desperately to take a step back, but holding my ground and refusing to show any weakness to these bastards or acknowledge the excitement that is currently running through my veins.

"We'll be going on a little hunt," Jude bursts out, practically bouncing in his saddle. I swing my gaze to him as his chestnut horse steps to the side and Jude has to tug the reins a little to regain control. *Serves him right.*

"And you are the prey," Tarl adds in his sultry voice. I shiver when I look into his hungry, mismatched eyes, even though it's a hot summer afternoon with no hint of a breeze.

"So, Dove?" Aeron demands, and I finally come back to him. Back to the dark glee that makes his ocean eyes sparkle.

"Yes?" I ask, my heart now thudding painfully in my chest, no longer exhilarated because of the fear coursing through my veins, and maybe, just a little, anticipation.

"Run."

✂

"YOU'RE THE ONE THAT I WANT" BY LO-FANG

TARL

We all watch as, with wide sparkling eyes, our pretty little bird takes flight, turning tail and running into the woods behind her.

"This is going to be so much fun!" Jude exclaims, and I take my eyes off the spot she disappeared into, casting them over him. He's bouncing in his seat, poor Maleficent—his mare named after one of his favorite Disney characters—whinnying and stamping her hooves underneath him.

I can't blame him though, the thrill of the impending chase runs through my own veins, making my entire body tingle. I've always loved a good hunt, and I've never had prey as delicious as our beautiful bird before.

"Fifty G's says that I get her first," Knox states, and I look over to see the same hunger in his eyes that I feel as he trains them on the place where she vanished.

"I'll take that bet," I answer, his gaze swinging to mine. We're all excellent trackers, we've been hunting Dead Soldier scum for the past decade, but I like to think that I have a certain edge, given my history, that the others don't.

"Deal," Jude adds in, and I can hear the excitement in his voice.

"Deal," Aeron agrees, and I look to our leader to see he's got it just as bad as the rest of us, his eyes sparkling as he, too, watches where our pretty bird took off. An alarm goes off on his watch, loud in the quiet. "Showtime."

Jude takes off with a holler and whoop, the sound echoing in the forest and causing the birds to take flight from the trees as Maleficent's hooves kick up clods of dirt when he crashes into the forest. Laughing, I follow suit, directing my horse—named Tiam on account of her beautiful soul-filled eyes—in his wake at a slower pace. I'll see more if I don't rush, the sweetness is in the anticipation, after all.

I don't hear the other two behind me, clearly, they've decided to see if they can cut her off and go around. A smart plan, but not one that will win them the prize.

Looking around, I spot broken twigs to the left and my lips tilt upwards. Clever bird. Pulling Tiam to a stop, I swing my leg over and get off, landing silently on the dirt path.

"I'll catch her better on foot, *aziz-e delam*," I whisper as I stroke her soft muzzle. "Go find some nice grass."

Turning her to face the way that we just came, I give her a light tap on her rump so that she walks towards the fields beyond. Then, I head toward the broken undergrowth, ready to catch my bird.

"SANCTIFY" BY YEARS & YEARS

LARK

My heart pounds as I rush through the woods, twigs snagging in my braid, pulling it apart and scratching my face. My entire body tingles, and I jump when I hear a shout and whooping, then the thunder of hooves behind me.

Fucking psychos. Who hunts someone with horses?

The Tailor boys apparently.

I veered off the path almost straight away, deciding that I stand a better chance if I'm not an open target for them. Not hearing anything too close, I pause, hands on my knees as I catch my breath.

My cardio is shit, Knox, thanks for asking.

It's a shame that I'm being hunted, because this forest is beautiful, with towering trees and birdsong all around. They've not even paused in their cheerfulness, regardless of the hunters that stalk their woods. *Fucking traitors.*

Straightening up, I go to take a step forward, only to have one powerful arm clamped around my upper torso and the other around my waist, making my pulse skyrocket.

"Caught you," Tarl whispers in my ear, and his cardamom scent wraps around me as my heart ricochets inside my chest.

"Goddamnit," I breathe out, sighing as I accept defeat and relax in his stronghold. "Couldn't you have at least pretended to give me a bit of time? Just so I felt like I had a chance?"

Regardless of my words, my body sinks back into his even more, and the delicious hardness that pokes me in the lower back makes my thighs clench together.

Hello, my name is Lark, and I'm a sucker for Tailor dick.

"But then I wouldn't get to enjoy my prize while the others are still looking for you," he murmurs, and I hiss when he licks a scratch on the side of my face, the sharp sting causing my nipples to harden. I never knew that I craved pain at the hands of my lovers. That's some fucked up shit right there, and I wonder if it's something that I need to worry about. Or maybe it's just how I process the trauma of being taken against my will for most of my sexual life?

The arm around my waist shifts, pulling me from my dark, self-critical thoughts, as Tarl's hand strokes down my stomach, sending tingles racing across my body and hardening my nipples further until they ache and beg for his attention.

"Tarl," I moan as he dips below the waist of my jodhpurs, the tight fit of the garment ensuring that I feel each movement as he pushes lower.

"Yes, *Koshgelam?*"

He finally reaches the apex of my thighs, and a swipe of his finger over the bundle of nerves there has me groaning long and low. He chuckles, exploring my slick folds, my hands coming up to grasp his forearm, which is still wrapped around my upper chest in a vise-like hold. My hips move of their own accord when he kisses and nips my neck, and my knees threaten to buckle with the bliss that's rolling across my body.

"Aw, you started without me."

I blink to see Jude leaning against a tree, a pout pulling down his pillowy lips. The outline of his hard cock is clear in his tight jodhpurs, and a small sound escapes my lips at the sight of him so ready for me. Tarl doesn't stop, just carries on, circling my clit with his fingers, bringing me closer to an edge that I want to fucking leap off.

"Join us, Brat," Tarl says to him, his touch moving back over my swollen bundle, and I whimper. "You can fill that naughty mouth of hers while I take her delicious pussy".

Wetness floods between my thighs, his words and the visual they create enough to send me tumbling over the edge into the blissful abyss. My nailless fingers dig into his skin as I thrash with my release, my thighs clamping around his hand with the force of my orgasm.

Fucking hell.

I melt into him, opening my eyes to see Jude now standing before me, his ocean-deep eyes eating up every twitch and shiver.

"So beautiful, Nightingale."

I whine when Tarl removes his hand, my exhale sharp when he brings it up near Jude's lips.

"Suck," he commands, and Jude obeys, his eyes rolling as he licks and sucks my climax off of Tarl's fingers.

"Fucking delicious," he moans, cleaning the digits thoroughly.

"Good boy," Tarl praises, and hoe my god that shit right there almost has me coming a second time. "As wet as our pretty bird is," Tarl continues, removing his hand from in front of me. "I think I'm going to need some more lube, Brat."

My brows furrow, wondering if Jude keeps a bottle of lube about his person all the time, when the psycho in question bends down and pulls a fucking hunting knife from his boot.

"What the fuck?!" I rear back, much like Samson did earlier, as the blade glints in the dappled sunlight.

"Don't worry, *Koshgelam*. It's not for you," Tarl soothes, and I watch wide-eyed as Jude brings the knife to his palm and slices across it. Jude lets out a pleasured sigh when blood immediately wells in the gash, covering a line of scars that I just manage to catch a glimpse of, and drips down his fingers. Tarl shifts me a little to the side, enough so that his dick isn't pressing into my back anymore and he's more to the side of me, his arm still around my upper chest. Bloody big bastards, the lot of them. "Take me out, Brat. Slick me up."

Oh.

Oh!

Sweet mother of all things hotness.

I watch transfixed as Jude reaches forward and pulls Tarl's tight jodhpurs down, his thick length springing free. Metal glints at the tip of his mushroom head, and I lick my lips, remembering how good Aeron felt inside me, the piercing adding an extra sensation.

Jude soon covers Tarl's cock with his palm, and the sight of his blood coating it does something to me that makes my heart race and more wetness slick down my thighs. Tarl moans in my ear, his grip on me tightening as Jude pumps his fist up and down, twisting it at the top, a bead of pre-cum glistening and mixing with all that red.

"Does that feel good, sir?" Jude asks, his voice deep and breathy.

"You know it does, Brat," Tarl answers in a low moan, and I get lost watching the movement of Jude covering Tarl's length with his own blood. I must whimper because they pause, and I look up to see a smirk on Jude's face.

"I think our birdie wants some too, sir," Jude says, and my heart gives a thud.

"Then who are we to deny her?"

Jude lets go of Tarl, who steps back behind me, releasing me from his embrace only to yank my jodhpurs and panties down a second later, leaving them around my lower thighs and me teetering. He steadies me with a firm grip on my hips, one hand coming up between my shoulder blades and pushing down until I'm bent over, my hands trying to find purchase.

"Grip onto me, love," Jude murmurs in a husky, low voice. He helps to guide my hands up to his hips, and my fingers immediately dig into the firm, ink-covered muscles. I can feel the scars underneath my fingertips, and I find myself tracing them.

Moments later, I feel the nudge of Tarl's head at my entrance, and with a slow, controlled thrust, he surges inside my heated channel. The cry that leaves my lips startles the surrounding birds, making them take flight from the trees around us. I was right; the piercing feels fucking mind-blowing.

"Open your eyes, Nightingale," Jude coos, and I do as he says to see his own cock coated in red and his metal gleaming before my face. Grabbing the base of his dick, he presses it against my lips and I open at the silent command, tasting the tang of copper alongside the musk of Jude as he pushes inside my mouth, not stopping until he hits the back of my throat. The piercings make for an interesting change; the metal clacking against my teeth as it passes. I gag, and Tarl groans behind me.

"She tightens when you hit her throat, Brat, and it feels fucking incredible."

Jude holds still, letting me suck in tiny amounts of air as Tarl moves behind me, pushing Jude deeper into my throat. I moan around Jude's cock as the drag and pull of Tarl's sends me spinning, my fingers digging into Jude's flesh with ecstasy.

"Are you ready to be ruined, Nightingale?" Jude asks, his bloody fingertips trailing a wet path down my cheek. I roll my eyes upwards, and give a slight nod, our position making it impossible for me to do much more. "Such a good, broken bird."

He pulls out, allowing me a gasp of sweet air, before he thrusts into my mouth once more, pushing me back onto Tarl who slides deeper into my cunt. The world around us spins and careens on its axis as he practically touches my cervix, and I whine around Jude's cock.

"Goddamn," Tarl rasps out, his fingers gripping my hips just as tightly as mine do Jude's.

"Does she feel good, sir?" Jude questions, his own voice strained as he repeats the move.

"Exquisite."

They do as Jude promised, ruining me in the middle of the forest, the gentle breeze caressing the overheated skin of my thighs as the sounds of birds singing returns, our moans and grunts adding to the melody. They build me higher, my body threatening to burst with the pleasure that they're forcing upon me, and a part of me never wants it to end, even as another craves the climax that I can feel just out of reach.

Snapping twigs draw me away from the dance we're doing, and I roll my eyes to the side to see Aeron and Knox standing there, chests heaving as they grip their dicks. I moan around Jude's cock, and he tugs my hair, my eyes rolling back up to him.

"Do you see how wild you make us all, Nightingale?" he grits out, teeth clenching as he keeps thrusting into my mouth, and I'd worry about him chipping a tooth with all that metal, but I'm too high off them to give a shit. "We're all desperate for you. You've bewitched us."

Another incoherent sound gurgles in my throat, my inner walls clamping around Tarl as I come so hard that I see fucking stars. My entire body stiffens, the pleasure that's fracturing my insides almost too much as they thrust harder, fucking me with wild abandon like savages.

I hear curses and scream when Tarl thrusts so hard into me it fucking hurts, but the pain just makes another orgasm rip through me, leaving me trembling and drowning in sweet agony. He holds me there, pouring his release inside me just as Jude shouts and my throat is full of him as he, too, fills me with his climax.

I'm held motionless, barely able to breathe as I hold them both inside me. The pleasure I feel with these men is tortured bliss, borderline painful, like having my insides rearranged until I no longer recognize who or what I am. Am I a Dead Soldier? Are we still enemies? Do I care either way?

I gasp when Jude slowly pulls out of my mouth, my throat aching with his vicious intrusion. A small moan leaves my swollen lips when Tarl withdraws, and Jude uses his grip on my chin to pull me upwards.

"So fucking beautiful," he sighs, licking the corner of my mouth and groaning. "And so fucking ours."

Jude slips his tongue inside my mouth, and like I did for his dick, I open up to him, relishing the taste of naughty deeds and intense highs that hits my tongue.

Tarl presses close behind me, turning my head and breaking my kiss with Jude, placing his lips onto mine so that he can kiss me over my shoulder. He makes a deep sound when his tongue invades, clearly tasting Jude in my mouth. Tarl tastes like sinful nights in hot climates, decadent debauchery, and things that heat your cheeks in the light of day. I can't get enough.

"Ours to ruin," he whispers when he pulls away.

My head turns again, Knox's hazel eyes bright and shining with the afterglow of an orgasm.

"Ours to hunt," he hums, placing his lips over mine and kissing me stupid. I melt into him, loving the taste of him. It's like flying on the back of a motorcycle down the highway. Like freedom.

"Ours to own and keep," Aeron adds from the other side, tangling his fingers in my hair and jerking my lips to his, Knox growling as I'm torn from him. "Ours to break and put back together again."

He whispers the last part against my lips, moments before his own close the minuscule distance. His kiss is an invasion. A possession. He tastes like invading armies that take what they want with no shame, pillaging the land and bending the people to their will.

I sink into it, allowing him his fill with no resistance as he conquers me completely. Everything disappears when they surround me like this. There is no gang war. No enemies. No Romeo and Juliet comparisons. Just them, and me, and us.

I wish with every fiber of my being that it could be like this always.

Just us against the world.

But wishes are like stars. Pretty to look at, yet unreachable. Unattainable.

And there are so many stars in our night sky that it sparkles.

CHAPTER SEVENTEEN

"PLEASE DON'T BREAK MY HEART" BY ESCAPE

LARK

The next few days pass in confusing bliss, leaving my head spinning and my heart yearning. Jude makes me watch every Disney movie known to man during the day, because apparently, my 'Disneycation' is woefully lacking. I spend each night in Aeron's or Jude's bed, lost in the passionate embraces of one or more of my Tailor boys.

Wait, when the fuck did I begin to think of them as mine?

Aeron strides into the room one morning, throwing open the curtains and making Jude, Tarl, and I all flinch as the light momentarily blinds us.

"What the fuck is wrong with you?" I hiss, shielding my face by burying it into Jude's neck and taking a deep inhale of his sweet, popping candy scent.

I squeak when the covers are thrown off, and yell a second later when the asshole known as the heir to the Tailors grabs my ankle and I'm hauled out of bed, landing in a naked heap on the floor.

"Morning, Dove." Aeron smirks down at me, holding a hand out, and I scowl, huffing as I let him help me get to my feet. He doesn't let go, pulling me close so that our bodies touch, and a shiver runs over my skin. There's something about having him fully clothed when I'm completely exposed that makes my pulse race.

"Morning, Devil Man," I whisper back, the last part said against his lips as he leans in and places them over mine. As always, his kiss claims me and destroys me in equal measure, leaving me weak-kneed and desperate for more.

"I like that nickname from your lips," he hums against my lips this time, the brush of our flesh making my breath hitch. "But I like my name being screamed from them when I'm deep inside you more."

Fuck me, he's out for the kill this morning.

Wetness slicks my thighs, his rude awakening forgotten as I try to press closer. He chuckles a deep manly sound that does nothing to ease the ache that he's created.

"Later, Dove. For now, it's race day and you need to get dressed as you'll be on my arm for all to see."

"Race day!" Jude yells, leaping from the bed and grabbing me out of Aeron's hold, spinning me around until I'm dizzy and giggling. "Why didn't you say that?"

We come to a stop and I see Aeron shaking his head, a smile playing at the corner of his lips. He looks at Jude with a softness that I rarely see directed at anything or anyone else. Except, perhaps sometimes, me.

"There's a dress for you in my room, Dove," Aeron says, and Jude plants a smacking kiss on my lips before running off to his bathroom to presumably shower, his peachy ass delicious, especially with my bite marks on it.

"Good morning, *Aziz-e delam*," Tarl greets me softly, kissing my lips gently before turning around and walking towards the door, his own ass taut and fucking edible.

"What does it mean?" I ask.

He turns back, his caramel-colored skin shining in the morning light. Like all the others, he, too, has ink covering parts of his body. Beautiful, swirling designs that ebb and flow over his taut muscles with what looks like some kind of scripture running alongside the lines.

"Dear of my heart," he tells me, a twinkle of mischief in his mismatched eyes.

"And what you called me in the woods?" My throat is thick, the implication that this is more than what our bodies crave making me all kinds of fucked up.

"*Koshgelam?* My dear." He stalks back towards me, a predator lurking in his eyes as he presses his hot, hard body against mine. I whimper when I feel his solid length between us. Cupping my face in both of his palms, he brings our foreheads together, my eyes closing at the rightness of being so close. "*Kharâbetam.*"

I swallow once. Twice.

"What does that mean?" I whisper, my heart racing as the blood rushes around my body.

"I am ruined for you."

Placing a light kiss on my lips, he releases me to turn back around and stride from the room, leaving me cold and bereft, tears stinging my eyes. Heat presses against my back, and my head whirls as my body sinks into the comforting warmth.

"We all are," Aeron whispers against my ear. "You are the Tailors' Ruin, Dove."

And you are mine, I want to say, knowing that truth in my very soul.

✂

"OCEAN EYES (ACOUSTIC)" BY SVRCINA

AERON

We wait in the living area for our Dove to emerge. *I wonder what she thinks of the dress I chose?*

We're all dressed to impress; top hats and tails, our dove gray suits—I thought that the color choice was apt—tailored to perfection. We are Tailors so it's expected, even though we have nothing to do with tailoring clothes unless you count using the businesses to clean dirty money. Jude of course has to add his usual flair; a bright blue waistcoat the exact shade of Dove's eyes, his shirt undone with his bow tie hanging loose. Plus a Mad Hatter-style top hat with feathers and playing cards tucked into the band. Tarl also couldn't resist deviating from the dress code, a blue, silk scarf tucked into the neck of his shirt, also the startling bright color of Dove's eyes, and Knox isn't much better, wearing his boots instead of the dress shoes we're supposed to be sporting.

I guess we're the Tailor boys so can do whatever the fuck we want. It's our race, after all.

We all pause and turn towards the stairs when we hear her tread, the sound of her heels ringing in the warehouse.

Fuck.

Me.

My dress choice was definitely the right one. She's covered from neck to ankle and wrist to wrist in snowy-white lace, a train of it dragging behind her as she walks. Under the lace is a white, mini underdress that skims the tops of her breasts and thighs. The dress both hugs her delicious curves and leaves teasing glimpses of creamy skin on display. Her auburn-red hair tumbles over one shoulder, a small hat covered in dove feathers perching on one side of her head.

She looks fucking exquisite.

"My lady," Jude says, rushing to the base of the stairs and holding his hand out for her to take. A dusky pink blush steals across her cheeks as she takes it, letting him guide her off the last step and towards us. "You look magnificent. My brother chose well."

A twinge of envy stabs my gut when he gets the first kiss, but then her sparkling eyes find mine.

"You could have found more comfortable shoes, Devil Man. I'm going to break my fucking neck before the end of the day in these."

My lip twitches at her rudeness. I like it when she talks back and challenges me. The almost-smile falls when she lifts her hem to show us her shiny, black, peep-toe Louboutin four-inch pumps.

"Show me the sole," I demand, my blood heating as she twists her foot to flash us a glimpse of red.

"You'll be wearing those later when I fuck you raw, Little Bird," Knox growls, blocking her from view and dipping his head. I hear her soft moan, and all that fiery blood rushes to my cock, hardening it in an instant.

Knox pulls away and steps aside, his mouth slashed with the red from her lips. I cast my eye over the ruin of her perfection, and decide that I like her better this way; looking like she's just been debauched and waiting for me to take my turn.

Unfortunately, Tarl beats me to it, but keeps it quick with a press of his lips to her cheek and whispers, "You look ravishing, *Eshgham.*"

He strolls away, and I step in front of her, my eyes devouring her.

"Knox ruined my lipstick, didn't he, Devil Man?"

I just smile, knowing that I'm living up to my nickname when her eyes widen. Dipping my head, I bypass her plush lips.

"Almost fucked looks good on you, Dove," I breathe, and I feel her entire body shudder as my hand comes to her waist. I jerk her towards me, relishing the gasp that falls from those lips and puffs against the side of my face. "But don't worry, I'll remedy that ache later, where everyone can see that you belong to us now."

"Wha—" she starts, the rest of the word a moan when I place my lips over her pulse point and suck. One hand comes up to grip my bicep, which flexes under her touch, her fingers digging in, and for once, I don't care that she's crinkling my suit. I don't give a fuck that I'll look untidy as I continue to mark her, wanting everyone to know who she belongs to.

I pull away, my breath heavy, as I straighten up and stare into her hooded eyes. My cock is practically screaming at me to sink balls deep inside her, but I've not lost all my control just yet. Though she definitely tests it.

"Time to go." I step away, adjusting myself in my slacks, her eyes darting down to track the movement, that delicious red coating her cheeks. It doesn't hide the hickey that I just gave her, standing out like a beacon on her slender neck. Good.

"That was hot as fuck, brother," Jude says, letting go of her hand when I hold my bent arm out to her. Rolling my eyes, I ignore him, taking an inhale when she slips her hand into the crook of my elbow. "Can you give me one? Pretty please?"

"Oh, for fuck's sake, Jude!" I glare at him over the top of Dove's head. Even in the heels, she doesn't reach beyond my shoulder.

"I think that would be pretty hot," comes a soft voice, and I look down at her, her cheeks blazing now.

"You want me to give my brother a hickey?"

She licks her lips, looking up at me, and I see the desire there, plain as day.

"I—I mean, there is something kind of horny about the taboo nature of it."

I consider her for a long moment, wondering how far I would go to make her happy. To turn her on.

"Let's go," I finally say, breaking our stare-off and leading us towards the door. I don't miss Jude's words as we walk into the sunlight.

"If anyone can convince him, you can, Nightingale."

Little fucker.

We arrive in style, it's what everyone expects, our vintage Rolls-Royces pulling up outside the entrance. Staff, in suits, rush out to open the door, and I step out, turning back to hold my hand out for Dove. The boys exit their car—I made them get the second car as I wanted our Dove all to myself for the ride over. Suffice to say, she looks even more disheveled, her eyes still have the desperation of someone who's on the edge of pleasure and has been denied a climax.

She may have ruined us, but I'm still a bastard and not above teasing her in retaliation.

She shies away when the flashes of the cameras blind us, but I keep a tight grip on her hand, pulling her into my side as the others come and stand either side of us, giving the vultures what they want.

"Who's the beauty, Aeron?" one shouts, and I just give my signature glare in the direction the voice came from.

"Is she your new plaything?" another voice yells, and Knox growls as Jude throws his head back and laughs.

"She's a beautiful toy, isn't she?" he asks the crowd, grabbing her hand and stepping forward, making her twirl for the cameras. Her posture relaxes at his antics, and when he pulls her into his side, I see him whisper something into her ear which leaves her blushing and smiling coyly.

"How's your father, Jude? Still in Dubai?"

"Yes, and having the time of his life finding some more race winners," Jude replies, his smile wide as he keeps our bird pressed to his side. "Speaking of, as lovely as it is chatting to you all, we must be off, otherwise, we'll miss all the action."

And just like that, he has them eating out of the palm of his hand as we walk through the tall glass doors into the reception foyer. I hear Dove's gasp as she takes in the floor-to-ceiling glass windows and the swathes of pink and white flowers and silk that decorate the vast space. It's busy, but not packed, full of the rich and elite, owners of the horses that are running today. The ladies sparkle, dripping with jewels, long-flowing dresses that cost thousands covering their surgically-enhanced bodies. The men are all in top hats and tails, thousand-dollar suits, and gold watches showcasing their wealth. Fucking sheep, the lot of them.

The manager of this venue, dressed to the nines in gray tails and a top hat, strides towards us, his face split into a wide grin.

"Boys!" he greets in a deep, booming voice, and I can't help the grin that tugs my lips upwards.

"Uncle Rick," I say, the breath whooshing out of me as he wraps me up in a bear hug.

"I swear you get taller every time I see you!" I roll my eyes at him as he releases me with a couple of slaps on the back.

"I stopped growing about ten years ago, Rick."

"How old are you?" Lark's shocked voice interrupts us, and I turn slightly to face her.

"Thirty-two, sweet Dove," I reply, holding her gaze as her eyes widen.

"That makes you ten years older than me, you fucking pervert!"

Rick's roaring laughter echoes around the space, people stopping their conversations to turn and stare at us. Lark's cheeks redden again, but I'm used to the attention.

"I like this one! She's got some gumption!" He closes the gap between them, holding out his hand for her to take. Without hesitation, she slips her much smaller hand into his palm, and he surprises me by bringing it to his lips and placing a kiss on her knuckles. "Rick Taylor, miss. At your disposal."

"Lark Jackson."

A breath whistles out between his teeth, but he doesn't let go of her hand. Nor does he try to hurt her, which is lucky for him as, family or not, we wouldn't let him lay a finger on our bird.

"You boys like playing with fire, huh? Fucking miscreants." He chuckles before releasing her hand to give Jude a hug, then shakes Knox's and Tarl's hands. "Come, let me show you to your box."

"The jockeys first, Rick," I tell him, and he gives a knowing nod, switching direction and taking us towards a door marked as 'Staff Only.'

I greet people along the way, walking next to Rick who does the same. They all give Dove curious glances, but only the tightening of her hand in the crook of my arm lets me know that she's uncomfortable. Her face is serene, fucking beautiful in the room's light, and I see more than one envious stare from the women. The men all look at her with desire in their eyes, and I'm man enough not to get pissed, but feel a sense of pride at the fact that I own this beautiful creature that others covet.

Passing through the door, we enter the back part of the setup, walking down a long corridor that takes us out towards the riders' area and stables. The sound of men jibing each other reaches my ears as we get closer to the breakout room, a place for the jockeys to relax before a race and for them and their saddles to get weighed to ensure a fair race. Well, as fair as any fixed race can be. Afterwards, they're expected to mingle with the crowd and to fuck the wives of the rich men that have placed exorbitant bets and are drowning their sorrows in Laurent Perrier.

"Stand lively!" Rick shouts as he throws open the door and the rush of bodies getting up to do his bidding has my lips twitching upwards.

I cast my eye over the brightly-colored small men, it always surprises me how tiny some of them are; one of the few sports where smaller is better. They're all standing to attention, giving me a respectful nod as I catch their eye. They know who runs this show.

"Morning, boys," I say, and I can see the quirk of several lips as many of them are approaching retirement—mid-thirties for a jump jockey—thus making them older than me. I'm an asshole and like to remind people of their place. "I take it you've got all you need for today?"

There's a chorus of 'yes, Mr. Taylor' and 'yes, sir'. I see my little Dove's lips twist, and turn my gaze on her, narrowing my eyes when she blinks up innocently at me.

"Something to say, Dove?"

"No, sir," she replies in a husky whisper that has blood rushing south to my dick. By the way that she smiles at me, she knows the effect she has when she calls me sir. No worry, I'll be punishing her for her teasing soon enough.

Giving her a wink that has her smile faltering, I turn back to the men and call one of them over.

"Good luck today, O'Sullivan," I say, placing my hand on his shoulder and bringing him closer. "Unfortunately, Bluebonnet is feeling peaky, so you'll have to pull back on the last furlow."

"Understood, Mr. Taylor," the jockey replies, a serious look in his eyes.

"I hear that your eldest just got a place at Harvard Law, congratulations. The dean himself told me only yesterday that he was looking forward to welcoming such a promising young man."

"T–thank you, Mr. Taylor, we hadn't heard anything yet," O'Sullivan stutters, his eyes widening as his cheeks flush.

"The dean is here today, I'm sure he'll want to give you the acceptance letter in person after the race," I tell him, making sure he understands the offer is conditional.

"Understood, sir, thank you." He gives another nod, not flinching when I slap him on the back.

"Take a few bottles of champagne home to celebrate," I tell him before releasing my hold and letting him return to the others.

"What was that all about?"

I look down to see Dove's stare on me, her auburn brows slanted in a frown.

"Hm?" I ask, knowing full well what she's asking about.

"That. The telling him to pull back, and then the whole thing with Harvard?"

"It's how we clean the money, Nightingale," Jude interjects, coming up behind her and wrapping his arms around her. I find I like the way she sinks into him with no hesitation, relaxing in his hold. I roll my eyes at him, but figure that we're not letting her go so where is the harm?

"Clean the money?"

"We place huge bets on the horse with the best odds, most likely to win. Sometimes it does, but sometimes it doesn't," Tarl says from next to us, and she looks to the side at him.

"Why would you want it to lose?"

"Bookies keep the bets, Little Bird," Knox adds, and her head swivels to look at him, Jude still hanging around her.

"And...you own the bookies..." she trails off, her eyes going wide as realization hits. "So either way, you clean your money and make some money. No wonder you're so fucking rich."

I laugh.

"It's not the only way we make money, but yes, it can be a very lucrative venture," I tell her, holding out my hand for her to take again. She places her smaller hand in mine, and electricity runs up my spine at the contact. She really is the Tailors' Ruin.

"How else do you make your money?" she asks as she steps away from Jude, and I indicate to Rick that we're ready to go.

"If I told you, then I'd have to kill you."

Her brows shoot up into her hairline at my words.

"Holy shit, Aeron! Did you just make a joke?!" she teases, and I give her a blank look, my left eyebrow arching, but can't stop the way my lips try to copy her smile.

"Hell has been known to freeze over occasionally, Nightingale," Jude says, and I switch my glare to him. Like the fucker he is, he just laughs and skips ahead.

She groans when we reach the base of a staircase, the one that leads to our owner's box.

"Fucking seriously? In these shoes?"

I don't have time to make a smart remark as no sooner are the words out of her mouth than Knox sweeps her up into his arms. She shrieks, the sound turning into a giggle that has us all straightening up, even Rick.

"She's a rare one, that's for sure," he comments when we follow her peals of laughter as Knox jogs up the stairs. "Where has old Rufus Jackson been hiding her?"

The mention of Lark's father's name has my teeth grinding, remembering exactly how he's been treating his daughter for the past ten years, and then an evil smirk tilts my lips upwards.

"Are our guests all settled?"

"In the box next to yours as you requested," Rick replies, a dark eyebrow lifted in curiosity, but he doesn't question me further, keeping his thoughts to himself as we walk through the doors into the Tailor box.

Dove is no longer in Knox's arms. Instead, she's standing frozen as she gazes out of the window towards the balcony next to ours.

"D–dad?"

CHAPTER EIGHTEEN

"BLOOD//WATER - ACOUSTIC" BY GRANDSON

LARK

My entire body is still, ice flowing through my veins as I stare at the embodiment of my ruin. All else fades away as I look at the man who was meant to shelter me, protect me, but instead gave me away like yesterday's trash. I don't feel hatred like I do when there is a distance between us. I don't feel the usual fire of anger burning inside me. No, I'm numb from the cold, frozen to the core.

As if he can feel my glare burning into the back of his head, my sperm donor turns, his blue eyes so like my own, locking onto me. It doesn't matter that there's glass between us, I want to recoil, I want to run away from the acid in his gaze, but I'm rooted to the spot, unable to move like so many times before.

Helpless.

"Come, Little Bird," Knox brushes his fingers down my arm, and I feel my body shiver, though it doesn't penetrate the frost that coats me. "I think we'll all need some Dutch courage for this."

Usually, I'd wonder what he means, but I can't. Not while *he* stares at me like that. Like I'm his worst mistake.

I let Knox tug me away, but I can feel *his* eyes on the back of me, scoring me with the burn of ice.

"Here, drink," Knox commands roughly, shoving a glass of amber liquid into my hand. There are ripples on the surface as my whole body trembles.

Why is he here?

I bring the glass to my lips, knocking the whole thing back in one go. The burn of alcohol going down my throat finally breaks the spell, and I cough, blinking and seeing our surroundings for the first time.

Like downstairs, the dusky pink and white swathes of flowers and silk decorate the space, the cream carpet so fucking thick and plush that my heels sink into it. *That's what she said.* A hysterical laugh almost slips past my lips, but I somehow hold it in just as I feel someone come up behind me.

On instinct, I smash my glass against the bar that Knox dragged me to, brandishing it in front of me as I whirl around. To give the eldest Taylor brother credit, he doesn't even flinch, just pauses and gives me a sardonic look, one dark brow haughtily raised.

"And what do you plan to do with that, Dove?"

"Why is he here?" I seethe, my lips pulled back as I bare my teeth at him. My entire body still trembles, but my hand is steady as I step closer, pressing the glass to his jugular. A bead of red slides down the sharp edge, and I blame these fuckers for the fact that my core clenches.

"I wanted him to see that you belong to us and that he couldn't touch you now without serious repercussions," Aeron calmly says, cool as a motherfucking cucumber. I blink, my arm dropping slightly as the realization hits.

"You're claiming me?"

He scoffs, taking a step into me. Hurriedly, I move the sharp glass edge away, successfully nicking his neck more and blood drips from the wound.

"I'll claim you in front of this entire fucked up world if that's what it takes to keep you safe, Dove." His voice is fierce, and tears sting my eyes, my chest tightening. No one has ever been in my corner before. Not even Rook. It wasn't his fault, he's younger and had a dick so didn't know how they treated me. What they subjected me to.

"Oh."

"Yes, oh," he repeats. "If you don't stop pointing your guns at her, I will empty them down your throats."

I frown, my gaze darting past him to see lots of big guys dressed in black hastily tucking weapons away. *Oops.*

"I hurt you," I gasp, reaching out to his neck which has a line of blood running down the side.

"I've had worse, princess."

I don't stop to think, just lean forward and lick the line with a slow swipe of my tongue. His hands are immediately on my waist, tugging me closer as he groans low. The metallic tang of his life force sits on my tongue, and my eyes roll at how delicious it is to have this part of him.

Fixing my lips over the wound, I suck, gently at first, then harder when his grip tightens, and he grinds his hardness into me.

"Fuck, Dove. I'm gonna cream in my pants if you keep that up," he rasps, and I finally release him with a small giggle. My lips pull up in a smile at the large, red hickey on his neck.

"Now we match," I tell him, looking into his eyes, entranced by the stormy sea that rages in them.

"Our souls matched long before today, Dove."

My breath stutters out of me, one hand cupping his cheek, the other resting on his lapel.

"Sorry to break up you two kinky lovebirds," a gruff voice inter-rupts. "But the race is starting in five and I need to head down there."

"Of course, Rick," Aeron replies, still not taking his eyes off mine. "See you later." I hear soft footsteps getting quieter, and assume their uncle has left when the door closes a moment later. "Let's go watch the races, Dove."

Aeron steps out of my embrace, taking my hand and tugging me towards the glass balcony. As soon as he does, I freeze up again, seeing the hateful way my father stares at me, and my cheeks flush as if they've caught me with my hand in the cookie jar. Or my lips on the neck of our enemy, same difference, right?

"Ignore him, Nightingale," Jude says, slinging an arm around my waist and helping Aeron drag me to the doors. Fucking heels, I'd totally be able to resist them if it wasn't for these fucking shoes, pretty as they are.

"We won't let him near you, *Azizam*," Tarl adds, placing a hand on my lower back, the warmth of his touch calming me a little, and urging me forward. "Never again."

They completely fucking overpower me, so I give up, and straightening my shoulders, I take a deep inhale and decide to put my best tit forward and stride out like a badass bitch.

The noise of the crowd hits me like a wave as soon as I step out of the doors, and when we reach the balcony edge, I look down to see that we're pretty fucking high. I love it, feeling a sense of freedom even with the looming presence of my sperm donor as I look out over the racecourse.

Aeron steps away, only for Knox to replace him at my side, Jude on my other side, and Tarl next to him. I feel a warmth at my back, Aeron's fresh cotton mixed with amber and vanilla scent engulfing me as he steps so close that our bodies touch all the way from my shoulders to hips. I grind back a little into his hard length, just able to reach it, and he chuckles darkly.

"Do you want me to make good on my promise to claim you in front of all these people, Dove?" he murmurs into my ear, and I swallow hard. "Do you want your father to know exactly how much you belong to us?"

Like before, I don't think.

"Yes."

He growls and shivers cascade over my skin at the primal sound.

"Be very fucking sure, Dove. It's not just me. Each of us will take our turn, take you until our cum runs down those pretty thighs, and they'll hear your cries in the stands below. Your father and his crew will know that we are fucking you, and their dicks will never be inside you again."

"Please," I beg, not pausing as I squirm more against him, his words making me burn. This time, unlike my father coating me in ice, my entire body is alight, on fire for him. For them.

He doesn't ask again, doesn't hesitate as I feel the back of my skirt being lifted, the cool breeze tickling my legs as he draws it higher.

"Don't worry," he assures as he lifts it higher, "no one will see anything that belongs to our eyes only. The boys will make sure of that."

I look to the side, seeing Knox facing me, his back to my father's balcony and blocking me from view. Turning to glance at the other side, Tarl and Jude stand side by side, blocking the people in the next box from seeing what we're up to.

A soft sigh falls from my lips, their combined scents and the caress of Aeron's fingertips on my sensitive flesh making me forget our surroundings, my father, everything apart from the Tailor boys. My Tailor boys.

"Jesus, Little Bird," Knox hisses out.

"Naughty, Nightingale. Not wearing any underwear just to tease us," Jude hums, and I turn to see his eyes devouring my exposed flesh.

"She just knows how we like it, don't you, Dove?" Aeron asks, gently stroking my backside, sending tendrils of electricity across my skin, his fingers getting closer to the place that I really want him to be.

"Yes," I whisper, arching my back and sticking my ass further out as I lean over the railing, hoping that it will encourage him. He just laughs darkly.

"Look at how she glistens for us, how her pussy drips for us," he comments, swiping a finger through my slick folds, and I gasp at the explosion of pleasure that threatens to overwhelm me already.

"Please," I moan, pushing back further. "Please, please, please."

Suddenly his hands leave my body, a whine of protest starting in my throat but cutting short when I hear a buckle being undone. My body tingles, my fingers gripping the railing tight, and my heart pounds as I wait for that first delicious stretch.

A hand grasps my chin, and tugs me to the side, bright hazel eyes full of fiery lust boring into mine.

"No one but us will ever touch you again, Little Bird. You are ours now until we decide to end you, and even then we won't let the devil have you." His voice is low, full of violent promise and a pleasure I can't even imagine, and I long for the end that I know now only they can give me.

Without giving me a chance to answer, although fuck knows what I'd say to his dark declaration, he slams his lips onto mine just as Aeron thrusts inside me. Knox swallows my scream, made up of part pleasure and part pain as Aeron's piercing drags against my inner walls, sending sparks shooting straight to my core. Aeron gives me no time to adjust, not even a moment to get used to his length and jewelry as he pounds into me, Knox inhaling every cry and whimper that leaves my lips.

My body flashes hot as a hand reaches around the front of it, fingers toying and playing with my swollen, aching clit, another snaking around my throat and squeezing tightly. I want to scream that it's too much, that I can't take them all like this, but I have no voice. They've all stolen it as they brand me with their claiming, doing exactly as they promised and showing the world that I am property of the Tailor boys.

Knox finally releases my mouth, and we're both panting, his lips puffy with my kisses. He moves slightly, and ice-cold, blue eyes catch mine, dousing me like a bucket of cold water.

But at that moment, someone pinches my clit hard, and holding the gaze of my father, I come harder than I ever have in my entire life.

CHAPTER NINETEEN

KNOX

I watch as our Little Bird comes undone right in front of me, and it's the hottest fucking thing I've ever seen. Her cheeks are flushed, her body frozen in ecstasy as Aeron continues to pound into her from behind, a vicious snarl on his lips, his suit jacket wrinkled, as he looks in the same direction she does.

Glancing behind me, I can't help the smirk tugging my lips upwards when I see the fire in Rufus Jackson's eyes as he watches his mortal enemies fuck his only daughter. His gaze flicks to mine, and my grin widens as I lift my chin and mouth one word at him.

Ours.

His jaw tightens, and I hope he cracks a fucking tooth, as with a slight lift of his upper lip, he spins around and storms out. My breathing catches as an older teenage boy, perhaps eighteen, who has flame-red hair and startling, blue eyes stares at our group. Rook Jackson, Lark's brother.

It's not seeing him for the first time that makes my heart suddenly gallop, or the eerie resemblance to our Little Bird. It's the look of confused hunger in his eyes as he watches his sister clearly get fucked that sets my teeth on edge.

Swelling my chest, and stepping so I block his view—I'm a big motherfucker and I know he can't see past me—I turn back to her to see how she's reacting to seeing her brother, but her eyes are closed, and by the blissed out, slightly pained look on her face, she didn't notice him. Good.

"Come again for us, *Eshgham*," Tarl commands, his hand tightening around her throat. Luckily, he's got a long reach, having to stretch past Jude who has his hand buried in between her legs and shows no sign of giving up that treasure.

I watch as her lips part, the lower one quivering as her eyebrows furrow.

"I–I c–can't," she gasps, voice barely above a whisper.

"You can and you will, Dove," Aeron snarls, a sharp clap sounding as he smacks her ass hard.

"Fuuuuck!" she yells, her hands gripping the rail so tightly that her knuckles turn white as she climaxes again. Aeron pounds into her, his hands clamping her hips so tightly that I can already see the bruises blooming on her pretty, porcelain skin. She marks up so beautifully for us.

With an animalistic roar, he thrusts powerfully, seating himself inside her as he comes.

"Tarl, swap," I growl, the need to be inside her consuming me suddenly until it's all that I can think about. He must hear the desperation in my voice, as he lets go of her throat with a lingering caress, and then joins me so that I can step away without her being revealed any more than she has been. Jude turns his body so that he's fully facing her again, blocking her on the other side.

I place my hand on Aeron's shoulder, already taking my rock-fucking-solid cock out of my suit pants.

"Yeah, yeah, give me a minute," he grumbles without any heat behind the words, and I would chuckle but he leans forward and places a gentle kiss on the back of Lark's neck, whispering something in her ear that has a shiver running through her body. He pulls out, giving me a nod as her lace skirts flutter back to the ground.

"Turn around, Little Bird," I order, palming my aching cock and giving it a slow pump. Pre-cum already beads at the slit, and I use it to smear across my head. She follows my decree, and goddamn, she's a fucking vision, freshly fucked but ready for more. "Good girl. Lift your skirts."

"Yes, Daddy," she answers in a breathy voice, and I'm not the only one who groans at the nickname she uses for me.

I'm fixated on her hands as she inches the fabric up, slowly teasing me until she finally reaches the apex and I see her red and swollen cunt, Aeron's cum coating her inner thighs.

"Thanks for the lube, brother," I joke, my voice so deep it's almost a growl. I look back up at her face, studying her intently. "Do you trust me, Little Bird?"

"Yes."

She doesn't even fucking hesitate, and my grin turns positively feral as I step closer to her.

"Good."

Letting go of my dick, I dip down, grabbing her under each thigh and lifting her up as I take a step towards the balcony. Her arms immediately wrap around my neck, pressing her luscious body closer to mine, and I hum in appreciation.

"K–Knox! What the—"

"You said you trusted me, Little Bird," I admonish, stepping closer until I can perch her pretty ass on the railing. I'm tall enough that it's not too high for me to reach that sweet cunt of hers.

"I–I do, but, it's just so high," she stammers out, looking to the side and down, swallowing visibly. I chuckle.

"I won't let you fall, Little Bird," I assure her, leaning in to nuzzle her neck. God, she smells fucking delicious, sweet and soft like a summer breeze. "I'll always keep you safe."

I take one hand off her thigh, and I use it to help line myself up with her soaked opening. She gasps and then moans low as I push inside, my way eased by Aeron's cum. Letting go of my cock, I grab her hip, my fingers digging into her soft flesh over Aeron's prints, groaning with how divine she feels.

"Shit, Knox," she gasps, hooking her ankles behind my ass—those fucking red-bottomed heels digging in just like I told her they would—and pulling me closer. "You feel so fucking good."

"So do you, Little Bird," I groan out, pushing in the last couple of inches and having to pause to stop myself from exploding right the fuck now. "You were made to take this cock, baby."

I can't see all that well, her dress bunched between us, but I sure as shit can feel how she clenches around me, trying to strangle my cock with her pussy. God, I would happily spend the rest of my days buried balls fucking deep inside her.

Slowly, teasing myself as much as I am her, I pull out, feeling every squeeze of her inner walls as she refuses to let me go.

"Don't worry, Little Bird," I say with a chuckle. "I'm not going anywhere."

Her cry rings out across the stadium as I thrust back inside, hard.

"You have balls of steel, Daddy," Jude's voice whispers in my ear, and my heart pounds as I feel his hand reach around and cup said balls. "One day soon, I want them slapping against my ass cheeks as you fuck me as hard as you're going to fuck her."

"Jesus, Jude," I rasp, pushing inside our Little Bird more as his words make my blood heat to a fever pitch. I lose all control I was working to hold on to and start thrusting into her so fucking hard that she can't make a sound, just little gasps of air as our bodies collide. He holds my balls, squeezing and massaging them, whispering dirty scenarios into my ear that just wind me up tighter.

Letting go of her with one hand, I trace the spot on her bicep, the slightly raised part that I know is her birth control implant.

"I wanna cut this out of you so fucking bad, Little Bird," I snarl, pressing against the object buried in her arm as I fuck her hard. "Then watch as your belly swells with my child."

"Oh–God–fuck–shit–cunt–Knox!" Lark mumbles, her fingers digging into the back of my neck as her walls clamp down around me. Jude chooses that moment to give me a firm squeeze, and lightning erupts across my skin, my orgasm tearing through me with the force of a fucking freight train.

With a deep growl, I push all of my dick inside her, hot ropes of cum spurting and coating her inner walls as stars fill my eyes.

"Good, Daddy," Jude teases, removing his hand, and I open my eyes to see him step next to us, licking his sticky fingers.

My head drops to her heaving chest as I try to remember how to fucking breathe. Her lace-covered breasts rise and fall with her pants, and if we were anywhere else, I'd snuggle into them and fall into a blissed-out sleep.

"Our turn, brother," Tarl's accented voice comes from behind me, and I blink my eyes open to see him standing next to Jude.

"Did someone say threesome?" Jude sings, clapping his hands with excitement, his pupils lust-blown and wide.

"Up against the balcony, Brat, pants down, cock out," Tarl demands, and my dick twitches at the thought of Jude doing my own bidding.

With a deep inhale and gathering together strength that I didn't know I possessed, I step back, keeping our Little Bird pressed to me until she can slide her legs down. I slip out of her as her high-heeled feet touch the floor, and she whimpers like she misses me already.

Leaning down, I press a kiss to her red, puffy lips.

"Ours," I purr against them.

"Yours," she breathes back, and my heart swells in my chest at her admission.

✂

"POISON" BY FREYA RIDINGS

LARK

Theirs.

Am I theirs? Do I now belong to these hard men?

They have claimed me, publicly now, and as I look at Knox's softening dick, covered in my ecstasy, I know that I've claimed them back.

"Are you ready to be owned by us completely, *Aziz-e delam?*"

Mismatched eyes gaze into mine, a fire burning in their depths, the rest of his face unreadable, yet there's a fierceness about him that makes my already pounding heart thud painfully in my chest.

"Yes."

It's the only answer that I can give. The only word that falls from my tongue with ease.

Tarl steps up to me, his hand coming out to caress my chest in a featherlight touch that, like a ripple on the surface of a lake, leaves shivers cascading all across my skin.

"*Kharâbetam*, Pretty Bird," he whispers, his eyes tracking over my features as if he's committing them to memory. "We are all ruined for you, just as we will ruin you in return so that no one else will ever have you." My eyes fall closed as his lips touch mine, and it's like he can't help himself, his tongue coming out to tangle and tease mine. His taste is addictive, like exotic nights and deeds done only in the dead of night. He completely decimates me with his kiss, leaving me begging for more as he pulls back. "I'm going to take that dress off you now, beautiful as it is, I want you bare before me, your owner," he tells me, and a flare of panic makes my already trembling legs weak.

"B–but–"

"Shhhh, no one but us will see you," he breathes as I feel the small pearl buttons on the back of my dress being popped open. I glance behind me to see Jude standing there, his sweet-popping candy smell putting me at ease. I relax more when Aeron stands on one side of us, Knox on the other, penning me in their circle.

In a whisper of lace and silk, the dress slides down my body, Jude helping it when it sticks to the parts that are now slick with sweat. I can feel the blush rise from my chest as they devour me with hungry eyes, and a sense of power leaves me with a head rush. I have this effect on these powerful men, men who strike fear and awe in equal measure.

"Brat."

"Yes, sir?" Jude answers, his voice low and deep and missing its usual teasing quality.

"Impale her on your dick from behind, make sure we can see."

"Yes, sir."

I inhale sharply as he pulls my hips backwards, my ass cheeks spread, and then Jude thrusts hard inside my dripping pussy.

"Shit, Nightingale," he says, his voice gruff and gravelly, pumping his hips back and forth, leaving me reeling and grasping with my hands. "I can feel their cum coating my dick."

"Juuude," I sigh, the sound broken and full of desperate need.

"We're just getting started, my little broken bird," he replies, fucking into me like he needs it to live.

"That's enough!" Tarl shouts, and I look up at him, gasping as Jude suddenly pulls out. A small whine escapes my lips, and while a part of me worries that I'm giving them too much power over me, another knows that it's too late. "Don't worry, *Eshgham*," he tells me, cupping my cheek and bringing me upright. "He was just lubing up so he can fuck that pretty little asshole of yours while I'm buried in your sweet cunt."

No fucking words. I have no response to what he's just told me.

"Told you," Jude singsongs from behind me, bending down to hook one of my legs over his elbow. I wobble as he straightens, my heeled shoe making me teeter, but three sets of hands steady me, holding me up as I'm forced to stand on one leg. My hands grip their arms, my fingers digging into Aeron and Knox's forearms.

"Deep breath, Dove," Aeron says, his voice calm, and I look to see an almost indulgent look on his face, softening his usually harsh features. Don't get me wrong, his pupils are blown, and his suit is all messed up, his now-hard dick standing proud.

Nodding, I do as he says, taking a gulping breath when I feel Jude pressing against my tight ring. No prep or anything, the bastard, but as he pushes past my entrance, I can't deny that the sharp pain makes my pussy drip with the need to be filled as well.

"You're doing so well, *Koshgelam*," Tarl praises, and my heart flutters at his words. "That's it, take him all."

"Fuck, she's so fucking tight," Jude grits out, pushing further in until his entire length is inside me. "You feel fucking incredible, Nightingale."

I pant as he moves, his thrusts shallow until my body gets used to him, and my hips undulate in time with each one. His piercings drag against the inside of me in a way that I've never experienced before, and I'm fucking dripping for him.

"More," I keen, looking up at Tarl. "Please, Tarl. I need you inside me too."

His lips quirk up in a suggestive smile at my words, a sensuous flame in his beautiful eyes. "Since you asked so nicely, Pretty Bird."

He steps closer, Jude pausing as I watch Tarl line up his dick with my cunt. His metal flashes as it catches the sunlight, then he disappears inside me, and I can't even think as I'm stretched between them. My brain up and leaves, and all I can do is feel, trying to ride out the intense sensations of having Tarl and Jude inside me at once. Sweat breaks out across my skin, and it has nothing to do with the warm summer's day.

"Such," Tarl bites out, sinking deeper. "Such a good fucking girl."

"You guys need to try this," Jude states, his voice strained as Tarl bottoms out. They pause, and we stand there, locked together and just existing for a moment. Connected.

The heat burns inside me again, and they chuckle when I wiggle, desperately seeking friction.

"Do you want us to fuck you hard, Pretty Bird?" Tarl asks, one hand around the back of my neck, the other gripping my hip.

"Yes, please. A thousand times yes!" I gasp out, the tips of my still mostly nailless fingers sinking further into the boys' arms.

"As you wish," Jude answers, but I don't get time to appreciate The Princess Bride reference because, in the next moment, he pulls almost all the way out only to slam back into me. Sparks fly from our point of connection, Tarl groaning when I clench around him.

They find a rhythm, a push and pull where they use me as a rag doll, and I just hold on for dear life, both of their piercings adding an extra texture that I didn't know I needed in my life. Occasionally, one will leave my body, only to thrust back inside as if they can't bear to be apart from me for that long.

"Put her leg on my shoulder, Brat," Tarl orders, sweat glistening on his caramel skin. My mouth waters at the thought of licking it off, but I can't move, trapped between them and their desire. He's still got his shirt on, though it's undone, and I can see his inked-up chest and abs gleaming in the sunlight.

I'm about to protest, to tell them I won't stretch like that, but then my ankle rests on Tarl's muscular shoulder and I'm screaming with how deep they can go with this angle. I know that I'm fulfilling Aeron's promise for the whole stadium to hear me, but I just can't contain the pleasure that's filling me up right now. It's too much for a mere mortal to handle.

My cries turn into whimpers and gasps as they build me up, pushing me over the edge and into the abyss as an orgasm crashes over me, my body trying to seize as waves of intense pleasure roll me over and under like a piece of driftwood in a raging sea.

"I can't last much longer," Jude rasps between gritted teeth. "She's gripping me like a fucking vise."

"You will come when I tell you to, Brat," Tarl snarls, his movements becoming furious. "And you will come one more time for your masters, Pretty Bird."

"I–I c–c–can't!" I sob, tears gathering in my eyes as my orgasm lingers, easing up only slightly.

"Yes, you fucking will," Aeron commands, his tone hard and unwavering and I turn to face him. His arm is moving up and down as he pumps his dick, a deep furrow in between his thick brows. "Because we demand it, Dove."

"Prove to us you are ours completely, Little Bird," Knox says in a gruff voice from the other side, and I whip my head around to see him in a similar position to Aeron, large cock in hand as he pumps it furiously.

"Come all over me," I gasp, the thought of being covered in their seed making wetness seep out of me. "Show me I belong to you and no other."

His nostrils flare, his jaw grinding as his arm pumps faster. Jude and Tarl are grunting and cursing as they continue to fuck me hard, and I look down and watch as Knox's dick swells. I lick my lower lip, and it seems to be that which tips him over the edge as thick, hot ropes of cum shoot out of his shaft and cover my lower stomach. I moan with the feel of his hot cum hitting my skin, my pussy clamping down on Tarl as I almost tumble off the precipice with Knox.

"Look at me and open your fucking mouth," Aeron orders, and I twist my head to look at him, my mouth automatically opening. With a deep groan, he climaxes, and I flinch when the first spurt hits my breast, more hitting my chin and finally my mouth.

It's the salty taste of him that sends me over, white lights flashing before my eyes as I writhe and scream my release. It feels as though the world aligns, as though something momentous has happened when a snarl in front of me brings me back enough to see

Tarl come, thrusting deep inside me. Jude is quick to follow, burying himself in my ass as he orgasms, and their releases keep mine going, my legs twitching and the one holding me up threatening to buckle beneath me.

My eyes drift closed as I come down, my entire body, including my fucking teeth tingling. Vaguely, I feel Tarl and Jude pull out, my body protesting as they leave it, but I'm too tired, too fucked out to make a fuss, and soon I'm wrapped up in a jacket smelling of clean cotton, vanilla, and sandalwood. Knox picks me up, adding his motor oil, cloves, and leather scent as he carries me back inside the box.

I don't know what happens after that, allowing myself to succumb to the darkness that, for once, feels welcoming and not threatening.

CHAPTER TWENTY

"CONTAMINATED" BY BANKS

LARK

A beam of sunlight tickles my face, my eyelids fluttering open to the semi-darkness of a room which I don't recognize.

"Morning, Little Bird," a deep, husky voice says beside me, and twisting my head, I see Knox staring at me with softness in his hazel eyes.

"Do you often stare at women when they sleep?" I grouch, and he chuckles, the rasping sound making my core clench. I wince at the slight ache there, my body heating as memories from the balcony yesterday flit before my eyes.

"Only when they're beautiful birds in my bed," he replies, reaching a hand out to push aside some of my tangled hair. I'm actually feeling kind of fresh, which is a surprise considering our activities yesterday at the races.

"Why am I not more gross? More cum-covered?" I ask him, earning Knox's raised, dirty-blonde brows and a devilish grin.

"Our illustrious leader cleaned you up himself before he left last night after I called dibs."

"I'm not some fucking dog toy to call dibs on, you know," I tell him, my lips pulled down in a pout.

"That is what bothers you about what I just said? Not the part about you being unconscious and having someone clean your sweet pussy?" he asks, his fingers toying with the strand of hair that he pushed back before.

"I've had worse done to me when I've been unconscious, Knox," I say quietly, dropping my gaze to his bare, inked-up chest and trying not to fall into those dark memories when I would wake up with no knowledge of how I got the bruises on my inner thighs or the sharp ache in my cunt.

His fingers still, and I chance a glance upwards to see his jaw clenched so tightly I'm surprised that he doesn't crack a tooth. His gaze settles on mine, and I take a sharp inhale at the fire that rages in his eyes, hot enough to burn the entire world down. He drops my hair before cupping my face in his warm palm.

"I will kill them all, Little Bird. Every fucking cunt who touched you without your permission will drown in their own blood." His voice has dropped until it's the savage whisper of an avenging god, and my heart thuds in my chest at his vehemence.

I don't know what to say, how to process his words. I've never had someone on my side, a protector. Well, not since Mom passed away anyway. It's always been me, myself, and I up against the monsters that make up the Dead Soldiers. I swallow, deciding that it's too fucking early to process everything that's being thrown at me.

"What's the beef between you and Devil Man?" I ask, having noticed the tension between the two men frequently. He sighs, his exhale almost pained as it leaves his lips. His hand leaves my cheek, and runs through his thick hair, leaving it deliciously disarrayed.

"He blames me for June's death," he confesses with a slight hitch in his voice. Unconsciously, I reach my hand up and tangle my fingers with his, his own gripping mine tightly back.

"What happened?"

The skin around his eyes tightens, and it's only now that I can see he, like Aeron, is older than me by some years.

"She snuck out to meet me after Aeron forbade her to leave their home on her own, but June was full of fire, much like you are, Little Bird, and wouldn't listen. You two probably would have gotten on like a fucking house on fire." He gives a rueful laugh, and my lips tug up into a smile at his words. I would have liked a female friend. "Anyway, she was walking towards me, with that swagger she had that said 'fuck you' to the entire world. I don't remember seeing the car, but suddenly I heard gunshots, three—Bam! Bam! Bam!" His body twitches with each one, as if he's remembering each shot as if they were for him. "Then the squeal of tires as the car sped off. I had instinctively crouched down, hidden in the shadows of a building, but when I looked up, it was like the entire fucking world had stopped. Somehow, Jude was there, a crumpled and unresponsive June held in his lap. I scrambled up, dropping next to him, and there was so much blood, Lark. It covered her." His haunted eyes glisten, and my own fills with tears at the picture he's painting; of Jude holding his own twin as she died in his arms. I almost miss that he called me by name, my stomach dropping with the sound of it on his lips, like when you fall from a great height. "Jude was crying, screaming at me to just do fucking something, but the light in her eyes had gone. She wasn't there anymore, and there was nothing I could do. Fucking nothing."

"It wasn't your fault, Knox," I tell him, letting go of his hand and wrapping myself around his body, pressing our naked bodies close. "You didn't pull the trigger."

His body shudders, his arms encasing me and pulling me even closer so that not even a breath of air remains between us.

"I couldn't protect her when I needed to, Little Bird. I couldn't do anything but watch her bleed out, knowing that it was me she was coming to see." His voice is thick, like the words are being pulled from him after being trapped for so long.

"Knox, this happened around eight years ago right? After...after they shot my mom down?" He nods. "You need to forgive yourself for something that you had no control over. It wasn't your fault," I tell him again, willing this powerful man to believe it as I snuggle into his body, his pounding heartbeat under my cheek. "Shit happens that we can't control, that we can't do a fucking thing about apart from keep going and hope that one day, things will be better." Tears are streaming down my cheeks, landing on his chest and making his ink darken. I didn't know until this moment that's what I needed to do; admit that my mother's murder wasn't my fault. That everything which followed wasn't my fault.

"Hey, talk to me, Little Bird," Knox's gentle voice breaks through my sobs, his face coming into view as he pulls back a little. A pang of guilt at letting my trauma take over runs through me.

"T–this isn't about m–me," I hiccup, swiping at my cheeks.

"You've just helped me, beautiful. Let me help you," he pleads, his lashes dipped in moisture and his eyes sparkling with unshed tears.

"My mom snuck Rook and I out for burgers and milkshakes the day she was s–shot," I tell him, my lower lip trembling. "It was my twelfth birthday, and she wanted to treat me. She stepped out of the diner afterwards and I remember hearing what sounded like a car backfiring and then she was on the ground and there was so much blood." The memories try to resurface, but although they hurt, they don't overwhelm me like they once did. "I held her like Jude did with June, watched as she died. After that, well, you know the rest."

"Oh, baby." Knox's voice is thick again. He pulls me back into him, and I sink into the comfort he's offering, even though a part of me knows I shouldn't. That this can't—won't—last. "I'm so fucking sorry, Little Bird."

I draw strength from a man for what feels like the first time in my life as we hold each other, and the guilt doesn't feel as all-consuming as it usually does.

However, a new guilt rears its ugly head, leaving me with a pain in the back of my throat and a tightness in my chest that no amount of air will ease. It's for something that is yet to pass, something which I also cannot stop.

A fter spending the morning dozing in Knox's arms, hunger forces us to leave the cocoon of safety that his bed now represents, and we head downstairs, hands intertwined.

"Morning, Nightingale!" Jude hollers, bounding over to us and wrapping me up in his arms, taking a deep inhale of my hair like it's the first full breath he's taken all morning. "Morning, Daddy Knox."

Knox growls as I giggle, his hand tightening in mine.

"Is there anything to eat?" I ask Jude, placing a kiss on his scruff-covered chin. "I'm fucking starving."

"For you, my lady? Anything!" Jude declares, stepping back and giving me what I think is supposed to be a knightly bow, but his untucked, Hawaiian shirt and checkered pants ruin the vibe somewhat. "What would my Nightingale like?"

Before I can answer, Aeron comes storming in, phone pressed to his ear and his face thunderous.

"One second, Dad. I'm putting you on speaker now," he says, looking at me and placing a finger over his mouth in a 'be quiet' gesture.

He strides over to the kitchen island, and we follow, Tarl joining us. Knox has a firm grip of one hand, Jude the other as Aeron sets his phone down and hits the speaker icon.

"*Boys,*" a deep voice greets, and I shiver at the anger lacing the man's—clearly Adam Taylor, Aeron and Jude's father, leader of the Tailors—tone. *"Has our little bird sung yet?"*

All eyes flick to me, and my pulse picks up, my muscles tensing as if ready for flight. Knox and Jude squeeze my hands to reassure me, but it does little to quell the churning of my stomach.

"Not exactly, but we're close," Aeron replies, his ocean eyes trained on me as he speaks.

"Well, that is a shame for her. This morning I had a report that they targeted the stables last night, blown to all fucking hell by Dead Soldier scum." Sharp intakes follow his words, and my eyes widen, still caught in Aeron's stare. *"We've lost some prize horses, including Blue."* Jude stills next to me, and it takes a moment for me to register the name. Blue, or Bluebell, their mother's horse. A breath rushes out of me at the memory of the beautiful, gentle creature, and her, no doubt, grizzly end.

"And we know it was the Dead Soldiers?" Aeron asks, and I wonder how many other people it might be. How many other enemies they have.

"They left their calling card wrapped around Jim's bloody neck," his father replies, and I bite my lips just in time to stifle my gasp of horror. Jim was so kind, and now like so many before him, he's dead at the hands of my father's gang. I know what the calling card is; army tags my father likes to drape around the slit neck of his victims. *"So, we need to know where these scum are hiding, where they scurry off to, and that little bird of yours needs to fucking tell us."*

I'm still trapped in Aeron's stare, and for a moment I swear it turns pleading, begging me to tell them. A pit in my stomach opens at that look because I can't. Not until I've secured Rook's safety, which he's refused up to this point.

"We will get the information," Aeron tells his father, his voice tight and jaw clenched. My body stiffens, all my muscles screaming at me to run, far and fucking fast.

"I don't doubt you, son, but I've sent Earl along to help give some... support, perhaps add to your persuasion."

I shiver at his words, bile stinging the back of my throat. Earl, as I later found out, was the one who opened up my back, and my wounds there twinge as if in memory.

"When will he be here?" Aeron asks, his voice sharp and cutting, like when I first met the heir to the Tailors.

"*About an hour, maybe less,*" Adam Taylor answers. "*Get the intel for me, boys, and let's take those fuckers down once and for all.*"

"Yes, sir," Aeron says, the others mumbling the same as they all stare at me, sorrow shining in their eyes.

My legs feel weak, and my breaths saw in and out of my throat, the threat of pain leaving me trembling. The warmth and safety from this morning, of lying in Knox's arms, evaporates like smoke, leaving just uncertainty and terror in its wake.

How much will they hurt me? How far will they go? And how far will I go in order to protect my brother?

CHAPTER TWENTY-ONE

AERON

Fuck.

FUCK!

My mind spins and whirls as I try to figure out what the ever-loving fuck we're going to do. How do we protect her?

The call ends, and for just a moment, one small millisecond, I close my eyes and breathe, my fists clenching and unclenching by my sides.

"Please," I rasp, my pained whisper loud in the quiet. "Please, Dove, tell us where the Dead Soldier's HQ is."

I open my eyes, my heart sinking when I see her trembling body, but the fire in her eyes tells me she won't give us what we need to keep her safe. Not yet.

"You know my price, Devil Man," she says back, and fuck, I fall harder at her stupid fucking strength that underlines every word, even if I know that she's terrified.

"Rook," I answer, heaving a great sigh. "I can't promise his safety, Dove. Anything else I might be able to do, but to leave the heir to your father's kingdom alive is fucking foolish. Signing our death warrants."

She straightens her spine, letting go of my brother's and Knox's hands as she steps away from them. I can see Knox shut down, his face going hard, but he can't hide the agony in his eyes. As our punisher, this will be worse for him than the rest of us. Tarl too. Jude looks fucking devastated, his shoulders curling as she walks around the island towards me. She whips Knox's shirt over her head and lets it drop to the ground, leaving her beautiful body naked and exposed.

"Then we understand each other perfectly." Her voice is barely above a whisper, and it takes everything inside me not to drop to my knees and fucking beg her not to make us do this. Not to make us hurt her. We stare at each other, my jaw working as my breaths claw in through my nose, my brain fucking failing to give me any other options. "It's okay, Devil Man. It was a beautiful dream, but people like us don't get to live in dreamland for too long," she says quietly, reaching out to cup my cheek in her soft palm, and I clench my teeth so hard that I feel my jaw crack.

She's too good for us, and how she ended up being so astounding living under Rufus fucking Jackson's roof is beyond me.

A knock sounds in the warehouse, making her flinch, and my body instinctively moves as if to protect her. A fucking joke considering it's us she needs protection from.

"Tarl, Knox, take her downstairs," I order, my tone strained and the words hurting as they pass my lips.

"But—" Knox starts, and I snap my gaze to him, daring him to argue. He bares his teeth, the skin around his eyes tightening as he glares at me. I'll welcome his anger later. For now, I just need him to do as I fucking tell him. I can't deal with mutiny now.

"Come, *Koshgelam*," Tarl says, swallowing visibly as he comes to take hold of Dove's bicep.

She leans forward, pressing a soft kiss on my lips before she allows him to lead her away, towards the basement, Knox following them. The ghost of her lips burns, and a raging inferno swirls inside me, my fucking soul at war with itself.

"Brother" Jude begs, and the glisten of unshed tears makes his eyes truly look as deep as the ocean.

"She's made her decision," I tell him, another loud knock at the front door sounding like a death knell. I take a deep inhale, turn my back on him, and head to the door, my steps feeling like the thud of nails going into a coffin.

I just wonder who's going to be buried.

"RUNNING UP THAT HILL (A DEAL WITH GOD)" BY LOVELESS

LARK

The cold of the basement causes goosebumps to pebble on my skin, my nipples hardening despite the fact that I feel no arousal. Fear makes my body tremble and quake, but I try to remain calm, knowing that nothing can change the impasse we've come to.

"Little Bird," Knox says as we step into the room, my glass coffin still in one corner, the cross in the other. There are more shapes and dark shadows under cloths that line the room, and I ponder which they will use on me first. "Lark! Fucking look at me!"

A strong hand wraps around my upper arm, tearing me away from Tarl and suddenly Knox's beautiful ruggedness fills my vision, his motor oil, cloves, and leather scent enveloping me. His eyes are wild, the whites showing around the hazel irises, bright with panic.

"Please, baby. Just tell us what we need to know, and we can go back upstairs."

My body softens in his hold, and the need to sink into his warmth, to give him what he's asking is so strong that I have to take a deep, steadying breath.

"What would you do to keep Tarl safe?" I ask in reply, his brows furrowing. "To keep Jude alive? Aeron?" I watch as his lips press together in a hard line, his mouth opening only to close a second later. "That is why I can't just tell you, Knox. I need a guarantee of Rook's safety. I can't settle for any less. He's all I have left."

"Rook may be my only heir, Lark, but my crown doesn't have to go to my blood. Brings those boys in and Rook will get to wear it. Don't and..." My sperm donor's words from before I left all those weeks ago flash through my mind, leaving an empty feeling in my stomach.

"You don't know what you're asking me to fucking do, Little Bird," he whispers, and I can see in the slump of his shoulders that he understands before he hisses and lets go of my arm to storm away.

I can't reply, as a moment later, the door swings open, and a man who I'd hoped to never see again walks in.

Fucking Earl.

I study him as he swaggers over to me, my heart racing enough to leave me drawing shallow breaths. His face is lined with age, placing him around fifty if I had to guess, a scar bisecting his left eye and making him look so much like a cartoon villain that I have to hold back a hysterical laugh, but it's the cruel smirk on his thin lips that makes the sound die before it's even had a chance to form. The sick delight in his eyes reminds me so much of my father's men that I have to swallow bile.

"Hello, little songbird."

My head whips to the side as sharp pain blooms along my cheek. I take a moment to realize that he's just backhanded me. I hear shouts above the ringing in my ears, and feeling liquid dripping down my chin, I watch a drop of red spread on the concrete floor.

"Touch her again, Earl, and I'll fucking cut off each of your hands while you watch," Tarl snarls, and I turn back to see Earl surrounded by my guys a step or two away from me, Tarl nose to nose with him.

"My bad, boys." Earl chuckles, the sound slithering across my skin like an oil spill. "I've always found the best way to get information is going in hard and fast."

"Well, you're here to observe," Aeron interjects coolly, Tarl stepping back so Aeron can stand in front of the older man. I shiver at the ice in his tone. It's like a frozen wasteland, ready to steal your last breath. "Leave this to us. Understood?"

I watch as something dark flickers in Earl's beady eyes, his nostrils flaring as if he would challenge Aeron.

"Understood," he replies after a few tense moments.

Aeron stares at him for a second longer, then gives a sharp nod, turning his back and dismissing Earl as if he were no one of importance. I watch as Earl's fists clench, Aeron's move pissing him off royally. Good, but Aeron best watch that one.

The heir to the Tailor throne turns his icy stare onto me, and it takes every ounce of strength I possess not to flinch.

"Tarl, the gurney."

I hear Tarl walk past, his fingers brushing mine, and then the sound of wheels fills the space. I swallow, unable to look away from the swirling tundra of Aeron's eyes.

"On the gurney, Dove."

Taking a moment, I hold his gaze. Then, spinning around, I see a metal gurney behind me with thick, leather ankle and wrist straps dangling down its sides.

"It'll go easier for you, *Koshgelam*, if you comply without a fuss," Tarl tells me, his accent more pronounced than usual, his voice choked. He holds out a hand, like an old-fashioned gentleman would offer to a lady to help her into a car.

Not saying a word, I step towards him, taking his hand and

pausing for a second to let its heat lend me strength. Using it, I move to sit up on the cold metal, a breath hissing from my parted lips as the chilly surface touches my bare ass.

"Could have warmed it up first," I joke, but no one laughs, the silence of the room oppressive and heartbreaking.

Tarl helps me to lie back, then with a touch as gentle as if he were tucking me into bed, he buckles the strap around one wrist. Then my ankle, the other ankle, and finally, my other wrist.

"I truly am sorry for what is about to come, *Eshgham*," he whispers, his mismatched eyes full of anguished sadness. I just nod, swallowing the lump in my throat, unable to say a word.

My head turns as Jude comes into view on my other side, his ocean eyes glistening. I watch as a single tear tracks down his stubbled cheek. He doesn't wipe it away, instead; he places a cloth over my face, his fingertips brushing the side of my neck in a soft caress.

Tremors wrack my body, my concealed lips trembling as I hyperventilate.

"Begin," Aeron's impersonal voice says.

I take in a frightened breath, which proves to be the absolute worst fucking thing to do as my mouth and nose suddenly fill with ice-cold water. Spluttering, I thrash against my binds, my lungs screaming as I cough and hack, trying to breathe.

Shit, this is so much worse than I expected. Sure, there's no excruciating pain, but being unable to breathe, the cloth making any attempt futile, sends my body soaring into panic mode, which just makes me inhale more water.

Water fills my mouth and nose, and every attempted inhale feels like shards of glass as I also take in the water and drown on dry land. Just as spots dance across my vision, the stream stops, and the cloth is whipped away.

Turning my head to the side I vomit up watery bile and take huge, gasping breaths. Pain ripples across my head as someone grabs my hair, and my blurry vision fills with bottomless eyes, the color of the deepest parts of the ocean that no one comes back from.

"Anything to tell us?" Aeron snarls out, and this time I do flinch, his grip loosening as he swallows and for a second his eyes are full of such torment that my body leans towards him, instinctively trying to soothe it away.

"You going to give me my brother's safety, Devil Man?" My voice is croaky, each word painful and sharp. The grip tightens, and he bares his teeth at me.

"Again."

I have a moment to feel the relief of not having his painful grip on my hair, but then the wet cloth is over my face and I'm drowning again.

And again.

And again.

They waterboard me for what feels like hours, my body growing weaker the longer it goes on until I feel as though I might pass out. I must admit that they're good at this. Really fucking good. They know just when to stop, usually before I can give into the darkness that threatens the edges of my vision.

"I thought that the great Inquisitor had methods more effective than waterboarding?" Earl's nasal voice sneers, and I try to turn my head to give him a glare. Spoiler alert; I don't manage it.

"I usually go before that," Knox says to my right, and I manage to look at him. His entire body is tight, a fine tremble running across his body as his fists clench at his sides.

"Knox—" Tarl starts but cuts off at the shake of Knox's head.

"I'll share this burden, brother," Knox mumbles as he places a hand on Tarl's shoulder.

Tarl's entire body slumps, his eyes shining as he nods, and I feel sick at the thought that my refusal to speak is hurting them just as much as it's hurting me. Maybe more so, as mine is only a physical pain, whereas theirs is etched deep into their souls.

"Tarl, Jude, get her off and hold her up," Aeron orders, and even though I can't see him, the anguish in his voice is clear.

The buckles release with a clank, and then I'm being heaved off the gurney, my legs wobbling under me when my feet touch the ground. Strong hands grasp my upper arms, their grip painfully hard, and the mix of cardamom and sunshine surrounds me as Jude and Tarl hold me upright.

Struggling, I lift my weary head and look at Knox, seeing Aeron off to one side and that cunt, Earl, leaning against the wall, arms crossed with a big-ass grin on his ugly face.

My gaze returns to Knox, and my chest hurts at seeing him so distraught, the pain superseding that of the near drowning. He's staring down at his hands, his nostrils flaring as he flexes his fingers.

"It's okay, Knox. Do what you have to," I whisper, Rook's tearstained face flashes before my eyes, from the day Mom died and I told him it would be alright too. Knox's head snaps up to look at me with wide, terror-filled eyes. He gives a hard swallow, then his face goes completely blank.

"It will never be okay again, Little Bird."

CHAPTER TWENTY-TWO

"SAY SOMETHING" BY PENTATONIX

LARK

My breath whooshes out of me a second later, and I cry out, pain radiating down my arm, my exhausted lungs cramping as I struggle to draw in a breath. The boys pull me up, and every muscle protests as I try to curl in on myself, but they won't let me. The second hit to my other bicep is just as bad as the first, and I sag in the boy's grip as both arms go dead.

"I've seen you hit harder than that, Knoxy. You wouldn't be pulling your punches, would you now?" Earl questions, glee in his tone as Knox heaves just as much as I am, his knuckles white with how hard he's clenching his fists.

"Shut the fuck up, Earl," Aeron snaps, and I glance over to see his own hands balled up tightly, his eyes a maelstrom of emotions.

With a roar, Knox kicks my upper thigh, the intense pain

shooting through me like a bolt of lightning. Tears fill my eyes, a gasp leaves my lips as my leg gives out completely, and Jude makes a sound as he continues to try to hold me upright. Seconds later, Knox brings his knee up into my other thigh, rendering me immobile as I fall to a heap on the cold concrete, my hair falling over my face as my head bows.

Tears stream down my cheeks, and my entire body is one throb of anguish as I lie there, my heart hurting as much as my limbs. I know that there's no choice, that I'm giving them no choice but to do this, but it still hurts my soul more than I expected.

A firm hand reaches through my tangled hair, strong fingers clamping behind my ear and the upper side of my nose. A scream rips through my mouth as the most intense pain I've ever felt radiates through my head as I'm pulled upwards by the grip on my face. I can't think, only follow as it pulls me upwards, my broken cries echoing around the room.

"ENOUGH!"

The sharp pain immediately stops, and I fall back down on my knees as I'm released. My entire body trembles, my exposed skin slick with sweat and water. My eyes trace a crack in the concrete, my body wanting to curl in on itself and weep. The physical blows are only part of my devastation, it's the unseen blows to my heart and soul that hurt the worst.

Shiny, black shoes appear in my vision, then knees clad in navy blue slacks. A perfectly manicured hand appears next, stopping when I flinch. The fingers flex, as a deep, pained sigh leaves Aeron's lips.

"I will keep Rook safe, you have my word."

"You can't fucking promise that!" Earl shouts, and my head snaps up to see him step away from the wall, his face an ugly shade of purple.

"Take another step and it will be your last, my father's wrath be damned," Aeron calmly answers. My gaze swings back to him, and a full-body shudder makes the pain in my limbs flare as I look into his eyes and see the deadness in them that I hadn't realized had disappeared these past weeks.

"Y–y–you s–swear? W–whatever h–happens, y–you'll k–keep h–him s–safe?" I ask, my voice all kinds of croaky and fucked up.

"On my life," he answers, and my chest lightens as a breath puffs out of me.

"I'll have to take you there, be with you when you go. It's full of booby traps that only a Soldier, or a Soldier's Darling, would know," I tell him, begging him to believe me even though the words add to the queasy feeling in my stomach, the tang of them bitter and taunting. His jaw clenches and then he gives a single nod.

"Deal."

"That's it?! You're going to believe the word of this fucking whore, just like that?!" Earl spits out, and even I glare daggers at him, fucking prick.

"Tell my father that we have the intel, and will come up with a plan," Aeron states, not even bothering to look at the older man. "You're dismissed."

"Adam will hear of your insolent behavior, pup," Earl threatens before storming towards the door. He pauses, twirling around and I just know by the gleam in his eye that what he's about to say next will hurt. "And I knew bitches were stupid, but you must really be dumb to crawl into bed with the man who killed your mother."

My breathing stops, the air rushing past my ears as I look away from his hateful face and back to Aeron. He's frozen, still crouching down, but he's not looking at me, instead, his eyes trace the same crack that moments ago held my undivided attention.

"Aeron?"

His head slowly lifts, as if it's taking a gargantuan effort to do so.

"Oh, did you not know, girly?" Earl's voice is a harsh, malicious sound, and I feel he's moved closer, but I lock my stare with Aeron's, to the unshed tears that are making his blue eyes shine and sparkle like sapphires. "It was Aeron Taylor, heir to the Tailors, who pulled the trigger on your mom outside that diner. I was there and saw how she froze as the bullets hit home. Watched as she fell to the ground, your face a picture of confusion like you'd never heard a gun go off before."

"A–Aeron?" I ask again, begging him with my eyes to tell me that Earl is lying.

"Get him the fuck out of here," Aeron grits out, not answering me, and it's like one of Knox's blows, but this time I feel it to my very core. The noise of Earl being forced out by someone fills the space, but I can't take my stare off of Aeron.

"Did you murder my mom!" I shout, ignoring the flash of pain as I straighten up on my knees, adrenaline lending me the strength that I need to confront him.

"Yes."

And just like a marionette puppet whose strings have been cut, I slump down as that one word echoes around my head.

Yes.

"Nightingale—" Jude starts, reaching out for me, but I hold up a hand, looking at his face.

"Did you know?" I ask, watching as his hand drops and his face crumples.

"Yes, but we didn't know what happened afterwards, with your father and the–the others," Jude stutters, his ocean eyes pleading with me to understand.

"You all knew." It's not a question, and I can see the confirmation as I look at Knox and Tarl, both with fresh anguish on their tight faces. Of course they all knew.

Nausea swims in my stomach, and movement has my gaze settling back onto Aeron, who's now kneeling, his head bowed in supplication.

"I had no choice, Dove, but I beg your forgiveness and kneel before you like I vowed to do for no man when I passed my initiation into the Tailors." His voice is stilted, his words formal, and a part of me knows he speaks the truth. None of us have a choice in this gang life, it's part of the reason I have to get Rook and I out. Whatever the cost.

Using the little strength that I have, I push up to my feet, swaying slightly when the room spins, but holding up my hand once more when Jude and Tarl rush forward. Swallowing hard, I look down at Aeron, my soul feeling like they have torn it to shreds and broken me more effectively than anyone ever has before.

"You unleashed Hell on me that day, and because of your actions, they tore my innocence away, replacing it with pain and suffering for a decade. You took the only light I had, Aeron. The one person who protected me, who kept me safe. How am I meant to forgive that?"

His chest heaves, his shoulders rising and falling with what I suspect is a sob. I want to drop to my knees and cry with him, to scream at the injustice of a cruel world that would make me fall in love with the man, and men, who ruined my life.

Instead, I take a step away, then another, my stare locked on the open door. My arms wrap around my battered body, and although I can see them in my peripheral, none of the others reach out to help me. I'm not sure if I'm pleased or disappointed by that.

After what feels like a fucking age, I reach the door, resting against it for a moment, before stepping to the right, towards the cell I was first put in.

"Nightingale, you don't need to go down there. Stay in one of our rooms," Jude says, his voice strained as he reaches out to grab me, then stops before he makes contact.

"It's where I belong, I'd forgotten for a time, but now I know." My voice is hollow, just like my soul, and no one halts me as I move towards the cell, stepping inside, and shutting the door behind me.

I make it to the dirty mattress on the opposite side of the room before my knees buckle and I fall in a desperate heap. The sound of wailing fills the dark, dank space, and it takes a moment to register that it's me making the noise of a wounded animal.

Giving over to the sobs, I let my agony flow through me as I think

of my lost mom, my broken childhood, and the betrayal of the men
that I know now I am irrevocably in love with.

CHAPTER TWENTY-THREE

"LOVE IS GONE - ACOUSTIC" BY SLANDER, DYLAN MATTHEW

JUDE

Four fucking days our Nightingale has been in the cell. Ninety-six fucking hours of absolute torture for the rest of us. She wouldn't let Tarl help heal her and she's barely eaten anything that I've put in front of her, no matter how much I plead or beg.

Aeron is a fucking mess, spending most of the time drunk, with a glass of his favorite whiskey dangling from almost lifeless fingers as he stares into the distance, lost in the past and what that has meant for his future without him even knowing it. Knox is high off fuck knows what, racing off on his bike without a goddamn helmet, no doubt haunted by what happened in the torture room. Tarl is also plagued by the ghosts of his actions in that room; pouring water over her face—over the cloth that my trembling hands laid over her mouth and nose—until she couldn't breathe and helping me to hold her up while Knox beat the shit out of her. He may be known as the Inquisitor, but he's a healer at heart, and it broke something inside of him to use his torture skills on our beautiful, broken bird.

I know that the image of drowning my beautiful Nightingale will feature in my nightmares for years, and I feel sick every time I look at the hands that held her while Knox hit her. The only relief from the black fog I feel is when my blade slices across my skin, leaving a sharp trail of pain and remorse behind. There are ninety-six in total, one for every hour that she's been down there. It was hard to convince myself not to do one for every minute, but I knew that Tarl would kill me if he found out. He still might.

Dishing up a plate of pancakes, not giving a fuck that it's closer to dinnertime than breakfast, I try to think of a cheery song while I work. It's the same dish I made her that first morning, although unlike then, the Disney songs just won't come to me. Another reason to convince her to come back to us.

Walking past the guys in the living room, all heads turn to me, matching looks of sorrow in their eyes, but no one says anything as I open the door to the basement, then walk down the stairs. The skin on my exposed chest tightens the closer I get to her cell, the frigid air beyond our control as it really is a room intended for people who won't make it out alive, so why do they need to be kept comfortable?

"Good evening, Nightingale," I greet as I stride into the room. My brows dip when I see her shivering on that filthy mattress, naked back to me and completely ignoring the brand-new mattress and bedding that I bought the very first night to try and help keep her warm. "I've bought your favorite; Jude's special pancakes."

A huff and something mumbled that sounds a lot like my name taken in vain is my only response, but I'm taking it as a win as it's the first thing she's said to me since she walked in here. And like a fucking lightbulb, inspiration strikes and my lips tug up into a grin.

Taking a deep breath, I begin to sing "I see the Light" from *Tangled* and it takes all my effort not to fist pump the air when she stills and then turns over. The sense of triumph quickly dies when I see her red-rimmed eyes and the skin on her slender arms and thighs a mottle of blue and purple bruises. Marks that we're all responsible for.

Walking closer, still singing and holding the plate of pancakes, I sink down as she pushes up, tears making her blue eyes sparkle like the purest of diamonds. They drip down her cheeks, and I can't help my free hand reaching over and brushing them away. She doesn't flinch, and I can feel my eyes moisten at the knowledge that she's not afraid of me. That I may not have lost her.

Coming to the end of the song, I present the plate, and she sniffles, catching the hand that wiped her tears away and nuzzling her cheek into my open palm.

"Disney has a song for every occasion, huh?" she says, her voice broken and rough sounding, and my chest tightens at the sound of her pain. I want to hear her voice like that when we've forced too many orgasms on her fragile body, not like this. Not when we've hurt her physically, and possibly her heart too.

"It's what I've been saying for years, Nightingale, but no one ever listens to me," I tell her softly, my mouth suddenly dry and my hands trembling. "Not until you." A rush of lightness flows through me at the fact that she's talking to me. It makes me feel as though I could fly like Peter fucking Pan.

"J–Jude—" she starts, and I don't hold back, pulling her to me with the hand on her cheek and melding our lips together. She hesitates for just a beat, a fraction of a second, and then with a sob that I swallow greedily, she returns the kiss. Her arms wrap around my neck, her fingers tangling in my hair and she pulls me closer. I almost drop her brinner, managing to hold it up as I fuse our lips together, my bare chest chilled as she presses her freezing, naked torso against me.

It's like coming home after years spent in the cold. Like the moment you wake up after a nightmare to find sunlight pouring in the window, and realize that it was all just a bad dream.

"We're so broken without you, Nightingale," I whisper against her lips, unwilling to stop kissing her but needing to say the words. "We're like lost boys, and you're our Wendy Darling, our north fucking star, guiding us home."

I can taste the salt of her sadness as the tears drip onto my lips, and I lap each one, vowing to never make her hurt again.

"Jude," she moans, rubbing herself up against me in a bid to get closer. It's really fucking hard not to push her back and sink into her body, but my brothers need her too. She anchors us in a way that no one else has before, not even June.

"I want to do nothing more than give you all the pleasure you deserve, Nightingale," I tell her, reluctantly breaking our kiss. "But Aeron needs you, they all do. None of us have much choice in this life, broken bird. You should know that more than most."

I watch as she takes in my words, fresh tears spilling over her pale cheeks even as she nods slowly.

"...Okay," she whispers, a hint of the fire that made us all fall hard entering her stunning eyes. "But I want my pancakes first."

LARK

After I demolish the admittedly fucking delicious pancakes, Jude leads me to what turns out to be a bathroom further up the basement corridor, complete with a shower and fluffy bath robes and towels. I arch a brow, but he just laughs and swats my ass, avoiding any of my bruises as he turns the water on and encourages me to step into the glass cubicle.

I freeze, the sound of the shower taking me back to the near drowning the guys gave me five days ago. A warm, naked body presses into my back, and I spin to find Jude there, droplets of water beading on his beautiful, inked-up body. A gasp falls from my lips when I see lines of red scabs marring his upper thighs. I lose count, there are so many, and my eyes flash up to meet his.

"Ninety-six. One for every hour you spent down here," he tells me in a hoarse tone, and my chest tightens at his confession. His jaw is clenched, like he expects me to tell him off. To judge him for his coping mechanisms.

"Oh, Jude, love," I say softly, stepping into his arms and wrapping my own around his torso, resting my head right over his beating heart. "I'm so, so sorry."

He pulls me away, just enough to look into my eyes.

"Don't you ever say sorry to me, Nightingale. Never, you hear?" I nod, feeling a twinge in my chest, the knowledge of what I have to do lying heavy over my heart. Then his whole face lights up. "You called me love."

"It hurts here whenever I'm apart from you." I hold his stare as I place a hand over my beating heart and I repeat the words he told me not so long ago. "I feel rage here whenever I think about anyone hurting you," I continue, laying my hand over my solar plexus. "I feel calmer, safer here whenever you're near." I take his hand in mine and place it against my temple. "Now tell me, is that love?"

His jaw works, and I'm sure the droplets lining his eyelashes are not just from the running shower behind my back.

"I don't know who gave you to me, Nightingale, but I call dibs for fucking life," he says back, and I laugh, the water no longer bothering me like it did when I first got in. "Let me take care of you."

We spend a long time letting the steamy water warm up my chilled body, Jude washing away the trauma of five days ago, while I face the reality of gang life.

Jude was right when he said none of us have much choice in this life, and also correct to point out that I should be aware of that more than others. How can I blame Aeron for what he was forced to do? Maybe he'll learn to feel the same after...

One thing at a time, Lark.

I don't let my mind go there, to what will happen. They'll be fine. Instead, I focus on Jude's strong hands as he covers me with a shower gel that smells a lot like Tarl; all spicy and exotic. When I'm finally warm enough, my skin pink from the heat of the water, Jude steps out first, wrapping a thick, fluffy towel low around his hips in that sexy guy way before holding one out for me.

"Stop looking at me like that, Nightingale," he admonishes as he dries my body with as much care and gentleness as he took washing it.

"Like what?" I reply, batting my lashes and pulling an innocent expression, even while I drag my eyes over his sculpted torso.

"Like you want to fuck me raw," he answers, throwing the towel he was drying me with on the floor and grabbing a white, fluffy robe. "Or like you want me to fuck you raw."

"And if that is what I want?" I ask in a breathy whisper, my core heating at his words, at the visual they create.

"Then make up with Aeron like a good girl," he murmurs against my ear as he wraps the robe around me, tying the cord tightly. "And we'll both fuck you. Together."

My breath hitches and I have to swallow past the surge of lust that floods my body before I can speak again.

"Promise?" I ask, and he steps away, his towel now tented in the most distracting way.

"Scout's honor," he replies, making the Star Trek sign against his temple and smiling roguishly at me. *Fucking idiot.* We exit the bathroom, our fingers intertwined as Jude leads me towards the stairs. Once we reach the top, I pause, my heart thudding in my chest at having to face them all. It's always been easier with Jude, what if I get some kind of PTSD with the others? "You'll be fine, Nightingale," Jude whispers, clearly seeing my thoughts racing across my face. It's not lost on me that he reflects my own thoughts about them and what's to come back at me. Taking a deep inhale, I nod and then follow him through the doorway into the darkened room, a single lamp illuminating the vast space.

He steps aside and I see them all there, Tarl and Knox frozen as they look at me with anguish in their eyes, their faces tight with all that's passed between us. My chest tightens at the pain and sorrow in their eyes, but it's Aeron who holds my attention right now.

Aeron's gaze is not on me. It's lodged somewhere in the middle distance as a glass of amber liquid hangs from his long fingertips. He looks different; his jaw covered in stubble where he hasn't shaved, his slacks creased and his shirt unbuttoned at the neck and rolled up to his elbows. I don't hate it, but can see that it's a sign of the turmoil his mind is in.

Without letting myself question my actions, I walk towards him on bare feet, not pausing once before I climb into his lap, sitting sideways so I can bring my feet up and touch as much of him as possible. The sound of a glass shattering on the floor sounds before strong, warm arms envelop me, pulling me closer as he breathes a huge, shuddering exhale.

"I'm so fucking sorry, Dove." His voice is gravelly, sounding just as broken as mine did when Jude first came to me in the basement.

"I know, Devil Man," I reply, snuggling into him and breathing in his comforting scent. There's a heavy dose of whiskey added to the usual clean cotton, amber, and vanilla scent, but again, I don't hate it. Pulling my head back a fraction, I look up at him and wait until he's staring back at me. "I was reminded that we don't get much choice in this life, but I can choose forgiveness, and I choose to forgive you, Aeron. We belong together, come what may, and I won't let our pasts take that away, because then they win." I don't need to explain who they are; our fathers whose bitter hatred for each other started this godforsaken war long before we were born. "I choose you. All of you."

His arms tighten around me, his head dipping down to rest our foreheads together.

"I choose you too, Dove. You, and only you, for as long as I have left," he whispers, and tears sting my closed eyelids. "And I swear to you that I will protect you with my life, now and always."

His lips brush mine, and I sink into the kiss, a shuddering breath leaving my chest when his tongue sweeps into my mouth in a claiming that is all Aeron Taylor. He reinforces his vow with his kiss, pulling me as close as he can, telling me with his body that he will protect me.

We pull apart, breathing heavily and staring into one another's eyes with this newfound thing between us. It's fragile like a seedling, and I just hope that it cannot be destroyed. That it's able to weather the storm that will descend on us sooner rather than later.

"Hells yeah!" Jude shouts, making me jump and swing my gaze over to him. "Hashtag whychoose!"

A laugh spills from my lips as Aeron holds me close, Jude's words wrapping around me in a warm embrace. I look at Knox and Tarl, seeing the same feeling shining in their eyes as they stare back at me.

Whychoose for fucking life.

CHAPTER TWENTY-FOUR

"GET YOU THE MOON" BY KINA, SNOW

LARK

I stay in Aeron's lap, Jude deciding that we need to watch Frozen as in his words 'we need to let it go'. *Twat.*

Partway through, the warmth of Aeron's body lulls me to sleep, and I wake up as he shifts upwards, carrying me in his arms.

"Shhh, Dove. Go back to sleep and I'll tuck you in," he whispers, walking towards the stairs.

"But Jude made me a promise," I grumble, my voice thick and husky as my core heats, remembering Jude's words from earlier.

"Oh?" Aeron pauses, and I tip my head back to look at him, a flush spreading across my cheeks.

"He promised that if we made up, I would get you both. Together."

His brows shoot up as his nostrils flare. "Did he now?"

"Scouts honor, bro," Jude adds, coming up behind Aeron and giving me a wink.

"I want to add Knox and Tarl too." Looking beyond Jude, I see the other two guys hesitantly rise to their feet, and the uncertainty in their eyes makes my soul hurt. "I want all of you."

"At once?" Aeron questions, his voice a deep, rasping sound, like limbs moving across silken sheets, and my nipples go hard.

"Yes."

The energy in the room changes, suddenly going heavy and laden with the promise of the pleasure to come. Aeron looks deep into my eyes, his arms tightly holding me to his body, and then his lips split into a decidedly masculine smile that has my thighs clenching.

"As you wish, little Dove."

He doesn't hurry as he carries me to the base of the stairs, but his steps are assured and confident as he takes me up them and heads in the direction of his room. I hear the others behind us, and my heart rate picks up with the anticipation of being touched by them all. My mind goes back to the races, to the exquisite pleasure that they gave me, one after the other and then all together.

Striding to the bed, Aeron sets me down gently on my feet in front of it, and as if he can't help himself, he cups my jaw tenderly and presses his lips to mine. With a sigh, I kiss him back, the heady feeling of his kiss making me feel as though I've just swallowed an entire bottle of champagne.

I feel the tug of my robe, and suddenly, my skin is exposed to the cool air in the room, instantly pebbling at the drop in temperature. I moan as hands caress me from behind, fingers cupping one breast while a hand dips down the front of me and finds my already damp slit. A hot body presses closer to my back, replacing the heat of the robe and I sink into the warmth.

Aeron swallows my groan as my lower lips are parted and a finger swirls around my clit with teasing moves. Sparks fly across my naked skin, a sense of rightness filling me up as I stand before them, naked and wanting, knowing that they will not leave me unsatisfied.

I gasp, breaking the kiss, as two thick fingers slide into my aching cunt.

"She's so wet and ready for us, brother," Jude's sensual voice says from behind me, his body pressing closer as he sinks his fingers deeper. "Such a good little Nightingale."

"Make her come for us," Aeron demands, and he releases his grip on my cheek to take a step back.

I watch as he begins to unbutton his shirt, exposing the tattoos on his torso that I've not had time to study properly before. He has their mark, the same scissors that I have burnt into my lower back, tattooed over his heart, and they're beautiful, the edges looking wicked sharp as they dig into his skin. There are other, seemingly random pieces; a feather under his pec, a snake coiling around his bicep, script running along his hip, and several more. What makes me still though and has my breath hitching is the fresh-looking small bird that resembles a lark. It's sinking its claws into his skin and is placed opposite the Tailors insignia, on his right pectoral. My breathing speeds up, seeing that the bird holds an olive branch, and my eyes flick to his, a knowing smirk on his face.

"You own me as much as I own you, Dove."

My breath catches as Jude works his fingers inside me, fucking me with them and grinding his palm into my clit with every thrust. My hands grip his forearms hard as I try to keep myself upright against the onslaught of pleasure he's forcing upon me while his brother's words flow in and around me.

Waves of electricity shoot across my body, my gaze finding Knox, who is shirtless, the tattoos down his arms and across his chest stark against his golden skin. He has his beautiful cock in his hand, his dark jeans open but still covering his thick thighs. He licks his lips as he watches us, and it sends a spike of pleasure shooting to my core.

Movement on the other side of Aeron catches my attention, and I turn to see Tarl standing there, his caramel skin covered in swirling ink, almost glowing in the low light of the room as he grips his own dick, metal gleaming as he strokes himself.

"Eyes back on me, Dove," Aeron commands, and I immediately obey, groaning when I take him in, now fully naked and also stroking himself. "Good girl. You're going to come all over Jude's fingers, aren't you? Like a naughty little slut, getting ready to take us all, desperate to have our cocks inside your dripping pussy."

His words build me up, sending me spiraling into the fucking heavens as I do as he requests and come all over Jude's hand.

"Such a good, broken bird," Jude whispers as he keeps moving his hand, wringing out my orgasm until I'm twitching and gasping, my thighs trying to close when it becomes too much.

"Please." I don't know if I'm begging for more or for him to stop, my mind a hot mess as my hands hold onto his forearms.

"Listen to her beg for our cocks," Aeron says, swiping the tip of his dick and then stepping back to me, pressing his thumb to my lips. "Open up."

A moan spills from my parted lips as the salty flavor of his pre-cum hits my tongue, and I suck his thumb like it's the last fucking lollipop on earth.

"Do you want him to taste your sweet nectar, Nightingale?"

A deep keen leaves my lips this time, and I see Jude's wet fingers pass me and press against Aeron's lips. A rush of warmth heats my already scorching core when Aeron opens his mouth, holding my stare as he takes Jude's fingers into his mouth and sucks. His eyes roll at the taste of me, and suddenly, I'm so desperate to be filled that I feel like I might die if someone doesn't shove their cock inside me right the fuck now.

"Please," I say again, releasing Aeron's thumb. "I need you inside me, please."

Manly chuckles sound throughout the room, and I don't care that I'm begging for their dicks. It's become an all-consuming need that is making me shake with the force of its ferocity.

Jude pulls his fingers out of Aeron's mouth, a smirk gracing the latter's plush lips. "Since you asked so prettily, Dove. Jude, on the bed and let her ride you."

"Fuck yes!" Jude says, spinning me around and then letting me go as he scoots back on the bed, already naked and hard. Lying back with his hands behind his head, he gives me a mischievous grin. "Now come ride me like I'm your favorite Disney prince."

I giggle, getting onto the bed and crawling up to him, feeling powerful as his hooded eyes track the swaying of my breasts. "You'll always be my favorite Disney prince."

His mouth falls open as delight makes his dark blue eyes gleam.

"Personally, I always liked the Beast best, although I thought he was ruined when he turned back into the Prince, you know?" he asks, a slight frown marring his brow. Fuck, I just love this boy's fucking crazy.

"Agreed," I answer, climbing over him and grasping his pierced member in my fist. He makes a choked sound as I pump him a couple of times, relishing the feel of his silken shaft in my hand. "Ready for me to fuck you raw, my prince?"

All I get in return is a deep groan as I position him at my soaked entrance and slowly sink down his length, feeling every piece of metal as they rub my inner walls.

"Goddamn, Nightingale," Jude grits out between clenched teeth, his hands grabbing my hips and squeezing hard. The flash of pain has my cunt clenching around him, and we both moan at how fucking good that feels.

Placing my hands on his pecs, I use the leverage to help me slide up and down his length, gasping every time he hits that sweet spot inside me. He lets me use him this way, allowing me to chase my own release when sparks begin to fire behind my eyes and my movements speed up.

"Fuck, Jude, I'm so fucking close." I'm lost in sensations, the added element of the others watching building me higher and higher.

"That's it, Nightingale. Come all over your Prince's cock," he groans out, his jaw clenched with no hint of teasing as he helps to pull me up and down, using me like his own personal fleshlight.

Seconds later, he pulls me down so fucking hard that I explode, crying out as my entire body goes rigid and I can no longer move, but fuck me I can feel, and the pleasure that fills my whole being borders on painful in its intensity. It rolls me under, holding me captive as I clamp and squeeze Jude's cock like I may never get another chance to feel him inside me.

Slumping over him, I feel the slickness of our sweaty bodies as I relearn how to take air into my lungs as if for the first time. Jude's hands caress my back, not pausing when the bed behind us dips and another set of hands stroke me tenderly.

My body tenses when I feel another cock push against my already-filled pussy. "Shhhh, Nightingale. Let him in."

The smell of whiskey mixed with clean cotton, vanilla, and sandalwood tells me that it's the elder Taylor boy demanding entrance. Taking a deep inhale, I will my body to relax, gasping when he pushes inside, the sharp pain making me squirm.

As if on cue, Jude reaches between us and finds my swollen clit, swirling a finger around and over the bud until the pain is all but forgotten, and I'm struggling not to wriggle for another reason.

"Just a little more, Dove. You're doing so well," Aeron praises, and his words fan the embers of my desire, my skin tingling as he pushes the last few inches inside me. "Fuck, this is tight."

"Told you that it would feel amazing, bro," Jude answers in an equally strained voice as they let me adjust to having both of them inside me.

Jude doesn't stop playing with my clit, moving his fingers in a beat that has me clenching around them both.

"I think she's ready," Aeron growls out before slowly pulling out. "Jesus, those fucking piercings, Jude."

A bolt of red-hot heat sears through me when I realize that Aeron is feeling the Jacob's Ladder piercing on the underside of Jude's dick, and by the sounds of it, he fucking likes it.

"I would say that I got them for you, bro, but Tarl would tan my hide because we all know that he likes to feel them up his ass," Jude quips, the teasing tone back, if a little deeper than usual.

"Oh, I'll be tanning your hide alright regardless," I hear Tarl answer, and almost laugh at the fact they're having this conversation while the two brothers are balls deep inside me. I say almost laugh, because, at that moment, Aeron is clearly fed up with Jude's bullshit and thrusts all the way back in. Hard.

I keen as both guys curse, and that's the end of talking aside from the noises of our fucking while they strike up a rhythm inside me, destroying me from the inside out. It's all I can do to dig my finger-tips into Jude's biceps as I let them take their pleasure, giving me almost too much in return.

Jude continues to play with my nub, bliss shooting from his fingertips as they fill me over and over again.

"I knew from the moment I watched Knox fuck you up against that wall, your back bleeding down your thighs, that you would be my destruction, little Dove," Aeron growls in my ear, not pausing in his claiming of my body. "And I would gladly let you destroy me a thousand times if it means you will stay here beside me. Beside us." And there he goes claiming my soul.

Although, who am I fucking kidding? These men claimed it the moment they took care of me after that first night. I just wasn't ready to admit it. There's no time for the guilt to rush in, my orgasm beating it in a rush of heat and exquisite agony.

"All of me is yours, Aeron. It's belonged to you always."

I lose track of time, of breathing as it sucks me under, leaving me full of starlight and unable to move. My body is frozen in ecstasy, Aeron and Jude picking up their pace as they find their own releases, one after the other, deep inside my heat.

We're frozen, caught up in each other for what feels like eons, the evidence of our pleasure coating my insides and inner thighs before Aeron leans down, placing a gentle kiss on my shoulder. He pulls out and I hiss as he flops down on the bed next to us, his chest glistening and heaving.

"You're too perfect for words, Dove," he rasps out, one hand thrown over his forehead.

"Just perfect for us," Jude adds, his own voice a deep, throaty growl.

I whimper when the bed dips behind me again, Tarl's melodic voice shushing me. "Perfect for all of us, and you can take all of us, can't you, *Aziz-e delam?*"

"Y—yes," I whisper back, shivering as his gentle hands caress all over my sweat-soaked back, languorous waves of pleasure emanating from his touch.

"I knew you were, our perfect, beautiful bird," Tarl purrs, his voice low and seductive, and Jude chuckles when my thighs clench around him. "Jude, hand."

One of Jude's hands leaves my back, and his sharp inhale followed by the warm liquid dripping between my ass cheeks tells me that Tarl is using Jude's blood for lube again. And just like in the woods, it's hot as fucking hell.

Taking his time, Tarl swirls a finger around the tight ring of muscle, teasing me until the promise of what I know will be heady pleasure has my ass wiggling, begging for the intrusion. He obliges, pushing one digit in and a whine leaves my lips as I press my forehead into Jude, whose hand floats to the back of my neck, the warm wetness of his blood dripping down my skin. Pumping in and out, Tarl allows me to get used to the sensation before he adds a second finger to the first.

"Shit," I gasp, an incoherent moan following when I feel Jude harden inside me. "Jude!"

"You can't blame a guy when you're moving like that, Nightingale," he chides, and I look at him through hooded eyes to see a feline grin on his face.

I hold his gaze as Tarl pulls his fingers out, replacing them with the head of his cock. We mirror each other, mouths agape, as Tarl fills my tight rosebud and Jude fills my pussy.

"F—fuck," I breathe out, nuzzling into Jude's cut palm when his hand comes up to cup my face. I can't deny that I love the feel of him marking my body with his blood, there's something so primitive and raw about being branded this way. "I'm not sure I can come anymore."

"Of course you can, Nightingale. You were made to come all over our cocks, over and over again."

I can't answer him as both guys begin to move in a rhythm that leaves my head spinning and my fucking teeth tingling. My previously wrung-out body starts to shudder, the pleasure building quickly once more as they force me towards another orgasm. Tears gather in my eyes with the anguished pleasure they're stirring in my body, but I don't ask them to stop. I never want them to fucking stop.

"Come for us, *Eshgham*. Come for those who own you."

And I do. My orgasm rips through me with such force that I can't even cry out, only clutch Jude once more as I ride out the pleasure that borders on pain.

"Fucking hell, Nightingale," Jude growls, stilling as he pours his second release inside me. Tarl yells, clamping his teeth down on my shoulder as he thrusts so deep into my ass that I scream as it triggers a second wave of pleasure to tear me apart.

"*Âsheghetam*, Pretty Bird," Tarl whispers against my skin as I, once again, try to calm my racing heart and take in much-needed oxygen.

"What does it mean?" I ask him in a rasping whisper, only able to see his face in profile as he pulls out of me and flops down on Jude's other side.

He reaches a hand to stroke my damp hair away from my face, his own features soft. "I love you, Pretty Bird."

I freeze, my heart giving a painful thud as my stomach drops, you know like when you're at the top of the rollercoaster and free fall into space.

"I love you, Tarl," I whisper back, the words sliding off my tongue with a rightness that should feel scary but somehow doesn't. His face lights up, the smile that tugs up his lips the kind of thing that angels must weep over.

Jude finally slips out of me as I shakily push up, breaking away from Tarl's bewitching stare, and force Jude to scoot over so I can sit between him and Aeron. Luckily, this bed is fucking massive, so it's not too much of a squeeze.

My eyebrows squish together when I look around and see Knox, still standing back, not coming forward. He looks as if he's at war with himself, his teeth clenched and not meeting my eyes.

"Knox?" His head snaps up at the sound of my voice, his usually bright hazel eyes full of unshed tears, and my body heats, but not in the same way it was moments before. "What's wrong?"

He shakes his head. "I—" I watch as he swallows, his eyes briefly closing and then he looks at his hands, opening and closing them as if they don't belong to him. "I hurt you."

My vision blurs, his beautiful body swimming as I try to blink the tears away. Shuffling down the bed, I ignore the wetness of our combined releases that drips down my thighs as I shakily make my way over to him. Grabbing his large hands in my own, I bring them up to my lips, kissing the knuckles of each one. Then, placing them on my waist, I cup both of his cheeks in my palms and tip his face up until he's looking at me.

"Make love to me, Knox."

"I. Hurt. You," he grits out between clenched teeth, and my chest aches.

"Then kiss each strike better, make me feel pleasure where there was only pain," I tell him, my voice soft as I try to make him see my forgiveness. There was no choice, not with Earl there, and not while I needed to secure Rook's safety.

His head sinks, bringing our foreheads together. "I never want to hurt you again, Little Bird."

"Then love me instead."

His entire body stills, his head coming up and his eyes darting between mine, searching for something. He must find it because seconds later his lips are on mine and he's pushing us back towards the bed. Just when I think he's going to throw me down, he breaks the kiss.

"Get on the bed, Little Bird. On your back," he orders, his voice deep and sinful.

Holding his stare, I do as he commands, the others giving us room but staying on the bed either side of me. Kneeling between my parted legs, Knox leans down and gently takes hold of my thigh, turning it slightly so he can see the bruise of his kick. He pauses, taking a deep shuddering inhale before lowering his lips and placing the softest of kisses on the spot.

A sigh escapes my lips, my body suffusing with warmth as he traces the sore patch with his tongue, peppering it with light, teasing kisses before he releases that leg and moves to the other. My breathing becomes heavy as that thigh gets the same treatment, and a whine leaves my lips before I can stop it, my ass shifting as I attempt to gain some friction on my suddenly needy clit.

"Just three more, Little bird," he tells me, settling his hips between my thighs as he brings my arm to his lips and starts tracing the bruise on my bicep with his mouth. Tingles race from the path his lips and tongue take, and I can't help squirming against his dick which nudges my opening tantalizingly.

Chuckling, he unhurriedly releases that arm and moves on to my other, repeating the same, gentle attention until my whole body aches with need.

"Knox, please."

My heart thrills at the look of smug satisfaction in his eyes, brightening them to their usual hazel. Gone is the lost look of agony from moments before.

"Patience, princess," he teases, rubbing his body along mine as he pushes forward until his lips can reach the spot on the side of my nose that he used to lift me up in that excruciating pressure hold five days ago. He presses a light kiss there, dragging his body back down and then leaning on one forearm as his hand tilts my head to the side. My nerve endings feel like they're on fire, and my hands grasp his broad back as he begins to nuzzle, kiss, and suck the spot just behind my ear.

"Knox," I moan, my hips moving of their own accord, seeking friction against his hard dick that is pressed up against my lower lips. He doesn't stop kissing my neck and the line of my jaw, but his hand moves between us, and I want to fucking weep with relief when he lines himself up and smoothly thrusts inside me.

"Fuck, I'd forgotten how good you feel, Little Bird." He leisurely pumps in and out of me, his hips moving in a rolling motion that leaves me fucking brainless. I grab handfuls of his peachy ass, making him chuckle in my ear as I urge him to go harder, faster. "Beg me, Little Bird. Beg your Daddy to fuck you hard."

Fucking Hell in a handbasket.

I nearly explode just from his dirty words.

"Please, Kn–Daddy. Please fuck me hard." I realize that I don't give a flying fuck when it comes to these men, these Tailor boys. I will beg and plead for their dicks to fill me up until the cows come home. "Please, please, please."

"Always, my love," he sighs in my ear, the affectionate nickname making my breath stutter just as he picks up the pace and slams into me.

"Yes! Fuck yes, Daddy!" I cry out as he sets a punishing rhythm, and I open my eyes to see Tarl staring at us with hooded eyes, his hand tangled in Jude's hair as he forces him to swallow and choke on his cock. *Shitting Hell that's hot.*

"Eyes on me, love," Knox growls out, and I turn back to be ensnared in his ardent gaze. "I swear to you, with every fiber of my being, that from this moment, I will protect you with my life if I have to."

My whole body shudders with his declaration, tears filling my eyes once more as he holds my stare and fucks me into the mattress.

"Fuck, Knox!" I cry out, the way he's moving his body inside mine driving me to new heights of insanity. "I'm yours, Daddy. Now and always."

He makes an animalistic noise in the back of his throat, reaching down to hook one of my legs over his arm and pounding into me with such force that I practically feel him in my fucking cervix. His pace is relentless, his eyes wild and ferocious, and I can't hold back any longer, my limbs stiffening as my climax sweeps over me, leaving me devastated.

It only takes a few more hard thrusts for Knox to find his release, but I'm too lost to my own pleasure, to the swirls and eddies of the sheer bliss to take much note of his roar.

"Little Bird," a deep voice purrs, and I mumble softly, my eyes closed, when a nose nuzzles my neck, kissing the sensitive skin there.

"I think we finally broke her," Jude says, and masculine chuckles echo around the room. I'd be a bit pissed to be the butt of their joke, but I can't bring myself to rouse out of my orgasm stupor.

"Let's clean her up, then we all need some sleep," I hear Aeron say, and I whimper when cold air meets the front of me as Knox pulls away.

"Shhh, Little Bird. I'll be right back and I plan to sleep in between those pretty thighs of yours," he whispers, his voice dark and husky.

I let their quiet conversation lull me to sleep, soon losing myself to darkness, knowing that I'm safely nestled in amongst my Tailor boys. All thoughts of anything else, the past and the future forgotten as I lose myself to their comforting embrace.

CHAPTER TWENTY-FIVE

"365" BY MOTHER'S DAUGHTER, BECK PETE

LARK

The warmth of hot bodies wakes me, and I come to slowly, reveling in the heat as I'm surrounded by the guys. By my Tailor boys.

Did we really just confess our feelings only last night?

It feels like forever since I arrived in this warehouse, though it's not been longer than a smattering of weeks, and so much has changed in that time. I've gone from being a tortured prisoner to... this. I nibble my lip as I consider what I am to them and what they are to me.

We're an impossibility, Jude was not far off when he quoted Romeo and Juliet at me. Our fathers have been at war for longer than any of us can remember. If either discovers how deep our love runs, like it's etched into our very bones... I shudder at the thought and my hands find Knox's head, resting on my stomach just like he promised. Sinking my fingers into his thick, blond hair, I use the contact to try and calm my racing heart.

But I can't stop the ache in the back of my throat at what will happen soon. What I will do to these guys who have become as essential to me as breathing.

There's no other way, not if you want to be free and save Rook, just like you promised.

"What has that beautiful face of yours frowning, Dove?" Aeron's deep voice is made even huskier by sleep, and I turn to face him, the weight on my chest unrelated to the man lying on top of me.

"How will this work, Aeron? Our fathers hate each other, our gangs are locked in a fucking war that started before we were even born. If my father ever found out—"

"Shhhh," he soothes, reaching out a large palm and cupping my cheek. Warmth from his touch has me nuzzling into it, my eyes briefly closing at the comfort it brings, something which, until meeting these men, I'd never experienced at a man's touch. "No one will ever hurt you again. Not now that you're ours. We protect what belongs to us."

A trembling exhale falls from my lips; I've never been claimed before, not in any way that made me feel safe and treasured.

"But who will protect you? I don't want him to hurt you." Even I can hear the panic in my tone, the idea of my father getting a hold of them making bile leave a sour taste at the back of my throat.

There's no choice, Lark.

"I might get offended by how you seem to think we can't take care of ourselves, Little Bird," Knox says, his voice a deep rumble as he pushes up and covers my body with his in a single, smooth move. "How *soft* you think we are." He punctuates the word 'soft' with a thrust of his hips, demonstrating that there isn't any softness to him this morning.

"Knox! Fuck's sake, I'm being serious."

"So am I, princess," he growls, dipping his head to take my nipple into his hot mouth.

"And I need a piss, so unless you're into golden showers..."

"We've already talked about that, Nightingale," Jude pipes up from the other side of me, and I turn my head to see the mischief making his ocean eyes dance and sparkle in the morning light filtering around the curtains.

"You're not helping, Devil Prince." I point an accusing finger at him, which backfires when he sucks it into his mouth.

"He never does," Tarl grumbles, grabbing a fistful of Jude's thick hair and pulling his head back, my finger falling from his mouth with a pop as his neck is exposed. "But he enjoys being punished too much to stop, don't you, Brat?"

Jesus fucking Christ, someone save me from the pussy-dripping vibes these two exude.

"As much as I would like to take this where it seems to be going," Aeron drawls on my other side, and I swivel my head, Knox nibbling the side of my neck as he tries his best to distract me. "We need to visit Mount Pleasant today."

I feel the rest of them go still, and it takes me a moment to connect the dots and remember where I'd heard that name before.

"To see your mom?" My stomach rolls, as if a kaleidoscope of butterflies has just taken flight.

"Will you come with us, Dove?" His dark brows are raised, his gaze full of a vulnerability that I don't often see on the heir to the Tailors' face.

"Of course," I reply, and the boyish smile that he gives me has those damn butterflies doing a fucking jig.

"Get the fuck off her, Knox. We need to shower and get ready." Knox grumbles but does as Aeron orders and with a parting kiss, heads to his room to get sorted. Jude and Tarl both kiss me sweetly, then walk out as well, leaving me alone with Aeron. "Let's go, Dove," Aeron says, holding out his hand for me as he gets off the bed. I wait a beat, admiring his naked body, the hard lines and ink making my heart flutter for an entirely different reason than my nerves at the prospect of meeting his mom. "Now."

"I'm coming," I grumble, taking his hand and untangling myself from the warm blankets with a pout.

He pulls me to him, so close that our bodies are flush and I can feel each of those hard plains that make up Aeron Taylor. "You will be now that I have you to myself." His husky whisper tightens my nipples and has my thighs trying to clench as he leads us into his en suite.

Not too much longer later, we come down the stairs to the smell of waffles and I groan as the kitchen island comes into view and a plate stacked high with yummy goodness awaits.

"Tell me I'm not your favorite, Nightingale?" Jude asks with a smirk, not even flinching when Aeron hits him upside the head.

I shake my head at them, but seeing the brothers together sends a pang through me at the thought of Rook, and the fact that I haven't seen him in so long. I worry our sperm donor will be sinking his claws into him now that I'm not there to provide a buffer. *Hold on, Rook, I'm on my way.*

"Hey, where did you go just then, *Eshgham?*" Tarl asks in his lilting, melodic voice from beside me, and I turn to give him a sad smile.

"I was thinking about Rook, and how I've not been there to, I dunno, stop Rufus from being Rufus." His face softens, and he gathers me into his arms, surrounding me with his spicy, cardamom scent.

"We'll get him out, *Aziz-e delam.* A Tailor never breaks his word, and you have Aeron's, and also ours."

I breathe out a sigh, Knox catching my eye as I snuggle into Tarl. Knox's brows are furrowed before he sees me looking, then his face transforms into its usual bright smile.

"Best eat up, Nightingale," Jude tells me, and I reluctantly step out of Tarl's embrace. I walk over to the stool in front of the plate of waffles, which are smothered in what smells like Nutella and bright red strawberries.

"Thank you, my prince," I say around a giggle, Jude's eyes going wide with delight as I sit down and begin demolishing the food.

"Fuck me, if she keeps making those noises I can't be held responsible for making us late," Knox groans, and a blush heats my cheeks when I look around to see all four of them staring at me like *I'm* a plate of chocolate and hazelnut spread waffles.

Oops.

I eat the rest with less vocal appreciation, and we're soon heading to a door down a corridor that I've not really noticed before.

"Where are we going?" I ask, stepping through and then pausing at the sight before me.

Gleaming supercars fill the garage space, as well as a few trucks and motorbikes, and I know my mouth is hanging open, but fucking hell. I knew the Tailors were rich, far more wealthy than the Soldiers, that's for sure, but I had no idea the extent of their wealth. It's fucking obscene.

"You're with me, Little Bird," Knox whispers in my ear, grasping my hand in his and leading us over to the motorbikes before grabbing a leather jacket off the hook on the wall.

He hands it to me, and I can't help the smile that tugs my lips upwards when I put it on and realize that it fits perfectly. I like that they pick my clothes, that they choose things they want to see me wearing. I've always had secondhand clothes, buying whatever was cheapest at the thrift store and helped hide my body from the predators that make up my father's gang. Not that it ever did much good, they still took what they wanted.

Huffing out a breath to rid my mind of those morbid thoughts, I smooth down the soft, buttery leather with my hands. Luckily, I went for jeans and a long-sleeved top today, thinking that now we're heading into cooler weather with the approach of fall, I'll need the extra warmth. Knox then hands me a sparkly, burgundy-colored helmet, and I marvel at the beautiful painting of a lark in flight on the side.

"No fucking reckless driving, Knox. I mean it, take care of her," Aeron barks as he strides over and helps me zip up the jacket.

Knox rolls his eyes. "I wouldn't put her in any danger, you know that."

Aeron takes a deep inhale before replying to him. "I know." He turns to me then, pulling me in for a deep kiss that sets my toes curling. "See you there, Dove."

"I'll be fine, Devil Man," I tell him, and his lips quirk up into that half smile which he reserves just for me, and I'm breathless all of a sudden, heat radiating through my chest as I gaze at him.

He gives me a nod, then releases me to walk over to a sleek, black sports car, Tarl getting into the passenger side. I try to ignore the way I feel bereft at the loss of his body heat.

"How's Jude getting there?" I ask, and squeak when arms wrap around me from behind, my body melting into the embrace instinctively even as my heart pounds.

"You didn't think I'd let Daddy have all the fun, did you?" Jude purrs in my ear. Knox clears his throat as his nostrils flare. "Maybe we could stop on the way and show him how much we like that leather jacket?"

My pulse picks up, and Knox grips his own helmet tight as he looks at us.

"Fuck's sake, Jude. Now I have a raging boner and that's just fucking uncomfortable when riding."

Jude laughs like the loon that he is before releasing me to don his own jacket and helmet, and heads over to a beautiful teal and cream bike, an Indian if I'm not mistaken. He slings his leg over, turning to give me a wink before tearing out of the garage with a deep rumble noise.

"Ready, Little Bird?" Knox asks in a pitch not unlike that of Jude's motorbike, and I see that he's gotten on his own bike, a matt black Indian that makes him look hella sexy.

My lips split into a wide grin as I approach, taking up the position behind him and wrapping my arms around his waist as my thighs tighten either side of his.

"Ready."

"Hold on tight, princess."

It's all the warning I get before he starts the engine, the vibrations beneath me doing things that they really shouldn't, as he also peels out of the garage in a squeak of tires.

I scream in delight as we race down the road, the sound lost in the roar of the engine and the whistle of the wind as we make our way out of town, and soon we're surrounded by forest with the mountains in the distance and the early fall sun beating down on us. I take a huge inhale of the sweet, fresh air, letting my lungs fill for what feels like the first time.

The freedom of being on the back of Knox's bike, the wind rushing past us is heady and unlike anything I've ever experienced. Before I can think better of it, I let go of Knox's waist, gripping tightly with my thighs and holding my arms out either side of me.

"Fuuuuuck!!!!" I scream into the wind, feeling Knox chuckle in front of me, his body adding to the vibrations of the engine.

The mountains and forest soon turn to rolling hills, and then we're pulling into a gravel drive, stopping in front of a beautiful, old-looking building that's painted a soft, sage green. Tall leafy trees line the curving drive, and there's a huge columned balcony that makes up the front entrance. There's so many large cream windows covering the front that I lose count. The whole place has a calm and peaceful feel, and as I take my helmet off, swinging my leg over the back of the bike to get off, I can't help but take a deep inhale of floral-scented fresh air.

"It's beautiful here," I whisper, and strong arms wrap around me from behind, the scent of cloves and motor oil surrounding me.

"I love seeing you so free, Little Bird," Knox murmurs in my ear, pulling me in closer as he presses a light kiss to my temple.

Turning in his arms, I bring mine up and wrap them around his neck. "Thank you, Knox."

"Anytime, princess."

He lowers his face, his lips teasing me for a moment before he presses them to mine in a kiss that tastes like freedom and adventure. I kiss him back hard, inhaling everything he's offering and letting it fill me up like a life-giving elixir.

The growl of an engine interrupts us, and I break the kiss to look over as Aeron's sports car pulls into the spot next to Knox's bike. The car has barely parked when the driver's door flings open, and Aeron leaps out, storming over and yanking me away from Knox, gripping my upper arms tightly.

"Hey—"

"Don't you ever fucking behave so recklessly again, Dove. Understand?" Aeron's eyes are wild, and he's trembling with fury. Or perhaps it's more akin to fright?

"Hey," I say again, more softly this time as I free one arm, bringing my hand up to cup his cheek. "I'm okay, Devil Man." His jaw works, his usually pristine hair ruffled as he stares at me. His chest is heaving against mine, and a twinge of guilt makes my own ribcage tight. "I'm sorry."

He closes his eyes whilst taking in a deep inhale. "No, Dove, I'm sorry. I just—" He cuts himself off, opening his eyes to look deeply into mine. "I can't lose you. Not now."

My breath catches and my throat constricts. I'm not used to this sort of affection, the kind that doesn't come in the form of a backhand across your face. "You won't."

Won't he?

I shut that bitch down, not ready to face that reality just yet. I'll have to soon, freedom comes at a price after all, but not now.

He looks at me for a beat longer, then drops his lips to mine in a bruising kiss. Tingles race across my skin as he devours my mouth, and my hand moves into his hair, clutching it for dear life as he defies anything to try and take me from him.

Just as suddenly as he started, he stops, pulling away but keeping his firm grip on my arm.

"Let's go."

Blinking, my panties fucking ruined, it takes me a hot minute to process his order. His hand slips down my arm, tangling our fingers as he holds my hand, still staring at me.

"S–sure," I stutter out, licking my lips and feeling a flash of heat in my center when his dark eyes zoom in on the gesture.

"It's your own fault, Nightingale." Jude laughs, grabbing my other hand. "You make him go all alpha possessive. It's hot as fuck, right?"

"Firstly, where the fuck did you come from?" I ask as we start walking, Aeron giving a deep chuckle on my other side. "And secondly, how the fuck is his needing to piss all over me like a dog claiming his territory my fault?" A growl from said alpha has my core tightening. *God-fucking-dammit.*

"I got here first before all you slow pokes," Jude answers as we approach the huge glass-paned doors and walk through. "And I don't know if you know this, Nightingale, but you have this whole broken bird that needs rescuing vibe."

"You kidnapped me!" I screech, my eyes going wide when several heads in the lobby turn and stare at us with slack jaws.

"Not technically us," Tarl says on the other side of Jude, a shit-stirring grin on his face.

I clench my teeth. "Semantics."

"The devil is in the details, Dove," Aeron adds, striding towards the front desk with a confidence that is too fucking hot.

"You'd know all about that, wouldn't you, Devil Man?"

A bark of laughter falls from his plush lips, the others guffawing, and my heart swells in my chest at the normalcy of this. Of us just poking fun at each other. It's...nice. More than nice. Sure, it's about my kidnapping, but whatever, it's still more normal than I've had in a long fucking time.

"Good morning, Mr. Taylor," a cheerful voice greets us as we stop in front of a light, wooden reception desk. "And Mr. Taylor, Mr. Johnson, Mr. Ahmad." She's older, with light blonde hair cut in a cute bob and a bright smile plastered on her lightly made up face.

"Good morning, Janet," Aeron smoothly replies. "Looking beautiful as always."

I press my lips together to suppress the surprised smile that wants to form at his flattery. I've not seen this side of him before, and I find that I love it.

"Oh, you!" She blushes, laughing and flipping a hand in his direction. "Flattery will get you everywhere. Mrs. Taylor is in the Orangey this morning."

"Thank you, Janet," Aeron says, squeezing my hand before leading me towards a set of double doors.

I barely get to take in the bright, airy opulence of the foyer before I'm pulled through the doors and into a light hallway lined with windows and landscape paintings.

"This place is unreal," I say, gazing with wide eyes at the beautiful worlds in their gold frames.

"It's the best money can buy," Aeron states, his voice oddly without emotion and I look up to see the lines around his eyes are tight, his mouth turned down into a frown. Still holding my hand, he leads the way, Jude not letting go of my other. "She's very...comfortable here."

The way he says the last part has a knot forming in my stomach, the early fall sunshine doing nothing to chase away the chill his words leave.

We soon arrive at another set of double doors, the glass in them showing a glimpse of an illuminated room beyond, the huge windows that make up most of the walls letting in every scrap of sunshine. Aeron pauses, so we all do. I watch as he takes a deep breath, squaring his shoulders as if he's preparing to face his demons, and then pushes the doors open.

I blink at the brightness of the Orangey, and it takes a second for my eyes to adjust enough to make out the frail figure sitting in a rattan chair, swathed in blankets.

"Mom?" Aeron's voice is softer than I've ever heard it, his grip on my hand painfully tight as he holds it like it's the only thing keeping him tethered to this world.

"Oh, boys. How lovely to see you." Her voice is like the fluttering of a small bird's wings, light and barely there.

"Hey, Mom," Jude says, also keeping his voice low. He lets go of my hand before walking over to her and pressing a kiss on her cheek.

I study her; she's beautiful in an ethereal kind of way. She's probably around fifty, although it's hard to tell as sadness lines her face and hunches her shoulders, so she could be younger. She's thin, painfully so, and a thick shawl is draped over her shoulders even though the room is warm. Unlike the brothers, she has startling, blue eyes and blonde hair that is dry and brittle-looking but still falls in loose waves around her.

"Hello, Mrs. Taylor," Tarl greets, also stepping up to her and kissing her softly on the cheek.

"Tarl, so nice to see you, dear boy." She cups his cheek, looking him over. "Have you been sleeping enough, you look tired." Jude snorts at that, knowing exactly why Tarl might look tired after last night. *Fucker.*

"Hey, Heather," Knox says, walking over until I'm left with just Aeron.

"Knox! I hope you're still keeping these boys in line for me." She laughs, and I want to wince at the broken noise. Her eyes go distant in an instant, her face dropping as if she's thinking of something sad. My heart aches at that look of desolation.

"Mom?" Aeron questions in that soft, calm tone he used before. She turns to look at him, a small smile coming onto her face. "I wanted you to meet someone."

He tugs me forward, and my heart beats wildly in my chest as her gaze fastens onto mine, her eyes widening.

"Julie?"

My mouth drops open, no words escaping as I hear my mother's name for the first time in years.

"They told me you'd died. Oh, Julie!" Tears fill her eyes, making the blue sparkle as she reaches out with both arms, her shawl slipping down to expose bony shoulders protruding through a white blouse.

"Julie was my mom," I tell her finally, shifting on my feet as I see the confusion on her face, her arms dropping and hands resting in her lap. Aeron's grip gets tighter. "I'm Lark, her daughter."

"Lark? Her little songbird?" she whispers, her eyes drinking me in. My stomach bottoms out at the old nickname, one my mom always used as I loved to sing when I was little before I knew the horrors of growing up. "Come here, let me have a look at you."

Taking a deep breath, I let go of Aeron's hand and go to her, this unknown connection of my mother's. She grabs both my hands when I step in front of her and pulls me down so that I'm kneeling on the hard tile under our feet.

"How did you know my mom used to call me that?" My fingers tingle where she's crushing them in her own, but I don't care. I just want to talk to someone who knew my mom.

"You look so much like her when she was your age." Her voice is full of soft wonder, and she releases one of my hands to cup my cheek. Her skin feels almost papery and her hand cool, but the touch is still comforting. "She loved you so, so much, Lark. Used to talk nonstop about how wonderful you were whenever we could sneak away to meet."

"You used to meet up? How?" My head spins with everything that she's revealed so far. How could the wives of the two rival gangs be friends? She chuckles, a dry rasping sound that has me wincing again.

"We were friends long before we met our husbands, and before they went to war," she tells me, her stare going far once more. "And we kept up our friendship over the years, meeting and talking when we could, trying to soothe things between the men. Of course, it all changed that night—" She swallows, the motion visible in her bird-like neck.

"After what night?" I'm afraid to ask, there's been so many fucking atrocious things happening between our families for so long.

"After your father caught us, letting his men punish us both for our friendship," she says, her voice barely above a whisper, but I can tell by the tension around me that the guys have heard. Tears fill my eyes, knowing exactly which night she's referring to.

I remember my mom coming back broken, bloody, and whimpering as she was dragged through the main room at our home and dumped onto the thin carpet floor. I was only eleven and a half; it was six months or so before my mom was killed, and I remember spying from the top of the staircase, feeling afraid as I heard their jeers and cruel laughter. It was the first time I truly feared my father and his men, and I ran to my room, shoving my pillow over my head when her screams became unbearable.

She couldn't leave her bed for days afterwards, and my father tasked me with nursing her back to health, as though it wasn't his fault that she was in such a mess. I'd heard about the Taylor lady, the men not caring of my child's ears when they talked about how she screamed for them as they each took their turn. Sex was never something that was hidden particularly well with the Soldiers. Everything was always out in the open, regardless of any innocent children present.

"It's okay, little Lark. It was a long time ago now," she murmurs, and I blink when I feel her touch, her frail fingers swiping my tears away while she smiles down kindly at me, even if her pain is visible in the tightening around her eyes. "I'm sorry we took your mother away from you not long after."

I bite my lips to try and hold back the sob, but it's useless. The guys have opened the floodgates within me with their soft affection, and I could no sooner hold back my desolation than stop the stars from shining.

Without saying another word, she wraps her thin arms around me, pulling me into her body that smells floral and so similar to my mom's old perfume that I just cry harder. My own hands clasp her back, and I can feel her blouse becoming wet under my cheek as I soak it with my sorrow; the sadness of a child who lost a parent and her innocence in a scant twenty-four hours overwhelming me.

"You'll be alright, little Lark, you're here now, and my boys will take good care of you," she hums softly, and it's enough to enable me to stem the flow a little, and pull away to look into her own tear-filled eyes. "I promised your mother that if anything happened to her, I would look after you. I've been too lost in my own sorrow to fulfill that vow, but I know my boys will. They'll protect you from now on, darling."

Fresh tears spill as I catch Aeron's gaze and he gives a sharp nod, his brow furrowed in concern as he takes us in. I can see in the way his jaw is tight that he doesn't like this, our sadness upsets him, and my heart flutters at the thought that he cares enough to be upset when I am. That he wants to make it better.

"She belongs to us now, Mom," Jude states matter-of-factly, and I feel the blush stain my cheeks at the implication of his words. Heather doesn't miss them either, if the knowing look in her eyes is any indication.

"Then you will keep her safe, even from your father." It's not a question. More of a command, and I see a glimmer of the Tailor lady inside her, the force that helped run their successful empire for so long.

"Even then," Aeron agrees, coming closer and holding his hand out for me to take. With a soft kiss on my cheek, she lets me go, and I use his grip to get to my feet, albeit shakily.

"Good," she says, a small smile gracing her thin lips when he wraps the arm around me and places a kiss atop my head. Warmth radiates from the spot. Jude, of fucking course, takes that moment to also wrap an arm around my waist, kissing my cheek and nuzzling into my hair. I can feel Tarl and Knox hover closer, and I cast a wary eye over to Heather, who just looks fit to burst into giggles.

"Off you go then," she tells us, sounding weary all of a sudden and waving them away when Aeron starts to let go of me and go to her. "I'm fine, just a little tired is all. I'll see you all soon?"

"Of course, Mom," Jude beams, darting away and pressing a kiss on her cheek.

"Will you come too, Lark?"

"I–uh..." I trail off, thinking of what's to come and that I may not be welcome again. "I'd love to." I settle on the words after seeing the hopeful look in her eyes.

"I'd love to talk more about your mother, and all the mischief we used to get up to."

"I'd like that very much," I reply, my chest tight and my soul soaring with this feeling of finally finding a family, a home, and knowing that soon, I will be the one to tear it all apart.

They do say the ones you love the most are the ones you hurt the most.

I just hope that they can forgive me for what I'm about to do.

CHAPTER TWENTY-SIX

"BODIES" BY BRYCE FOX

TARL

The drive back from Mount Pleasant is quiet, Aeron and I lost in our own thoughts, the swirling maelstrom of the past, and all the things we didn't know before today. The fact that his mother and Lark's were friends, and by the sounds of it long-time friends, was definitely not something any of us knew, Lark included.

"I've often wondered why dad and Rufus fell out," Aeron says, hands firm on the steering wheel of his pride and joy; his matt black Ferrari LaFerrari. "I'd always assumed it had to do with what the Soldiers did to Mom."

"And now?"

He huffs a sigh. "And now it seems like it stemmed from much earlier, and I'm wondering if all the fucked up shit we've done to each other was down to something far less noble than revenge for her rape."

I think on his words, they reflect my own thoughts. I've only really known the two gangs to be rivals, to be at war with one another, and I, too, believed the catalyst for it becoming an all-out bloody war was because of the attack on Heather Taylor.

But if what she said earlier was true, then they were fighting long before her attack, forcing the two women to keep their friendship hidden, and the fact that Rufus subjected his own wife to the same punishment...I knew he was a monster of a special sort, especially after Lark's confession, but it seems he was worse than any of us ever knew.

The thought of what Lark has had to go through makes my hands clench and unclench in my lap with rage. A feeling that courses through me like a drug and won't be satisfied until I can release it on Rufus, making him truly a dead Soldier.

Aeron's phone rings and he presses a button on the wheel to answer it.

"*Son,*" Adam's smooth voice floats around us, a warmth to his tone that is always present when talking to his sons. "*How was your mother?*"

Aeron's eyes flick to mine, a hint of warning that is unnecessary. I won't tell our leader that we took Lark, or that Heather confessed her friendship and vow to us.

"She was fine, pretty chatty actually," Aeron answers, his voice completely normal with no hint of the half-truth and I smirk. The best lies always hold a grain of truth.

"*Good, good,*" Adam replies, releasing a breath. "*Earl told me that our little bird sang, telling you that she can get you into Soldiers HQ?*" The memory of her mother's nickname flashes through my mind, and I find myself shifting in my seat when Adam uses it now.

My jaw clenches at Earl's name, and I shouldn't want to do all the horrible things that come to mind to him, what with Earl being the second-in-command and all, but I can't help it. He hurt my

Eshgham, and I blame him for what we had to do to her. How far we had to go.

"Yep, I wanted to come up with a plan of attack before I spoke to you."

"*And I'm sure that you will, son. Very clever to promise the safety of her brother to gain the intel. Of course, he will die with the rest of the Soldier scum, but she doesn't need to know that yet.*" The leather on the steering wheel creaks with Aeron's tight grip. "*But first, I have a job for you boys tonight. The wood for the rebuild is arriving, and I need you all there to take charge and ensure it gets to the warehouse.*"

He means the rebuild of the stables, Adam Taylor doesn't sit on his laurels. He gets shit done, and fast. He also refers to the deal that we, as the Tailors, are helping to facilitate between one of the biggest illegal arms dealers and his client. Think of us like the middlemen; we ensure no one is getting fucked over and we get paid a fuck ton of dirty money for our services. Luckily, we have a rather large racetrack to clean it.

"Of course. Send me the location and I'll make sure we're there."

"*I know you will, son. You're shaping up to be the perfect leader. The next generation of Tailors, ready to take us into the future. I'm proud of you, Aeron. Of you all.*"

I feel the swelling of my chest at his praise; this man who not only saved my life but gave me so much and treated me like one of his own. I can see Aeron do the same, sitting up straighter, even as a frown mars his brow.

"Thank you, Dad."

"*I'm sure that you have all of this handled. I trust you to be able to deal with the Soldiers in any way that you see fit. I want you to bring me their heads, son, Rufus's and the boy's. Preferably on a silver fucking platter.*" I shiver at the brutality in his tone, something I'd usually revel in, but unease makes me go rigid. How will we accomplish that without breaking our beautiful bird's heart? "*I've some business to take care of here, so I won't be back for several weeks. Make sure to take some of the men if you need them. Earl included. They're all under your command, and I'll make sure they know it. Speak to you soon, son."*

"Speak to you soon, Dad." The call ends, and once again, we sit in silence, both lost in our own thoughts.

"Are you going to do as he says?" The baring of Aeron's teeth as he looks at the road in front of us tells me he knows what I'm talking about. Rook, Lark's brother.

"She'll not forgive us for killing her only true family left," he replies, and I nod, my throat tightening with the thought that we're in between a rock and a hard place.

Do we kill Lark's brother and earn her hate? Or do we leave him alive and earn the wrath of Adam, as well as potentially a whole host of future problems?

Often, I'm glad that I'm not the heir to the Tailors.

We leave Lark at the warehouse, venturing out into the rapidly-cooling air of the evening as we take one of the trucks to the rendezvous point. We sit in silence, no one knowing quite what to say after Aeron told the others Adam's edict with regards to our bird's brother.

We're soon pulling up to the site of the stables, and our mood grows even more somber to see the scorched earth and little else left. All that remains of Adam's beloved stables is a light dusting of ash, and it makes my brows knit together with the thought of the suffering of those poor horses like Blue who were trapped. *Fucking Soldier scum.*

The site manager, a Tailor called Ralph, strolls over, greeting us before motioning to about a dozen other Tailors waiting to unload the wood ready for the contractors who are due in the morning.

"Everything is all set, Mr. Tailor," he says to Aeron. It should feel strange that a man in his late forties is showing such deference to someone over fifteen years younger than him, but Aeron, and to a lesser extent ourselves, have had this treatment for most of our lives, so it's become the norm now.

Soon after, a large HGV pulls into the lot, and our usual driver steps out alongside his son, walking over to us.

"Evenin' Mr. Taylor," Burt greets, dipping his head at Aeron, then the rest of us.

"Good evening, Burt. John." Aeron always remembers everyone's names, it was why it was so amusing that he purposefully called Lark Dove. "I take it you had no issues?"

"No, sir, everything was smooth as usual."

"Good. Why don't you take a little walk? Come back in, say, half an hour?" Aeron suggests, and they both nod, taking off towards the field next to us. "Ralph."

Ralph calls his guys over, and they get to work unloading the wood from the truck. They make quick work of it, calling quietly when they get to a piece that looks like all the others but is clearly lighter, the edge looking like several pieces stacked together.

"Thanks, boys," Aeron says, sending them back to the truck as he inspects the piece.

"Coffin concealment?" Knox asks, and Aeron nods.

"Looks like it."

"Worth a lot?"

"Three million."

Knox cracks his neck, blowing out a breath and going to open the trunk of the truck. He pulls out a slim crowbar, the moonlight glinting off the metal as he walks towards us and crouches down to run his palm over the wood. His forehead creases in concentration and then he smiles.

"Bingo."

With a care that should not be possible for such a large man— he's clearly the biggest of us all in terms of muscle and bulk—he gently slides the end of the crowbar into a tiny gap that I didn't see until that moment. With careful movement, he levers the crowbar, taking his time and not rushing until the lid of the piece pops off and slides to the ground, revealing the void underneath it.

Inside, wrapped in dark cloth is what I assume to be a square painting, something we're used to dealing in and what we were expecting. Knox opens the cloth to reveal the glint of an ornate, antique frame and a brightly-colored canvas.

"Load it in the truck. Rupert's waiting," Aeron tells us, arms folded over his chest as his eyes dart over to the Tailors still unloading.

Rupert is our crocked art dealer, a former auctioneer of Christies, London and now has his own fine art auction house here in Colorado. We won't be selling this through him, he doesn't deal in stolen goods, but he does help us to check their authenticity for our clients, to ensure that no one gets fucked over in a deal. It's one of the reasons why our reputation is so good as middlemen, we cover all the bases.

"Aye, aye, captain!" Jude salutes, and I'm not the only one having to press my lips together at his antics. Even Aeron's mouth twitches.

Jude and I gingerly lift out the painting, carrying it over to the truck where Knox already has the hidden compartment in the trunk open. We place it inside, ensuring that it's well padded and covered, then shut the compartment and the trunk.

We watch as Aeron speaks to Ralph, then leaves a large envelope of cash in the glove box before he heads over to us, his dark navy suit bringing out his stormy eyes. He really is beautiful, but has never swung my way so I've not pushed it.

"Let's go meet Rupert. I want to get back to our little Dove."

Me too, brother. Me too.

"GROWING UP CAN GO TO HELL" BY MARISA MAINO

LARK

I get bored right around the second season of Vampire Diaries, a girl can only take the poor decisions of Elena for so long. Like, why the fuck choose one brother when she definitely could have had both?! It's all about the brother sandwich, as I know now all too well.

Huffing, I decide to go exploring. The guys shouldn't have left me alone if they didn't want me to poke through their stuff. Swiping a bottle of what I always see Aeron drinking—a whiskey that I know is fucking extortionate—I pull the lid off and take a swig.

The burn hits my solar plexus like a punch, and I cough a little. It's been a while since I drank anything near this strong, mostly I used to steal the Soldiers' moonshine which tasted like shit but did the job of allowing me to escape my fucked up life for a little while.

Shaking those morbid thoughts away, I head up the stairs to the bedrooms. I've not been in Tarl's yet and color me curious. Pushing open the door, I'm instantly hit with the scent of him; all exotic spices and it makes me think of nights spent in carnal pleasure in forbidden lands with the heat of the breeze caressing your skin.

Taking a deep inhale, I draw the smell inside me as I step over the threshold and just stare around. It's beautiful and matches his fragrance perfectly. The walls are a deep gold color and the huge carved, four-poster bed is draped in sumptuous jewel tones, scatter cushions, and sheets that are all silk, if the sheen is any indication. The floor is covered in beautifully woven rugs piled atop each other so no glimpse of the original carpet can be seen. Lamps made from colorful glass are fitted around the room and cast patterned shadows on the walls as the light shines through them.

One corner catches my eye, and I walk towards it to inspect the array of interesting-looking instruments arranged carefully in the space. There are drums, of all shapes and sizes, as well as beautiful, wooden stringed instruments, a little like lutes, but with only two or four strings. I also catch a glimpse of what looks like wooden recorders, light-colored with intricate designs running all over them.

I remember Tarl telling me about where he came from, about his family before they all were killed. Iran used to be Persia, I think, and those rugs definitely look like what you'd call Persian carpets. The entire room has that whole *Arabian Nights* feel, with the silks and soft lighting. Tarl is still a bit of a mystery to me, as is Knox and where his family is. I shouldn't want to know more about them, but I want to know everything about them all, my heart at war with my head.

I spend some more time poking around his room, finding old, leather-bound books that are written in what looks like a Sanskrit of some kind. Seems Tarl is a bit of a history buff as well as a musician.

Deciding that I want to bring his scent with me, I head over to a beautifully carved, wooden chest of drawers, setting the bottle of whiskey on the top and rummaging around until I find a deep red T-shirt of his. Pulling it out, a bundle of battered envelopes comes with it, and I frown when I see all of the foreign postage marks on them. Biting my lower lip, I turn the package over in my hands. It's unusual to see letters in this day and age, and these don't look that old.

Being the nosy bitch I am, I open one to find a single sheet of paper, and what looks like a letter written in that same flowing language, Persian maybe? Placing the paper back in the envelope, I take another from the bundle to find the same thing; a single sheet of paper with the same cursive script on it. Curious, I open all the others to discover that they are all like that, nothing letting me know what the contents are.

Shrugging—for all I fucking know they're from some other family back in Iran that he's never mentioned—I put them all back in the drawer, in their bundle because only a fucking idiot doesn't cover their tracks. Then I take another sip of the alcohol before placing the bottle back down and stripping out of my long-sleeved top, bralette, and black jeans. Lifting the red stupidly soft T-shirt off the top of the drawers, I slip it over my head, Tarl's cardamom scent washing over me and making me feel all warm and fuzzy inside. All the guys are bigger than I am, so it falls to my mid-thighs and covers my lace underwear.

Grabbing my clothes and the bottle, I head out of his room, dropping the garments in the laundry basket in Jude's bathroom, before taking out some pink, fluffy socks that he bought me because I was always moaning about my cold feet. Now that it's getting colder, I must see about some other woolens, this bitch has poor circulation and I'm not about to turn into the only Smurfette once winter hits.

Putting the socks on, and heading back downstairs, I huff another sigh, looking around to see what I can interfere with. My eyes alight on another door off the living space that I've never ventured through, and an evil chuckle falls from my lips as I make my way over to it and turn the door handle.

"Fucking bastards," I grumble when it doesn't open, clearly having been locked. I pause, wondering if there is anything around here I can use to pick the lock. Unfortunately for me, my lock-picking kit is back at home.

Deciding that I'm a strong, independent woman who can be resourceful and won't be kept out of locked rooms, I walk over to the kitchen and start rifling through the drawers to see if there's anything I can use to break into that door.

"Motherfucking yes!" I grab the two paper clips out of the stuff drawer—*every kitchen has one right?*—and do a shimmy dance over to the locked door. "You're mine, bitch."

I mold them to my liking, bending them into the right shapes so that I can insert them into the lock and start jimmying. It takes a little while, but I squeal and do another dance when the click of the lock sounds and I can turn the handle.

The door swings smoothly open, and from the desk and book-cases, it looks to be an office. I go to bring the whiskey bottle back up to my lips, frowning when I realize I'm no longer holding it.

Searching the space, I see it sitting on the kitchen island and grumble as I walk slightly unsteadily over to it.

"Come to mama, big boy," I croon as I grab it, stalking back to the now open door and taking another drink. There's hardly any burn at all now, just that warm, fuzzy glow that comes from really good alcohol. Like a hug, a whiskey hug. I giggle at the thought of being cuddled by a giant bottle of alcohol, leisurely strolling around the office space once I've flipped the lights on.

There's a huge TV mounted on one wall, the wall itself painted a dark, forest green.

"Fucking always with the green in study spaces, eh?" I mumble to myself, running my fingers along the bookshelves. "Huh, boys know how to clean too do they?" They must do, I've never seen a cleaner around here, and this space is spotless. Unless someone has come when we've been out or I've been asleep.

Or when you've been held in a coffin, dumbass.

Yeah, well, whatever. The classics are all here, as well as some modern novels including *Fifty Shades* and the *Twilight Saga*. Fucking lols, I must ask what their opinion is of them. I've never read the books, the films were enough for me and I don't care how much of a heathen that makes me.

Leaving the books, making a mental note to come and grab a few later, I saunter over to the sleek, wooden desk and plop down heavily in the huge leather chair behind it. There's a silver iMac sitting on the surface, and I tut.

"Out of seven colors to choose from, you get the boring silver one. Typical."

Of course, it's password protected and I grunt in annoyance. The drawers are locked, and I can't seem to locate my handy dandy paper clips to open them.

"Motherfucking, cuntish fucktards," I murmur, getting up from the chair. The room sways, and I plant my hands on the table, waiting for it to right itself before grabbing the now, much emptier bottle and stalking from the room.

Frustrated and bored, I bring up the bottle to my lips as I stomp over to the TV.

"Alexa! Bitch, I know you can hear me!" I shout, her robotic voice pissing me off. "Play 'growing up can go to hell' by Marisa Maino." I command her to turn the volume up until the song fills my eardrums, and leaping onto the couch, I use the bottle as my microphone as I belt out a performance worthy of the Super Bowl.

I'm just finishing the second chorus when the front door flies open, crashing against the wall, and I spin around and there stands an amused-looking Tailor boy.

"Honey, we're home."

CHAPTER TWENTY-SEVEN

"PLAY WITH FIRE (ALTERNATE VERSION)" BY SAM
TIMMESZ, RULLE, VIOLENTS

KNOX

"You're back!" our Little Bird yells, launching herself off the back of the couch. Luckily, being part of the Tailors taught me to expect the unexpected, so I dart forward, catching her in my arms. My face splits into a wide grin as she giggles up at me and wraps her arms around my neck. My smile grows when I see the empty whisky bottle she's left on the couch, one of Aeron's favorites and costs a pretty penny too. "You were gone so long and I was soooo bored," she whines, and I chuckle as Aeron comes up next to us, scowling when he catches sight of the bottle.

"So you decided to finish my twenty-five-year-old single malt whiskey imported from the Isle of Skye, did you, Dove?"

My nostrils flare at the way her nipples poke through the soft fabric of her borrowed shirt. Clearly, she likes being told off by our fearless leader.

"Finish? I didn't—" She looks over at the empty bottle, her brows dipping. "Oops."

"Good evening, Nightingale," Jude says, kissing her on the head softly, his lips twitching as he fails to hold in his smirk. "And good work on the office door."

"I thought so," she preens, sticking out her tits which are becoming too distracting as I stand here holding her bridal style in our living room. My mouth waters at the thought of sucking them, my tongue darting out to lick my lips.

"What did you do, naughty Little Bird?" I ask, dipping my head and kissing her smiling lips instead.

"She broke into the fucking study, using two paper clips by the looks of it," Aeron growls, storming back towards us from the direction of the office. "Find anything interesting, Dove?" His tone might be hard, but his eyes are sparkling. He loves when she challenges us.

"No," she huffs, her bottom lip sticking out in a pout. Fuck me, I need to bite it, like now.

"But you found my shirt?" Tarl interrupts, his lips also tugging upwards in an indulgent smile.

"Oh!" she exclaims, wriggling out of my arms and stumbling into Tarl. He studies her, and she giggles again, a sound that goes straight to my rapidly-hardening cock. "Your room is definitely my favorite. Can I sleep in there tonight? Pretty please with a pussy on top?"

"Of course, *Koshgelam*," he says, wrapping her in his arms and kissing her soundly. She melts into him, and a flare of white-hot jealousy sparks in my center, just for a moment. She suddenly breaks away, spinning to look at me.

"Where are your parents?"

I can feel the color drain from my face and my cock deflating as dark memories of the time before Adam Taylor took me in tries to rush to the surface. I tamp them down, as I always do, and answer her, my voice monotone.

"I never knew them. I was in foster care until Adam adopted me when I was eight."

Aeron catches my eye, his own eyes swirling and lips pulled into a tight line. He knew me when I was just a mess of rage and hurt, lashing out at everyone and everything around me.

Her mouth parts and she wobbles her way over to me, stumbling into my arms and placing her hands on my cheeks.

"Why do you look so sad? So haunted?"

All I can see are her bright blue eyes, drilling into my very fucking soul as if to drag out all my darkest secrets and fears.

"I don't like to think about the time before I joined the Tailors. It was...unhappy." Inwardly I scoff. Unhappy doesn't even begin to cover the shit I went through before Adam saved me. Shit that not even the guys know. She considers me, a frown making her eyebrows dip. She leans in, encasing me in her arms.

"Why do I feel like we share a similar pain, Daddy?" she whispers into my ear and my breath stutters in my chest.

"Like recognizes like, I guess," I answer, my voice thick, pulling her closer and breathing in her sweet summer and cherry blossom scent mixed with Tarl's spicy fragrance. It's a heady combination and one that I take in deeply.

"I'm here if you need to talk." She pulls back, placing a soft kiss on my cheek before grabbing my hand and tugging me towards the couches. "Let's play a game!"

"Ohhh! I love games!" Jude exclaims, following us as Tarl fixes us all some drinks at the bar. "How about spin the bottle?" He brandishes the bottle that Lark drank from, and she looks at the couch as if wondering how it disappeared. Still drunk then.

"As long as I don't have to kiss or fuck my brother or any of you, I'm in," Aeron states, and I chuckle, pulling our Little Bird into my lap as I take a seat. I need her close as the dark memories of my past still swirl around me. Aeron takes up his usual armchair, Jude snuggles up next to us, and Tarl hands me a beer and then takes his place on the other couch.

"I'll go first!" Jude cries out before reaching over and placing the bottle on the metal and glass coffee table, then spinning it. I watch as it spins, arching a brow when it lands in my direction. "Yes!" Jude fist bumps and then turns to Lark. "How do you want to do this, Nightingale?"

She bites her lip, her pupils already widening, and from that look alone, my cock begins to stiffen again in my black jeans.

"I want to watch while you give Knox head."

Fuck. Me.

"Done," Jude replies, sliding off the couch and sinking to his knees in between my splayed thighs, looking up at me with wide, deep blue eyes that sparkle with mischief. "Will you choke me, Daddy?"

My breath hitches, Lark slipping off my lap to the side of me, kneeling on the cushion so she has the best view. I'm rock-fucking-solid as Jude unbuttons my pants, getting me to lift my hips so that he can slide them down my thighs and to my ankles. I'm bare beneath—because fuck boxers—so my hard length springs free, slapping me on my abs as it bobs in front of his face.

"Can I taste him first, Jude?" Her voice is husky and I feel the pre-cum leaking from my tip as her words register.

"Ladies first," he offers, holding out his hand and indicating that she can have the first taste.

"I'm not a fucki—" The words are cut off with a deep groan as her wet lips wrap around my head, her tongue teasing the slit. She moans in her throat, the sound going straight to my fucking balls, as she slides lower, taking almost all of me in her hot, slick mouth. "Fuck, just like that, baby. You're such a good girl for your Daddy."

The words spill from my lips as she slides up and down, my hands tangling in her luscious, flame-colored hair as she works me into a frenzy, the muscles on my thighs twitching.

"My turn," Jude says in a husky voice, and I watch as she pops off my cock, the length glistening with her saliva. She sits up, my hands releasing her hair, her lips swollen and looking so fucking delicious that it takes monumental effort not to claim them.

But my attention is stolen by the man between my legs, the guy who I've often been curious about but never had the balls to take it further. Not until our Little Bird entered our lives anyway. Holding my gaze, he places his lips around me and then sinks down. And down. And down.

"Fucking Hell, Jude!"

He chuckles, the vibrations making my hips fucking twitch as he holds me in his throat. Sparks flash across my skin, my nerves firing as he slowly draws up, only to sink back down again, his lips pressing around my hilt as he swallows me fucking whole.

A feminine moan next to me has my hooded stare leaving Jude's to find Lark naked and impaled on Tarl's cock from behind. I see we've given up on the bottle. Can't blame the fucker. Her new ink looks stark against the pale alabaster of her skin, and I thrust into Jude's mouth at the sight of our marks covering her. Claiming her.

Tarl pushes down between her shoulder blades, forcing her beautiful tits to swing from the force of his thrusts, her face twisted in lines of stunning agony. My hand reaches out, gently grasping her slender throat as Jude continues to suck and gives me the best fucking blow job of my life.

"Are you going to be our good fucking girl, princess?" I ask her, my voice husky and deep. My other hand comes down to Jude's head, grabbing a fistful of his thick hair and jerking him down hard, impaling his mouth with my cock. He groans, clearly enjoying the rough play.

"Yes, Daddy." Her eyes are as hooded as my own, her voice rasping as her breath gasps out of her with every forceful thrust of Tarl's. I turn down to look at Jude, using my grip to bring him up. Tears run down his face, his lips plush and dripping with his own spit.

"And are you going to be a good little boy for me?" He whimpers.

"Yes."

"Yes, what?"

"Yes, Daddy." His body trembles and I find a smile lifting up my lips.

"Then choke on my cock like you promised, and if you're good, I'll give you my cum." He groans at my words, his eyes fluttering. "But you don't touch yourself. You save your release for our little cum slut."

"Yes, Daddy."

He opens up as I force his head down, fucking his mouth mercilessly, the sounds of him gagging and choking driving me closer to my climax. My hand clenches around our Little Bird's throat, her strangled cries and gasps adding to the symphony of our fucking.

I can hear Tarl murmuring about fucking her bloody, about coating her sweet cunt in Jude's blood, and it's that image which sends me over the edge, thrusting into the back of Jude's throat and holding him there as I roar out my orgasm. He swallows, prolonging the electricity that races across my body until I finally pull him off of me and slump back, my hand still gripping Lark's throat.

I roll my head to look at her shuddering through an orgasm as Tarl buries himself balls deep inside her, his caramel skin glistening with sweat as he fills her with his release. My grip loosens, but I use it to pull her in for a kiss, stealing the small puffs of breath that leave her lungs.

She kisses me back, quivering, and I realize that she helped to chase the darkness of my past away. Her and Jude.

She pulls back, only for her lips to be caught by Jude, and a low groan sounds in her throat as she licks inside his mouth, tasting me on his tongue no doubt.

A throat clears, and I turn to look across at Aeron, swirling his drink around in his cut glass tumbler, a wicked smile on his face.

"You want to be filled up with Tailor boy cum, Dove?"

CHAPTER TWENTY-EIGHT

"DO IT FOR ME" BY ROSENFELD

LARK

"*You want to be filled with Tailor boy cum, Dove?*"

What little breath I had in my lungs catches, a small gasp leaving my lips when Tarl pulls out of my dripping pussy.

"Yes." My voice is a heady whisper, my throat raw from Knox's tight grip, but there was no stopping my answer.

The merry buzz I felt from Aeron's whiskey has been fucked out of me, to be replaced by the afterglow of my orgasm, and the anticipation of more.

"Then crawl to me on your hands and knees like our good little slut. Show me you want mine and my brother's dicks to fill you up until you can't breathe."

My breathing picks up as I get to my feet, my legs trembling with the adrenaline that pumps through me. Holding Aeron's stare, I slowly sink to my knees, then place my hands on the floor, grateful for the soft, Persian rug that covers this part of the concrete floor.

"Now that is a beautiful fucking sight, pussy swollen and leaking cum," Knox states, his voice low and gruff. More of Tarl's release and my own slicks my thighs at his words. These boys know how to rile a girl up until she's fucking desperate for dick.

"Such a beautiful, fuck doll," Jude whispers next to me, his lips ghosting over my naked shoulder and sending shivers skittering across my skin. "Purple really is your color." His fingers skim the bruises on my arms, marks that Knox left with his fists less than a week ago. "I can just imagine a necklace of these gracing that long neck of yours, Nightingale."

I swallow hard at the suggestion, my thighs clenching at the thought of it.

"She likes that idea," Tarl comments, his voice lazy behind me. "Look how her cunt flutters at the thought of hands wrapped around her beautiful throat."

Oh lordt.

"Come to me, Dove, and if you're really good, maybe we'll see about that necklace," Aeron orders, his tone confident and drawling. He's sitting in his chair like a king on a throne, knees wide like he needs all that space for his dick.

Spoiler alert; he does.

Licking my lips, I do as he says, crawling on my hands and knees, giving the others the perfect view of my soaked pussy. I hold Aeron's gaze as I do, coming to a stop between his splayed thighs and sitting back on my heels.

"Good girl," he praises, and it's like a fire has been lit inside me, my body warming at his words. "Now, take me out and use your mouth to tell me how desperate you are for my cock."

With fumbling fingers, I reach forward, undoing the belt on his navy blue slacks, letting it fall to the sides as I unbutton and then unzip his pants. The room is silent aside from my panting breaths as I reach inside his black boxer briefs and wrap my hand over his hard, velvety length. God, he really does have a fucking nice dick, the piercing at the end glinting as I pull him out, leaving his pants and underwear on. Seems I'm following orders tonight.

Leaning forward, I bring my mouth to his head, my tongue darting out as if on instinct and licking up the warm, salty drop of pre-cum. A low purr sounds in his chest, so I repeat the move, licking and lapping at just the head until it glistens.

"Fucking hell, Dove," he rasps, that warm, fuzzy feeling in my center returning at how I can make this powerful man come undone with a few swipes of my tongue. His fingers dig into the arms of the chair, his drinks glass on the small side table, forgotten. "That tongue." I roll my eyes upwards and look as his hooded eyes watch me with rapt attention. Not looking away, our stares locked, I open my mouth and take him inside, using my tongue to massage him as I swallow him down. "Fuuuuck!" he growls, and then there's a warmth at my back, fingers tangling in my hair as someone pushes me further down, making me gag as my lips meet Aeron's base.

"That's it, Nightingale. Swallow all of my brother's cock. Let me use your head to fuck him like you're his personal toy." Jude's voice is coaxing, his tone soft and at odds with the way he uses the grip on my hair to pull me up, then slams me back down on Aeron's dick.

"Shit, Jude," Aeron moans, and tears stream down my cheeks as I watch him tip his head back. My hands grasp his thighs, which are as solid as the cock in my mouth as Jude makes good on his word and fucks Aeron with my mouth.

He pauses, my head pulled back enough to allow me to draw some air into my screaming lungs. I moan long and low when I feel Jude at my entrance, pushing his way inside my heated channel with ease.

"Tarl lubed you up real good for me, Nightingale," he grits out, his own voice strained as he seats himself fully.

I whimper as he moves inside me, pulling out only to thrust back in. He has one hand on my hip, holding me steady for him as the other pushes and pulls my head on his brother's cock. Delicious sensations of rapture start to wash over me, sweeping across my entire body, and I relax, letting the Tailor brothers use me as they like.

Curses and grunts add to the slapping of our bodies, filling the room with the obscene sounds of our fucking, and I know that I'll be lucky if I can talk or walk tomorrow with how hard these boys are fucking me.

Aeron suddenly goes rock-solid in my mouth, his hands coming up over Jude's as he forces my head all the way down. With a shouted curse, he comes, pouring his release down my spasming throat.

"Your turn, little broken bird," Jude murmurs in my ear, his hand leaving my head to find my clit. He wastes no time, rubbing and flicking as he fucks me from behind, and soon I'm screaming around Aeron's cock as I crash into a sea of bliss.

Jude keeps up his assault on my body, prolonging my pleasure until I'm whimpering and twitching when he finds his own climax, pushing into me a final time and filling me up with his cum. Just like Aeron promised.

Aeron finally pulls out, and I take a huge gasping breath, my whole body flickering with pleasure like a light bulb about to blow. He chuckles, the sound deep and I open bleary eyes to see the smug satisfaction on his face.

"What's so funny?" I ask, my voice a croaking whisper that makes me cringe with how abused my poor throat is.

"We owe you a necklace, Dove," he tells me, leaning forward to skim his fingers along the column of my neck. "But we still managed to choke the air out of you, so that's something."

"You're all fuckers, you know that?" I grumble, swallowing against the pain in my throat.

"I'll make you some honey, lemon, and ginger tea for your throat, *Eshgham*," Tarl says as he passes us, pausing to brush a kiss to my head.

"More talk like that out of you, Dove," Aeron growls, grabbing my chin and pulling my face upward so he can whisper the last part against my swollen lips. "And I'll bring your coffin up into my room for you to sleep in tonight."

My eyes widen as he pulls back with a sexy fucking smirk, but I keep my mouth shut, knowing that he'd do it in a heartbeat. I mean, I might like the idea a little, but maybe not tonight. I'll save it for another day.

Not many left, Lark.

It takes everything I have not to let the thought show on my face, and I'm not sure if I manage it all that successfully when Aeron's brows dip slightly.

"Sorry, sir," I say quickly to cover the moment, and he considers me for a beat, then leans in and kisses my mouth softly.

"Good girl. Let's get you cleaned up and into bed, shall we? It's getting late and we've got a busy few days of planning ahead of us."

My stomach clenches, my skin achingly cold as he helps me up, Jude having pulled out when Aeron gave his coffin threat.

My mind whirls as he guides me upstairs, his hand in mine gripping tightly as if he knows what's coming and is trying to deny it as much as I am.

It's the only way, Lark. The only way to be truly free. To save Rook.

I just wish my heart would agree with that.

CHAPTER TWENTY-NINE

"PLAY DIRTY" BY KEVIN MCALLISTER

LARK

The next day we all get ready, and I can't help sensing the tension in the air, like bees buzzing around you, ready to swarm. There's a tightness in my gut that I can't seem to shake, no matter how hard I fucking try.

They'll be okay, they're some of the biggest bad out there.

"Hey, Little Bird. Nothing bad will happen to you or us," Knox tells me, wrapping his arms around me from behind, and the knot in my stomach tightens until I feel sick.

"That's right, Dove. We'll take care of you," Aeron assures me as he steps into my front and cups my face in his large warm hands. I have to swallow back tears, feeling like the blackest of devils. "And your brother," he adds after a beat. I can't speak, just nod and kiss him back with trembling lips when he presses his to mine. "Let's go meet the others and you can explain everything, okay?" His voice is softer than when I first met him, kinder too. The darkness that lived in his deep blue eyes is still there, but he doesn't look as pained as he used to, and that just makes me hurt more.

We get into one of the trucks, Knox driving, with Aeron and Jude on either side of me, Tarl on the passenger side. They all keep shooting glances my way, brows furrowed, and I know I'm doing a shit job of hiding my apprehension, but I can't seem to rein it in.

All too soon, we're pulling up in front of what I know is one of the many office buildings owned by the Tailor gang. I huff a laugh.

"What's so funny, little Nightingale?" Jude asks, bringing our clasped hands up to his lips and placing a light kiss on my knuckles.

"I was just thinking that only rich assholes like you would hold a meeting about the eradication of another gang in a smart office block. Will we get pastries and coffee?" Am I using sass and sarcasm to hide my misery? You bet your ass I am.

"Freshly baked from one of our bakeries," Aeron whispers in my ear, and fucking hell, that boy could make a shopping list sound sexual. It's almost enough to make me forget the sick feeling in my stomach.

"Only the best for us, Nightingale, and world domination is a hungry business, you know?" Jude says completely deadpan and without a hint of teasing. Of course he's fucking serious, bloody psycho.

Someone in a smart uniform comes towards us, opening the door for Aeron, who gets out and then leans back in, holding his hand out for me to take. Feeling shaky, I place my palm in his and allow him to help me from the car, grateful for my boots and a sweater now that we're entering into fall. The sun still shines like a traitorous bastard, like nothing terrible is about to happen. I just wish that sometimes my mood was reflected in the weather, like it should be stormy and blowing a gale outside like it is inside me right now.

Knox tosses the uniformed lackey his keys, and we make our way up to the modern glass doors which open with a swish as we approach.

"Good morning, gentlemen," a very attractive blonde woman greets us, her eyes pausing over me. "And miss. Your boardroom is ready."

"Thank you, Jessica," Aeron replies, still holding my hand, which he tucks into the crook of his suit-clad elbow as Jessica leads us down a bright and airy corridor. We stop before a large gray door, no windows to be able to see what we're walking into, and I can't help stiffening. "You'll be fine, Dove. We're right here," Aeron murmurs, and I look up to see him gazing down at me, a softness about his face that I'm coming to realize he only wears for me. "You're safe."

It's not me that I'm worried about, I want to scream at him before dragging them all back to the warehouse and hiding under the covers for the rest of our lives.

Rook.

The one reason that I can't do that. The one reason that I must keep going, even if it's like knives into my heart. Squaring my shoulders, I give him a nod and face the door again.

"Ready?" Jessica asks, and I nod again. If I keep this up, I'll be like one of the fucking nodding dogs that old people have in the back of their cars.

"Ready."

She opens the door for us, Tarl and Knox stepping in first, then Aeron and I follow with Jude behind us.

"Little songbird." The nasal voice crawls over my skin before my eyes even find him in the room. "I wondered if you'd be singing this morning."

"Shut the fuck up, Earl," Knox snarls, taking a step towards the older man who drops his smirk and retreats back into his chair. "You don't even fucking look at her."

Earl's jaw works, and I can see the fight in his eyes, the distaste clear on his screwed-up face. He's used to being top dog, but when his master is away, he has to obey new masters, whether he likes it or not. He gives a sharp tilt of his head.

"Good. Now that that is settled, shall we begin?" Aeron says, his voice unemotional and full of command as he leads me around to the head of the table where he takes his seat and then fucking drags me down onto his lap. *Asshole.*

I watch as the others come and sit either side of us; Knox on Aeron's left, with Jude and then Tarl on the right. A united front. There's a beat of hesitation, the five other Tailors looking at each other before sitting back down.

"Pastry, Nightingale?" Jude asks, reaching over to where a pile of freshly baked pastries and three steaming pots wait in the middle of the table. He grabs a small plate, piling several pastries onto it, before pouring me a steaming cup of what smells like hot chocolate and even adding some whipped cream and pink and white mini marshmallows.

A grin splits my lips, the thought that he knows not only do I prefer hot chocolate to coffee but that I love marshmallows in it too, making me feel all kinds of warm and fuzzy.

"As you know," Aeron starts, his hand splaying on my stomach as he pulls me closer to his body. I can't help it, I sink into him, placing my hand on top of his. "We have been looking for the Dead Soldier headquarters for years with no success." I see the other Tailors nod, and I notice that they're all dressed smartly, in suits that really make this feel like a business meeting, not the start of a killing mission. "Well, now we have our in, and this morning we will discuss the best course of action going forward."

"And we're going to listen to the Soldier whore? Just like that?" one of the Tailors asks, a young guy whose ears stick out from the side of his head, his closely trimmed, mousy brown hair doing nothing to hide them.

I jump when suddenly a knife is impaled in his shoulder, the handle bobbing as he screams before leaping to his feet. His hand goes to reach for it.

"I wouldn't do that," Tarl says, voice casual as fuck, and I twist my head to look at him as he watches the Tailor that presumably he just threw a knife at. "You'll lose blood quicker if you pull it out."

"Oh! Let's have a game!" Jude yells, jumping up out of his seat and fucking skipping over to the Tailor. Coming up behind him, he places his hands on both of the guy's shoulders and pushes him back into his chair. The guy whimpers at the rough touch. "If Dumbo here doesn't pass out before the end of the meeting, he can live."

The man, Dumbo, swallows as he shakes in his chair. "A–and i–if I do p–pass out?"

He looks at Aeron, missing Jude leaning down, right next to his ear on the side where there is a flower of blood blooming around the knife.

"I think even you can guess what happens then, can't you, Dumbo?" There's a wicked gleam in Jude's ocean eyes, and I can see his fingers dig into the man's shoulders as he grins. It shouldn't make my thighs clench, but I never claimed that I wasn't fucked up, and seeing these men defend my honor has my core heating. Aeron chuckles behind me, his other hand sliding up the inside of my jeans-clad thigh.

"Naughty, Dove."

With a final squeeze that causes Dumbo's eyes to roll, Jude saunters back to his seat, plopping down and grabbing a pastry before taking a huge bite. Fucking crazy bastard.

"You were saying, brother?" He turns to Aeron, his cheeks flushed and I know that he's also turned on by the violence, his arousal pressing against his canary yellow chinos.

"Dove?"

My body stiffens, all eyes on me and I have to swallow a couple of times before I can speak.

"Judy's Laundromat," I say, looking at Knox. "That's where Dead Soldiers HQ is."

"That's not—" Earl starts, falling silent as my guys twist to look at him. He pales ever so slightly, and to be fucking honest, so would I if they were all staring at me like they need no excuse to rip my throat out.

"Carry on, Little Bird," Knox encourages, and I turn to give him a small smile of appreciation.

"In the basement is an old speakeasy, from prohibition days. You can only gain access via the alleyway down the side of Judy's. There's a fire door, it opens into a lobby and from there down into the basement."

"Huh, didn't know Rufus could be so clever," Knox muses, looking a little impressed.

A hand comes up and grasps my chin, turning my head until Aeron's ocean eyes are staring into mine. It's almost too close, the position slightly uncomfortable, but I allow it, not protesting.

"And why can't we just break in through the fire door?"

"It's booby-trapped," I tell him, his hand lightening its hold so that I can speak more clearly. "There's a metal boot mat that's hooked up to the mains electricity as well as the door handle. It can only be turned off from the inside, and they watch the alley to make sure no one tries to walk in."

"So what's your plan? How can we get in?" he questions me, and my queasy stomach settles a little at the way he's taking me seriously, asking for my opinion as if it's as important as any of the others. I can see him trying to puzzle it out and can almost hear the cogs turning in his brain as he tries to figure out how to get in. I smirk, and his lips flit up for a brief second before they come back down into his usual serious expression.

"I was always an inquisitive child," I tell him, pausing when his lips lift again, as if to tell me that doesn't surprise him. "And one day I came across the old coal room, used as storage for all the product my father sells." Yep, that's right, as a kid, I wandered into a room full of drugs without anything to stop me. I mean, the door was locked, but that wasn't exactly a deterrent. "Anyway, I was poking around and came across what looked like an old coal chute. So, I climbed it, it's brick-lined so there were some handholds, and was able to push aside the broken manhole cover that covered it at the other end. It opens out onto a courtyard at the back of Judy's, and no one else knows about it. It's how I've managed to sneak out all these years, including the night your guys picked me up."

"Clever little Dove," Aeron praises, his thumb stroking the underside of my jaw. "Is it big enough for us?"

"I think so. I mean, if the girls can fit through, I'm pretty sure your big asses can."

His eyes dart down to where my breasts are pushing against my green sweater, a gift from Jude who seems to enjoy buying me clothes as my wardrobe keeps growing. He licks his lips, and my breath stutters at the look of heat in their depths.

"So we go down the coal chute, then what?" he questions, ever the leader, not willing to let himself be distracted for too long.

"The coal room is in a room down from the cages." I shiver at the thought of that room, the lack of windows, the metal cages that are solid iron, and a place that no one leaves alive. Aeron's arm tightens around me. "We'd need to go through that space and then there's a door which opens into the main room."

"Are there any guards?" Knox scrutinizes, and I twist to look at him.

"Honestly, no. My father doesn't think anyone will ever find him, so they're only watching the front. And they don't know about the coal chute."

"Okay, so we go down the chute, make our way up to the basement level, and then kill everyone inside. I like it!" Jude exclaims, clapping his hands.

"When is the best time to go? When are the most Soldiers there, Dove?" Aeron fires at me, ignoring his brother's outburst.

"Friday night," I tell them, looking around at the others in the room for the first time. Aside from Earl, who is not looking at me at all, the others all look like they're actually considering my words, nodding along. I lick my lips. "That's when all the Soldiers go there. It's mandatory. They discuss the upcoming week, initiate any new members and move others up the ranks, collect their product, and party."

I have to blink away the memories of those parties. Of all the times when I was forced to my back as members celebrated their promotions between my unwilling thighs.

"We'll kill them all, Dove," Aeron tells me softly, and I know that I didn't hide the memories fast enough. He turns me on his lap so that I'm sideways and he can cup my face with his hands and press our foreheads together. "Every fucking last one of them."

My eyes close, and I feel the tears slip down my cheeks, my attempt to hold them back as futile as trying to stop the sun from rising. He brushes them away with his thumbs, placing a gentle kiss on my lips, then tucking me into his neck.

"We'll meet in two nights' time, this Friday, at eleven PM, outside Danny's Diner. Don't be fucking late and don't allow yourself to be followed. Wear dark clothing that you can move in. Bring guns and ammo, any other small weapons that you can use, but nothing that will slow you down." He turns to look at one of the Tailors. "Nick, you need to stake out Judy's from midday. Watch who's coming and going into that alley, make a note of how many Soldiers will be at this meeting."

"Yes, boss," Nick nods, cracking his knuckles.

"They're really fucking paranoid, they'll notice if someone is hanging around all day," I tell him, glancing up and nibbling my lower lip.

"Don't worry, doll, I'm good at blending in," Nick replies with a wink and Knox chuckles.

"Yeah, Nick here has a face that even his own mother would forget."

I look at Nick and realize with a start that Knox is right. Everything about the man is average, unmemorable, from his brown hair to his nothing-special, gray suit.

"Knox, I want you round the back, keeping an eye on the coal chute," Aeron orders, and Knox inclines his head at Aeron.

"But—" I start, twisting to look at Aeron and shutting my mouth when he gives me a hard glare. I swallow hard. "I don't like being separated," I confess, my voice quiet and eyes pleading with him. His glower softens, his hand cupping my cheek.

"If you're coming with us,"—I nod, letting him know with my stare that no fucking way am I not coming with them—"which you're insisting on, then I want to make sure it's safe, and I trust Knox to ensure that."

My gaze flits to the man in question, and his lips are parted as he looks at Aeron, his forehead furrowed. I look back at Aeron and see him dip his head, his eyes on Knox too and it feels like something passes between the two men. Something that is almost like the beginning of forgiveness.

"Good. I believe, gentlemen and lady, that's our business for this morning concluded," Aeron tells the room, catching every man's eye and I'm struck by how much of a leader he is at that moment. He was born to lead, to steer others.

He shifts his arms, placing one under my knees and another around my back, and in a single, smooth motion, he stands, carrying me close to his chest. My arms fly to wrap around his neck, and I'd protest, but suddenly I'm so weary that I'm not sure I could walk out on my own feet. I glance down at the plate and cup on the table, still full as I hadn't managed a bite with my stomach churning so much.

I guess that's what betraying the men that you love does to you.

I look over his shoulder when I hear a pained sound, and see Jude holding the knife that was embedded in the clavicle of the asshole Tailor, Dumbo. Blood glistens on the blade, dripping from the tip.

"Good job, Dumbo. You didn't pass out." Jude claps him on the back, earning another wince and Dumbo looks like he's about to keel over after all.

Tarl takes the knife off him, and they both saunter over to us as Knox brings up the rear of our group. The door opens once more, Jessica waiting for us. She looks at me with concern, her forehead creased.

"Is she okay, Mr. Taylor? Do you want me to call a doctor?"

"No thank you, Jessica," Aeron replies, not pausing as he walks towards the front doors of the building. "She just needs to get home."

Home.

The word drags a sob from my chest, Aeron pulling me closer as we exit the building and walk towards the waiting truck. The word bounces around my skull, becoming a taunt as I break down in his arms, clinging to him as he gets us into the back and pulls me closer.

"It's okay, my love," he murmurs, and I feel Jude come up next to us, his hand rubbing soothing circles on my back. "They'll never hurt you again."

I just cry harder, knowing that it's not my past haunting me anymore, but my future.

And there's not a fucking thing I can do to change it.

CHAPTER THIRTY

"I FOUND" BY AMBER RUN

LARK

The guys stay close to me for the rest of the day, and we spend it curled up on the couches watching endless Disney movies at Jude's insistence. It's the healing balm that I need, yet know that I don't deserve, no matter how much I try to convince myself that I've put in fail-safes to ensure they're okay.

The next morning, I wake up, my stomach rolling and an ache in the back of my throat that won't go away, no matter how much water I drink.

"Let's go shopping!" Jude suddenly exclaims while I'm pushing bits of fluffy pancake around my plate, all of us sitting at the kitchen island for breakfast as it has become our routine.

"Shopping?" I ask, my head tilting upwards as he comes to stand over me. He bends down, framing my face in his warm hands.

"It always makes me feel better, spending lots of money on pretty things, and you classify as a very pretty thing, Nightingale."

I bristle. "You know that I'm a person right, Baby Devil?"

"Of course, a very pretty person," he replies, his brows dipping as if he doesn't get what the issue is. I huff out a breath that he inhales as his face is that close.

"I don't have any money, Jude."

"Yes you do, you have all of my money. What's mine is yours, Nightingale, and what's yours is mine. Especially that pretty cunt."

"Jude! For fuck's sake!"

Aeron laughs, the deep timbre of his voice distracting me from my misery and making my nipples harden. "He's not wrong, Dove. You can use our money, and we do own that beautiful pussy of yours."

"I am a person, assholes! Not just a hole for your dicks." I don't know why I'm so furious, my breath is coming in gasps, and I try to get up and break away from Jude's hold, but he doesn't let go, earning a frustrated growl from me.

"What's wrong, Nightingale? Why are you so angry and sad?" His deep blue eyes bore into mine, concern lacing his unblinking stare.

"I—" I cut myself off. I can't tell them one of the reasons, the biggest reason why my emotions are everywhere. I've worked too hard and come too far to ruin it now, but I can give them a little more of me, they deserve that much. "I've never been shopping." I can feel my cheeks heat, and I look away from Jude, unable to hold any of their gazes. *What twenty-two-year-old girl has never been fucking shopping?*

"Look at me, Nightingale." His voice has an air of command that can usually be heard falling from his brother's lips. I do as he says, lifting my eyes to meet Jude's ocean blue ones, full of compassion. No judgment. "Please let us take you shopping for the first time, and spend obscene amounts of our ill-gotten gains on you."

Tears fill my eyes, a small sob-laugh falling from my lips.

"Regular Robin Hoods, aren't you guys?"

"You know it, baby," Jude murmurs back, ghosting his lips over mine just enough to send tingles racing over my skin, then pulling back. "So, can we?"

"No posh twat shops."

"I solemnly swear not to take you into any posh twat shops. Scouts honor," Jude says, his voice and face deadly serious.

"Fine."

"Yes!" he exclaims before bringing my face to his and planting a smacking kiss on my lips. "I call shotgun with Nightingale in the back seat. I'm going to make her come at least twice before we get there."

My face flushes, my core tightening at his words.

Goddamit, Jude has the power to lighten any situation, turning my bad mood into good in the blink of an eye.

They take me to the nice part of town, where high-end boutiques with beautiful shopfronts line the street.

"You promised no posh twat shops," I grumble as we get out of the car, although there's not too much heat to my words on account of the post-orgasmic glow. Boy made good on his words and my entire body feels mellow and relaxed.

"This is not a posh twat shop, Nightingale. It's run by one of my favorite people," Jude admonishes me, bopping me on the nose. *Fucker.*

"Looks posh to me," I grouch as we go through the door, a bell chiming when we open it.

"Jude!" a feminine voice yells, and I stiffen when she comes barreling forward, wrapping him up in a tight hug.

"Roxy, good to see you, gorgeous," Jude greets back, keeping hold of my hand as he returns the hug one-armed. I can feel my jaw clench, and Aeron chuckles beside me.

"What's so funny, Devil Man?" I ask, and Roxy snaps her head to me and immediately releases Jude. Her brown-eyed gaze sweeps over me appreciatively, and my cheeks heat at her obvious interest. She's pretty with a heart-shaped face and messy brown hair, dressed in some kind of coverall in a bright floral pattern. It's a shame I don't swing that way.

"Well, hello there, beautiful," she purrs, and I bite my lips together when several low, menacing growls sound around me. Heat meets my back as the scent of leather fills my nose and a hand coils around my stomach possessively. Aeron grabs my free hand, stepping closer, and Jude's grip tightens on my other hand. Tarl looks about ready to step in front of me, blocking me from the small brunette's view.

"Mine," Knox growls out, and Jesus fucking Christ on a popsicle, my panties are decimated at his gruff tone.

"Jeez, can't blame a girl for trying, look at her!" Roxy holds a hand out sweeping it up and down in front of me, shrugging her shoulders. "I'm Roxy, owner of this fine establishment."

"Hi, I'm Lark," I go to hold my hand out for her to shake, but neither boy releases their grip. "Seriously, guys? I'm all about the peen, sorry, Roxy, so I'm not going to run away with her." She laughs, a tinkling sound that has the corners of my lips lifting.

"Damn shame that is, let me know if you ever change your mind," she says, a mischievous look in her eyes when the guys stiffen around me. I like this chick. "In the meantime, what can I do you for?" I laugh outright at that, especially when she waggles her eyebrows. More growls sound around me, and soon Roxy and I are crying with laughter.

"I knew you two would get on," Jude grumbles, like he wishes we'd get along less. *Too bad, sucker.* "Nightingale needs new clothes, anything and everything she wants." He pulls out a shiny, black card, handing it over to Roxy, who manages not to bug her eyes out unlike me. "I might have a look around too."

"Aye, aye, captain!" She salutes and I chuckle again. "Let's go find you all the pretty things, shall we?"

I pull out of Aeron's and Jude's grips, placing a kiss on each of their cheeks before spinning and doing the same to Knox and then Tarl. I give them all a pleading look.

"Don't be dicks, I'll be fine and you can watch my every move like good little stalkers, 'kay?"

"Watch it, Dove. I'm not above a public spanking," Aeron growls out, heading towards a pink velvet chesterfield and sitting down in it with more grace than I have in my fucking pinkie. *Bastard.*

We spend hours in the cute, quirky shop, and I find so many new and beautiful clothes that my head spins when Roxy rings them all up.

"Don't even think about protesting, Nightingale," Jude murmurs in my ear, his arms encasing me in a hug from behind. I can't help myself, I sink into him more, trying to breathe him in.

"But, it's too much," I say, nibbling my lower lip as Roxy swipes Jude's little black card. I've never spent anything on myself, trying to save everything I've ever managed to earn from my OnlyFans to aid our escape. My sperm donor would have gotten suspicious if I'd gone on big shopping sprees anyway, on account of him never giving me any cash. Any clothes that I had were given to me by Rook, occasionally bought at the thrift store, or given to me by some of the other women who hang around the Soldiers. They have the misguided hope that one day some gang member might make an honest woman out of them. They never did, but I can't fault them for dreaming, even if it's misplaced.

"Nothing will ever be too much for you, Nightingale. Nothing," Jude tells me, his arms tightening as Knox steps forward to grab the many bags that contain my new wardrobe. "You are worth so much more than a few clothes."

"Jude, I—" I can't finish, I don't know what to say, my soul tearing with every sweet word that falls from his beautiful mouth.

"Come," Aeron interjects, holding out his hand. "Let's go home."

Home.

There's that word again. A prayer and a taunt all rolled into one, causing a swirling inside me that threatens to pull my very being apart. I swallow hard, nodding and taking his offered hand, letting him lead me out of the store and back to the car.

Back to the only home that I've ever known. To the place that I hope will still be waiting for me one day, but know in the depth of my heart that will be closed to me the minute we break into my father's headquarters.

CHAPTER THIRTY-ONE

"SORRY" BY HALSEY

LARK

Friday rolls around all too soon, and I wake up with a headache and an empty feeling in the pit of my stomach. I'm sure the guys notice, especially when I can't eat much all day. They keep giving me furtive glances, pulling me close and whispering that everything will be okay after tonight.

How wrong they are. Nothing will be okay after tonight.

We're silent as we get ready, wearing all black. Knox left several hours ago, to take up point and watch the courtyard where we will make our entrance. I try to quell my racing heart as I pull on my long-sleeved black shirt and leggings, slipping my feet into black combat boots.

"Here, *Aziz-e delam*," Tarl says, his voice soft as he holds out a small knife encased in a leather thigh sheath.

"T–thank you," I reply, my mouth dry and the words hurting as they leave my throat.

"Allow me." He drops to his knees, holding my gaze. He turns his stare to my leg, taking the leather straps and wrapping them around my leg, doing the buckles up tightly. "Whatever happens tonight, it'll be okay." His voice is low, a whisper for only me to hear, and my entire body stills, my heart thudding painfully in my chest. *Does he know?*

I meet his mismatched stare, and his gaze is intense, like he's trying to delve into my very soul. I'm reminded that he's the Tailors' top man for gathering intel. That they call him the Inquisitor.

"O–okay," I whisper back, and we keep eye contact as he stands, so close that our chests brush. His hand reaches up, his dry, warm palm cupping my cheek as he leans in. My eyes close when I feel his lips hover over mine.

"I forgive you."

I can't react when he presses a soft kiss to my lips, my breaths ragged as chills sweep over my body. When I open my eyes he's gone, nothing but cold air where he once was.

"Are you ready, Dove?" Aeron asks, coming to stand where Tarl was moments ago. "What's wrong? You can stay here, it's not too late to back out."

"N–no, I was just..." My mind is racing, and I can't stop blinking, trying desperately to figure out why Tarl wouldn't say anything if he knows what my plan is.

"Just?" Aeron questions, leaning down to catch my eye. His hand cups the same cheek Tarl just did, and the warmth of his palm is enough to break me out of my frozen state.

"W–won't the cops stop us? We've a lot of weapons on show," I worry, my mind latching on something, anything to steer him away from my swirling thoughts. *Do the others know?*

"Not tonight, Dove. There aren't any patrols in the east side of the city tonight," he tells me, his face a blank mask but I can read between the lines. Whetstone PD is in the pocket of the Tailors, another reason for my father to hate them, but it doesn't mean that we can walk around with exposed weapons without fear of being arrested.

"Good to know." I take a deep inhale. "Are we ready to go?"

"Yes. As long as you are?" His brows raise, his face softening. I know that he'd rather I stay here, but he's also a good leader and knows that I have the best chance of getting them into the building and to my father.

"Then let's go kick some Soldier ass," I say, trying to lift my lips into a grin. It feels forced, and I know he notices because his forehead creases.

"Hells yeah!" Jude cries out, breaking the moment by grabbing me out of Aeron's hold and spinning me around. "Let's paint the east side red!"

A sour taste fills the back of my throat. I can only hope that it's not the blood of my men that coats the east side tonight, and I have to blink away the moisture that fills my eyes at the thought of any of them getting hurt. The plan is not for them to be harmed, they're leverage, but Rufus has never been a man of his word.

We meet the other three Tailors outside of Danny's Diner, the restaurant dark inside as it's closed for the night. Ironically, it's the place where my mother was shot by Aeron a decade ago and a fissure of pain freezes me for a moment as the memories try to rush in. I was worrying so much at the conference the other morning that I didn't realize this was the place we were meeting. I guess it's only fitting that my betrayal should start here.

A homeless man walks towards us, and I stiffen, blinking out of my impending panic until he pulls his large ragged coat off and Nick's face emerges.

"Report," Aeron commands in a low voice as Nick, the average Tailor, comes closer to us.

"I counted thirty Soldiers going down that alley, none coming out," Nick tells us, swiping grime off his face with a wet wipe he produces from a pocket.

"And Rufus?" Aeron demands, his voice hard as granite. A chill sweeps through me, making me shiver, and Jude wraps an arm around me, pulling me into his body. I try not to sink into him, try to resist the warmth, but it's like I have no control over my body anymore, and I do it anyway. Perhaps my body knows that I won't have many more chances after this.

"He's there. As well as his second and the boy," Nick tells him. I straighten, going rigid in Jude's arms.

"Hush, Nightingale. We'll get him out," Jude whispers against my ear. He places a soft kiss on my hair, and I have to take a few deep breaths to try and calm my pounding heart.

"Good work, Nick," Aeron nods, and I see the man stand a little taller at the praise. Aeron really will make a great leader one day.

If he gets that far.

I shut that bitch down, refusing to believe that I'm leading them to their deaths. It won't come to that.

The cold of the bright fall night surrounds us as we make our way to the back of the laundromat, all the guys looking around for any threats, any sign that we've been spotted. I know that even if we have, the Soldiers won't stop us. That's not the plan, after all.

A breath rushes out of me as we reach the broken fence that surrounds the courtyard, and Knox breaks away from the shadows. He jogs towards us, and when he stops, I can't help but wrap my arms around him and pull him close, my fingers cold from more than just the frigid air.

"Hey, Little Bird. Miss me?" His voice is teasing as he hugs me back, but he brings me closer anyway.

"Always," I say, my voice rasping and his arms tighten around me.

"I'm here now, love. No need to worry," he replies, his own voice soft. I hear a scoff behind me that sounds a lot like that cunt, Earl, but I ignore it, closing my eyes and breathing in Knox's leather, motor oil, and clove scent. God, the weight in my fucking chest is threatening to cave it in.

"Anything?" Aeron asks, his voice tight.

"Nope. Quiet as a nun's back door," Knox replies, and I cringe, pulling away.

"That's a visual I didn't need," I tell him, stepping back but he grabs my hand.

"But it made you smile so it was worth it." He pulls me back for a quick kiss before releasing me. My lips burn with the kiss, and I just want to pull him back to me and hide from what's about to happen.

"Let's go," Aeron commands, and we all follow as he goes through the hole in the metal fence. "Dove, where's the manhole?"

Letting go of Knox's hand, I look around the barren space, spotting the dark patch of the broken manhole cover and walking over. I bend down, reaching out with trembling hands to pull it off.

"Allow me," Tarl offers for the second time tonight, and I pause, staring into the side of his beautiful face highlighted in the moonlight, as if that will tell me all that he knows. As if that might tell me why he hasn't said anything to the others. He grabs hold of the edges, and in a swift yet nearly silent move, he pulls the cover off, placing it gently down next to it.

"I should go first, make sure no one is there," I whisper, and turn to see my guys frozen with clenched jaws. "It makes the most fucking sense, Aeron, and you know it."

"Fine," he grits out, his jaw tight. "But if you don't give the all-clear in two minutes, I'm coming after you."

"That defeats the whole point, asshole," I grumble under my

breath, Tarl's low chuckle reaching me as I lower myself into the dark manhole and find my first foothold.

Muscle memory takes over, my hands and feet finding purchase easily as I make my way down the short, pitch-black passage. This is the worst part, being enclosed in the dark, hands covered in old coal dust, but it's not long before I'm jumping down quietly onto the ground.

Glancing around, I see that it's pretty much the same as I left it, just with a few less packages of all the drugs, alcohol, and cigarettes that the Soldiers trade in. There's just the light from the coal chute, barely letting the moon cast its glow over the crates and packets.

Taking a final, shaking breath, I lean up into the chute and coo like a fucking Dove. Jude's idea of a joke.

The sound of the others coming down the tunnel fills the silent space, the rasp of their clothing against the sides as they make their way down seeming loud. I step back so the falling coat of dust doesn't get into my eyes, and soon dark figures are jumping down into the room until it's full of the Tailors.

My chest tingles as Aeron is the first to land, immediately coming over to me and pulling me to him. God, I feel like such a fucking asshole for leaning into him, taking the comfort that he's offering even though I don't deserve it.

"All clear, Dove?" he breathes against my ear, his voice barely a whisper. I give a sharp nod, not trusting my voice.

Taking his hand, I step toward the door and then kneel down, releasing him so I can pull out some lock-picking tools that Knox gave me.

With a quiet snick, the lock disengages and I get up again, Aeron leaning close as his fingers trail down my neck.

"Not just a pretty bird," he murmurs in my ear, and I have to swallow past the lump in my throat. I don't trust myself to speak, so I just turn my face and place a soft kiss on his cheek before reaching for the doorknob. His hand covers mine. "Sorry to break the rules of a gentleman, but I'll go first. Just in case."

Letting go, I step away as he opens the door a crack and peers out and I want to scream at him to run. For all of them to leave, that it's a trap.

My sperm donor's threat to my brother flits through my mind, so I don't say a thing. I keep my fucking traitor mouth shut and let them cautiously walk out, Jude placing me between him and Knox.

"What the fuck?" I hear Knox whisper behind me as we walk through the next room.

"The cages," I reply softly, my gaze raking over the two cages either side of us. They're huge, thick metal bars that run floor to ceiling that make them more like cells than animal cages. There are doors also made of bars, and I'm not sure if they were always here, or whether my sperm donor put them in, but I know that a stay in them is not pleasant. My father gave me that education several times throughout my teenage years when I would try to run away.

A shiver makes my skin pebble as we make our way silently past them, their outlines barely visible in the almost pitch-black, but it's the feeling of despair that rolls off of them in waves that makes the hair on the nape of your neck stand on end. You know bad things happen here. The kind of things that no one walks away from.

Another locked door is at the end of the narrow walkway, and I go forward to open it, once again standing back when the sound of the lock disengaging fills the silent space.

"You make a good member of the team, Nightingale," Jude says as I'm passed back to him, and it's as if a knife is lodged in my gut. Sweat breaks out all over my skin, my breaths coming faster as I watch Aeron open the door, peering through the gap and then opening it wider.

This time he lets Earl go first, then the other Tailors, and finally the rest of us. I can feel the tension, thick like molasses, as we enter the dark space. The main room where I assured them all that the usual Friday night party would be in full swing.

"What the—?" I hear just as I'm ripped from between the guys, a scream tearing from my throat as we're blinded by the lights suddenly being flung on.

"Boys!" The familiar voice of Rufus Jackson, leader of the Dead Soldiers and my fucking cunt of a father calls. Bile fills the back of my mouth as a knife is pressed against my throat. "Nice of you to join us."

CHAPTER THIRTY-TWO

"ARCADE" BY DUNCAN LAURENCE

AERON

I blink furiously, willing my vision to clear as Dove's scream rips my heart in two. The picture comes into focus slowly, the old speakeasy a complete shithole with Soldiers surrounding us, weapons drawn.

I ignore them all, searching for her, my whole body going ice-cold when I finally lay my eyes on her. Some Soldier scum has her pulled so close to him that I have to clench my fists hard to stop from storming over there and ripping his fucking hands off, but what makes terror fill my veins is the long, sharp blade against her beautiful throat. The blade that we gave her earlier.

I fucking knew we should have left her behind. Fuck, I should have tied her to the bed to keep her there.

"Boys!" The sound of that scum Rufus Jackson makes my jaw ache. "Nice of you to join us." Shit. He knew we were coming. I can see it by the delighted gleam in his fucking bright blue eyes, the same color as hers, our bird. I just wonder which of my men set us up. I'll rip their innards out myself when I discover who it was. No one fucking betrays the Tailors and lives. "You took so long, I thought that you'd never get here," Rufus continues, strolling over in our direction as if he doesn't have a care in the world. He looks like shit, like some wannabe MC president, in his leather cutoff and dirty jeans. Fucking disgusting, and I let the expression show on my face, curling my lip at him as he gets closer. His face tightens. "Always so fucking high and mighty, aren't you, little cunts? Always think you're better than the rest of us."

"That's because we are," Jude says, and I have to hold back a laugh as Rufus turns an ugly shade of purple.

"Bob," Rufus growls out, not looking away from me.

A feminine gasp has me darting my gaze behind him, seeing another Soldier step up to Dove, his arm moving in a flash. The sound of tearing fabric fills the room, and he steps away to reveal our girl, naked and now bleeding where the knife cut her as that dead scum cut off her clothes.

"You fucking piece of shit!" Knox roars, stepping forward, then grunting as two massive beasts of men smack him around the head with a baseball bat, forcing him to his knees.

In seconds, we're all being given similar treatment, pain lancing across my skull as a bat connects. My legs buckle as my knees are kicked out from under me, and I fight with all that I have, desperate to get to her, my rage lending me strength. A scream stops us all short. Her scream.

"No..." I whisper as I watch the knife pierce her side.

"Any more of that shit and I'll push it all the way in," Rufus snarls, holding the handle of the blade that is partway into our girl's porcelain skin. Red drips from the wound, and all I can hear is the thrash of my heartbeat in my ears as I see the pain in her beautiful, crystal eyes. "Better." She gasps as he pulls the knife out, her breasts heaving with her panting breaths. "Now that I have your full fucking attention, here's what's going to happen." He pauses for dramatic effect, and I want to spit at him, but I can't stop seeing the knife that's so close to my Dove. To our girl. Our soul. "Take their weapons."

All of us are roughly manhandled, Knox prostrated on the ground as four Soldiers divest him of his weapons. I don't move, just allow them to take mine, my eyes never leaving hers as two Soldiers hold my arms behind my back while another takes everything I have on me. Tears stream down her cheeks, and she's so fucking beautiful when she cries, but only if we're the ones making her do it.

My jaw clenches as a swift kick lands on my gut, my head snapping to the side as a brutal punch lands on my jaw.

"You said you weren't going to hurt them!" I hear Dove scream over the ringing of my ears, and I shake my head because surely I misheard her. "You promised, you piece of shit!"

I look back at her just as Rufus backhands her across the face, the knife at her throat nicking her and sending a trickle of blood down her neck.

"Nightingale?" The note of devastation in my brother's voice tells me I wasn't the only one to hear her.

I watch as her gaze swings to us, fresh tears spilling over her cheeks. Her jaw works, but no sound comes out, just silent tears as she looks at each of us.

"Of course!" Rufus claps, still holding that damn knife, stained with her blood, a wide smile on his face. "You don't know who your snake is, do you?" He stalks over to us, the gleam in his eyes turning malicious. "I'll give you a clue. We know her as the Soldier's Darling, but I hear that she's known as the Tailors' Ruin. Fitting name really, all things considered."

"Little Bird?" Knox rasps, barely able to get the words out. "What the fuck is he talking about?"

A sob leaves her chest. "W—we don't get much choice in this life."

I turn to look at Jude, his brow furrowing and then raising as his own words come back to haunt him. "Oh, Nightingale."

I turn back to her, the blood pounding in my ears as a guttural roar sounds from Knox.

"We could have fucking helped you!" he screams at her, and I see her flinch with every word he throws. "We were going to kill them all for you!"

Rufus laughs a dark and evil sound that sticks to my skin like fucking tar. "Kill us all, boy?" Chuckles sound throughout the room, and it sets my teeth on edge to hear the sound. "The eight of you against the eighty of us? Even a crook like you must see ten to one are not good odds."

I look properly around then, a heavy feeling in my stomach as I take in the sheer number of men, of Dead Soldiers that fill the room. He's been recruiting, heavily by the looks of it. It's like an ice bucket has hit my core, my very being frozen as I take in our situation. The situation that I led us into. I drop my gaze.

"I see you realize your position, boy. Just how much you've fucked up. Gotta grate a little, right? You being the future leader and all." My eyes raise to find Rufus standing in front of me, my head tilting back as I take him in from my knees. "But don't worry, I'm not gonna kill you boys yet. No, I'm gonna trade you for whatever the fuck I want from Daddy Tailor. I'll send him bits of you until he agrees to my terms, that's the sort of language you Tailors understand, right?" I don't answer, just narrow my eyes at him. "Take the four boys to the cages. Kill the others."

"No!" I try to lurch to my feet, but one of the men holding me pulls my arm up sharply until it feels like the bone will snap, and I'm fucking useless to stop them as I'm dragged away, watching as the four Tailors who joined me and the guys tonight are shot in the back of the head, their bodies crumpling to the ground.

Just before I'm pulled through the door we came through what feels like hours ago, I catch bright blue eyes, sparkling with tears as she tugs against her own captors, calling our names. The door shuts just as Rufus pulls his fist back and punches her in the stomach, making her double over and breaking our contact.

The beast inside me roars, desperate to help her, even though she betrayed us, and my soul feels torn in two as I think about her words.

"We don't get much choice in this life."

She's right, we don't. I didn't when I was forced to shoot her mother. Jude didn't when he held June in his arms as she died.

But Dove did have a choice.

We gave her a choice. We gave her the choice of freedom with us. Of a life with us. I even promised that I'd get her brother out. Yet she chose to betray us regardless.

And that is not something I can choose to forgive.

Not quite the end...

Want to know what happens next? Read Addicted to the Ruin now to see if The Tailors will ever forgive Lark.

To keep up to date with all my news, and read lots of yummy bonus content, sign up for my newsletter HERE.

AUTHOR NOTE

If you liked *Addicted to the Pain*, please consider leaving a review. They help our books get in front of new readers as they teach the algorithm that we're bloody awesome. You have that power, so use it wisely my fellow smut slut.

How are you feeling after that?

It was a rough ride right, and sometimes not the sexy kind but the rip your heart out kind am I right? These guys hauled me over the coals, and I can tell you that *Addicted to the Ruin* is just as painful.

But, it is a love story, and so must have a happy ending...right?

ACKNOWLEDGMENTS

I wouldn't be here, writing all the extra bits for my FOURTH FUCKING BOOK without the help of many simply wonderful people.

My gorgeous alphas and betas who give me incredible feedback, help the story to grow and tell me there is never too much sex. You are all so appreciated and your comments are more precious than gold.

My wonderful editor Polly who literally gives me life with her comments! She makes these books shine and I honestly would be lost without her.

I'd also be totally lost without Julia, my wonderful PA who does so much more than she gets paid for!

And my lovely Rosebuds and Darlings, my Arc readers and Street Team. You guys don't know how much you do, giving me awesome reviews and recommending my books. I love you all!

To my wonderful Patrons Jess and Nicola, you've been a wonderful support and cheerleaders for me since I started my Patreon and I can't wait to share more shenanigans with you!

And of course, my amazing husband who supports me in all that I do, and enjoys the benefits of being married to a steamy romance author (you all know what I'm talking about!). I genuinely wouldn't be where I am today, as a person, craftsperson or author without him.

Printed in the USA
CPSIA information can be obtained
at www.ICGtesting.com
LVHW040551091224
798490LV00001B/87

* 9 7 8 1 9 1 7 3 3 2 0 5 7 *